S0-BIW-213

Also by Lucia Berlin

A Manual for Cleaning Ladies (1977)

Angels Laundromat (1981)

Legacy (1983)

Phantom Pain (1984)

Safe and Sound (1988)

Homesick: New & Selected Stories (1990)

So Long: Stories 1987–1992 (1993, 2016)

A Manual for Cleaning Women: Selected Stories (2015)

Lucia Berlin

WHERE
I LIVE
NOW

Stories: 1993–1998

Black Sparrow Books

David R. Godine, Publisher

BOSTON

This is
A Black Sparrow Book
Published in 2017 by
DAVID R. GODINE, PUBLISHER
Post Office Box 450
Jaffrey, New Hampshire 03452
www.blacksparrowbooks.com

Copyright © 1999 by Lucia Berlin
Copyright © 2017 by the Literary Estate of Lucia Berlin LP

All rights reserved. No part of this book may be used or reproduced without written permission from the publisher, except in the case of brief quotations embodied in critical articles and reviews. For information, contact Permissions, David R. Godine, Publisher, Fifteen Court Square, Suite 320, Boston, Massachusetts, 02108.

ACKNOWLEDGMENTS

Thanks to the editors of the following publications where some of these stories first appeared: *Barnabe Mountain Review, Brick, Exquisite Corpse, First Intensity, Fourteen Hills, Gas, helicoptero, New American Writing, New Censorship* and *Sniper Logic.*

"The Wives" was based upon a play called "The Stronger," which appeared in *Acts II* and in *Phantom Pain* published by Tombouctou Press.

The poems in the story "Here It Is Saturday"
were written by Charles Clemons.

Thank you to my good friends and listeners: Jenny Dorn, Ivan Suvanjieff, Beth Geoghagan, Ashley Simpson and Dave Yoo. Thanks to Kenward Elmslie for comfort and delight.

ISBN: 978-1-57423-091-8

Black Sparrow Press books are printed on acid-free paper.

THIRD PRINTING, 2017
Printed in the United States of America

For Ed and Jenny, with love always

Contents

Let Me See You Smile

It's true, the grave is more powerful than a lover's eyes. An open grave, with all its magnets. And I say this to you, you who when you smile make me think of the beginning of the world.

VICENTE HUIDOBRO, *Altazor*

Jesse threw me for a loop. And I take pride in my ability to size people up. Before I joined Grillig's firm, I was a public defender for so long I had learned to assess a client or a juror almost at first glance.

I was unprepared too because my secretary didn't announce him over the intercom and he had no appointment. Elena just led him into my office.

"Jesse is here to see you, Mr. Cohen."

Elena introduced him with an air of importance, using only his first name. He was so handsome, entered the room with such authority, I thought he must be some one-name rock star I hadn't heard of.

He wore cowboy boots and black jeans, a black silk shirt. He had long hair, a strong craggy face. About thirty was my first guess, but when he shook my hand there was an indescribable sweetness in his smile, an openness in his hazel eyes that was innocent and childlike. His raspy low voice confused me even more. He spoke as if he were explaining patiently to a young inexperienced person. Me.

He said he had inherited ten thousand dollars and wanted to use it to hire me. The woman he lived with was in trouble, he said, and she was going to trial in two months. Ten counts against her.

I hated to tell him how far his money would go with me.

"Doesn't she have a court-appointed attorney?" I asked.

"She did, but the asshole quit. He thought she was guilty and a bad person, a pervert."

"What makes you think I won't feel the same way?" I asked.

"You won't. She says you are the best civil liberties lawyer in town. The deal is she doesn't know I'm here. I want you to let her think you're volunteering to do this. For the principle of the thing. This is my only condition."

I tried to interrupt here, to say, "Forget it, son." Tell him firmly that I wasn't going to do it. No way could he afford me. I didn't want to touch this case. I couldn't believe this poor kid was willing to give all his money away. I already hated the woman. Damn right she was guilty and a bad person!

He said that the problem was the police report, which the judge and jury would read. They would pre-convict her because it was distorted and full of lies. He thought I could get her off by showing that his arrest was false, that the report of hers was libelous, the cop she hit was brutal, the arresting officer was psychotic, evidence had definitely been planted. He was convinced that I could discover that they had made other false arrests and had histories of brutality.

He had more to say about how I should handle this case. I can't explain why I didn't blow up, tell him to get lost. He argued passionately and well. He should have been a lawyer.

I didn't just like him. I even began to see that spending his entire inheritance was a necessary rite of passage. A heroic, noble gesture.

It was as if Jesse were from another age, another planet. He even said at some point that the woman called him "The Man Who Fell to Earth." This made me feel better about her somehow.

I told Elena to cancel a meeting and an appointment. He

spoke all morning, simply and clearly, about their relationship, about her arrest.

I am a defense attorney. I'm cynical. I am a material person, a greedy man. I told him I would take the case for nothing.

"No. Thank you," he said. "Just please tell her that you're doing it for no charge. But it's my fault she got into this trouble and I want to pay for it. What will it be? Five thousand? More?"

"Two thousand," I said.

"I know that's too low. How about three?"

"Deal," I said.

He took off one of his boots and counted off twenty warm hundred dollar bills, fanned them out on my desk like cards. We shook hands.

"Thanks for doing this, Mr. Cohen."

"Sure. Call me Jon."

He settled back down and filled me in.

He and his friend Joe were dropouts, had run away from New Mexico last year. Jesse played the guitar, wanted to play in San Francisco. On his eighteenth birthday he was to inherit money from an old woman in Nebraska (another heartbreaking story). He had planned to go to London where he had been asked to join a band. An English group had played in Albuquerque, liked his songs and guitar playing. He and Joe had no place to stay when they got to the Bay area, so he looked up Ben, who had been his best friend in junior high. Ben's mother didn't know they were runaways. She said it was okay for them to stay awhile in the garage. Later she found out and called their parents, calmed the parents down, told them they were doing fine.

It had all worked out. He and Joe did yard work and hauling, other odd jobs. Jesse played with other musicians, was writing songs. They got along great with Ben and with his mother Carlotta. She appreciated how much time Jesse spent with her youngest kid Saul, taking him to ball games, fishing, climbing at Tilden. She taught school and worked hard, was glad too for help with laundry and carrying groceries and dishes. Anyway, he said, it was a good arrangement for everybody.

"I had met Maggie about three years before. They called her to our junior high in Albuquerque. Somebody had put acid in Ben's milk at lunch. He freaked out, didn't know what was happening. She came to get him. They let me and Joe go with her, in case he got violent. I thought she was going to take him to a hospital, but she drove us all down by the river. The four of us sat in the rushes, watching red-winged blackbirds, calming him down and actually helping him have a pretty cool trip. Maggie and I got along fine, talking about birds and the river. I usually don't talk much but with her there is always a lot I need to say."

I turned a recorder on at this point.

"So we stayed a month at their house in Berkeley, then another month. At night we'd all sit around the fire talking, telling jokes. Joe had a girlfriend by then and so did Ben so they'd go out. Ben was still a senior and he sold his jewelry and rock star photos on Telegraph, so I didn't see him much. Weekends I'd go to the marina or the beach with Saul and Maggie."

"Excuse me. This report says her name is Carlotta. Who's Maggie?"

"I call her Maggie. At nights she'd grade papers and I'd play my guitar. We talked all night sometimes, our whole life stories, laughing, crying. She and I are both alcoholics, which is bad if you look at it one way, but good if you look at how it helped us say things to each other that we had never told anybody before. Our childhoods were scary and bad in exactly the same way, but like negatives of each other's. When we got together her kids freaked out, her friends said it was sick, incestuous. We are incestuous but in a weird way. It's like we are twins. The same person. She writes stories. She does the same thing in her stories that I do in my music. Anyway, every day we knew one another more deeply, so that when we finally ended up in bed it was as if we had already been inside each other. We were lovers for two months before I was supposed to leave. The idea was to get my money in Albuquerque on December 28th, when I turned eighteen, and then go to London. She was making me go, said I needed the experience and we needed to split.

"I didn't want to go to London. I may be young but I know what she and I have together is galaxies beyond regular people. We know each other in our souls, all the bad and the good. We have a kindness to each other."

He told me then the story of going to the airport with her and Joe. Joe's belt knife and zippers had turned on the alarm at security, all three were strip-searched and Jesse missed the plane. He was hollering about his guitar and music being on the plane, got put into handcuffs, was being beaten by the police when Maggie came in.

"We all got arrested. It's in the report," he said. "The newspaper headline was "Lutheran Schoolteacher, Hell's Angels in Airport Brawl."

"Are you a Hell's Angel?"

"Of course not. But the report says I am. Joe looks like one, wishes he was. He must of bought ten copies of that paper. Anyway, she and Joe went to jail in Redwood City. I spent a night in juvenile hall and then they sent me to New Mexico. Maggie phoned me on my birthday and told me everything was fine. She didn't say a word about any trial, and she didn't tell me she had been evicted and fired, that her ex-husband was taking her kids to Mexico. But Joe did, even though she told him not to. So I came back here."

"How did she feel about that?"

"She was furious. Said I had to leave and go to London. That I needed to learn and to grow. And she was believing all the shit about her being bad because I was seventeen when we got together. I seduced her. Nobody seems to get that part, except her. I'm not your typical teenager."

"True," I said.

"But anyway we are together now. She agreed not to decide anything until after the trial. Not to look for a job or a place. What I'm hoping is by that time she'll go away with me."

He handed me the police report. "The best thing is for you to read this and then we'll talk. Come over for dinner. Friday ok? After you've read this. Maybe you can find out something about the cop. Both cops. Come early," he said, "when you get off work. We live just down the street."

Nothing applied any more. I couldn't say it was inappropriate. That I had plans. That my wife might mind.

"Sure, I'll be there at six." The address he gave me was one of the worst blocks in town.

It was a beautiful Christmas. Sweet presents for each other, a great dinner. Keith invited Karen, one of my students. I guess it's childish, but it made me feel good for him to see how much she looked up to me. Ben's girlfriend Megan made mince pies. Both of them helped me with dinner and it was fun. Our friend Larry came. Big fire, nice old-fashioned day.

Nathan and Keith were so glad Jesse was leaving that they were really nice to him, even gave him presents. Jesse had made gifts for everyone. It was warm and festive, except then in the kitchen Jesse whispered, "Hey, Maggie, whatcha gonna do when I'm gone?" and I thought my heart would break. He gave me a ring with a star and a moon. By coincidence we each gave the other a silver flask. We thought it was great. Nathan said, "Ma, that's so disgusting," but I didn't hear him then.

Jesse's plane was leaving at six. Joe wanted to come along. I drove us to the airport in the rain. "The Joker" and "Jumpin' Jack Flash" on the radio. Joe was sipping from a can of beer and Jesse and I from a pint of Beam. I never gave it a thought, that I was contributing to their delinquency. They were drinking when I met them. They bought liquor, never got carded. The truth was I was so much in denial about my own drinking I wasn't likely to worry about theirs.

When we got inside the airport, Jesse stopped and said, "Christ. You two will never find the car." We laughed, not realizing it would be true.

We weren't exactly drunk, but we were high and excited. I was trying not to show how desperate I was about him leaving.

I realize now how much attention we must have attracted. All of us very tall. Joe, a dark Laguna Indian with long black braids, in motorcycle leather, a knife on his belt. Big boots, zippers and chains. Jesse in black, with his duffel bag and guitar. Jesse. He was otherworldly. I couldn't even glance up at him, his jaw, his teeth, his golden eyes, flowing long hair. I would weep if I looked at him. I was dressed up for Christmas in a black velvet pant suit, Navajo jewelry. Whatever it was, the combination of us, plus all the buzzers that Joe's metal set off going through security... they saw us as a security risk, took us into separate rooms and searched us. They went through my underwear, my purse, ran their fingers through my hair, between my toes. Everywhere. When I got out of there I couldn't see Jesse, so I ran to the departure gate. Jesse's flight had left. He was yelling at the agent that his guitar was on the plane, his music was on the plane. I had to go to the bathroom. When I came out no one was at the ticket counter. The plane had gone. I asked somebody if the tall young man in black had made the plane. The man nodded toward a door with no sign on it. I went in.

The room was full of security guards and city police. It was sharp with the smell of sweat. Two guards were restraining Joe, who was handcuffed. Two policemen held Jesse and another was beating him on the head with a foot-long flashlight. A sheet of blood covered Jesse's face and soaked his shirt. He was screaming with pain. I walked completely unnoticed across the room. All of them were watching the policeman beating Jesse, as if they were looking at a fight on TV. I grabbed the flashlight and hit the cop on the head with it. He fell with a thud. "Oh Jesus, he's dead," another one said.

Jesse and I were handcuffed and then taken through the airport and down to a small police station in the basement. We sat next to each other, our hands fastened behind us to the chairs. Jesse's eyes were stuck shut with blood. He couldn't see and the wound on his scalp continued to bleed. I begged them to clean it or bandage it. To wash his eyes. They'll clean you up at Redwood City Jail, the guard said.

"Fuck, Randy, the dude's a juvenile! Somebody's got to take him over the bridge!"

"A juvenile? This bitch is in big trouble. I ain't taking him. My shift's almost over."

He came over to me. "You know the peace officer you hit? They have him in Intensive Care. He might die."

"Please. Could you wash his eyes?"

"Fuck his eyes."

"Lean down a little, Jesse."

I licked the blood off of his eyes. It took a long time; the blood was thick and caked, stuck in his lashes. I had to keep spitting. With the rust around them his eyes glowed a honey amber.

"Hey, Maggie, let me see your smile."

We kissed. The guard pulled my head away and slapped me. "Filthy bitch!" he said. Just then there was a lot of yelling and Joe got thrown in with us. They had arrested him for using obscene language in front of women and children. He had been angry when they wouldn't tell him anything about us.

"This one is old enough for Redwood City."

Since his arms were cuffed behind him, he couldn't hug us, so he kissed us both. Far as I remember he had never kissed either of us on the lips before. He said later it was because our mouths were so bloody it made him feel sad. The police called me a pervert again, seducing young boys.

I was disgusted by then. I didn't get it yet, didn't understand the way everyone would see me. I had no idea that my charges were adding up. One of the policemen read them to me from the counter across the room. "Drunk in public, interfering with arrest, assaulting a police officer, assault with a deadly weapon, attempted murder, resisting arrest. Lewd and lascivious behavior, sexual acts upon a minor (licking his eyes), contributing to the delinquency of minors, possession of marijuana."

"Hey, no way!" Joe said.

"Don't say anything," Jesse whispered. "This will work for us. Must have been planted. We had all just been searched, right?"

"Shit yeah," Joe said. "Plus we would have smoked it if we had it."

They took Jesse away. They put Joe and me in the back of a squad car. We drove miles and miles to the Redwood City jail. All I could think of was that Jesse was gone. I figured they would send him to Albuquerque and then he'd go to London.

Two nasty butch cops gave me a vaginal and rectal exam, a cold shower. They washed my hair with lye soap, getting it in my eyes. They left me without a towel or a comb. All they gave me to wear was a short short gown and some tennis shoes. I had a black eye and a swollen lip, from when they hit me after they took the flashlight away. The cop who took me downstairs had kept twisting the cuffs so there were open bloody cuts on both wrists, like stupid suicides.

They didn't let me have my cigarettes. The two whores and one wino with me let me have their last wet drags at least. Nobody slept or spoke. I shook all night from cold, from needing a drink.

In the morning we went in a bus to the courthouse. I talked through a window, by phone, to a fat red lawyer who read the report to me. The report was distorted and false all the way through.

"Advised of three suspicious characters in airport lobby. Woman with two Hell's Angels, one Indian. All armed and potentially dangerous." I kept telling him that things said in the report were total lies. The lawyer ignored me, just kept asking me if I was fucking the kid.

"Yes!" I finally said. "But that's just about the only thing I'm not charged with."

"You would have been if I had written it. Statutory rape."

I was so tired I got the giggles which made him madder. Statutory rape. I get visions of Pygmalion or some Italian raping the Pietà.

"You're a sicko," he said. "You are charged with performing sexual acts upon a minor in public."

I told him I was trying to get the blood off Jesse's eyes so he could see.

"You actually licked it off?" he sneered.

I can imagine what hell prison must be. I could really understand how prisoners just learn to be worse people. I wanted to kill him. I asked him what was going to happen. He said I'd be arraigned and a court date would be set. I'd come in, plead innocent, hope that when we went to court we got a judge who was halfway lenient. Getting a jury in this town is a problem too. Far right, religious people out here, hard on drugs, sex crimes. Hell's Angels were Satan to them and marijuana, forget it.

"I didn't have marijuana," I said. "The cop put it there."

"Sure he did. To thank you for sucking his dick?"

"So, are you going to defend me or prosecute me?"

"I'm your appointed defense lawyer. See you in court."

Joe was in court too, chained to a string of other men in orange. He didn't look at me. I was black and blue, my hair curled wild around my face and the shift barely covered my underpants. Later Joe actually admitted I looked so sleazy he had pretended he didn't know me. We both got assigned court dates in January. When his case got to court the judge just laughed and dropped the charges.

I had called home. It was hard enough telling Ben where I was. I was too ashamed to ask anyone to post bail, so I waited another day for them to let me out on my own recognizance. Stupidly I got that by having them call the principal where I taught. She was a woman who liked me, respected me. I still had no idea how people were going to judge me. It baffles me now how blind I was, but now I'm sober.

The police told me that Joe needed me to put up bond for him, so when I got out I went to a bondsman. It must not have been much, since I wrote him a check.

We figured out how to get to the airport. But it's like seeing Mount Everest. It just looked close. We walked in the rain, freezing cold, miles and miles. It took us most of the day. We laughed a lot, even after we tried to take a shortcut through a dog kennel. Climbing a fence with dobermans barking and snarling beneath us. Abbott and Costello. No one would pick us up when we got to the freeway. Not true, some guy in a truck finally did, but we were almost there, waved him on.

This was the worst part of the entire situation. I'm serious. Trying to find the damn car. We went all the way around every vast level, up and up and then back down round and round then back up round and round until we both were crying. Just bawling away from being so tired and hungry and cold. An elderly black man saw us, and we didn't scare him even though we were soaked through and crying like fools. He didn't even mind us getting mud and water in his spotless old Hudson car. He drove up and down and around over and over saying that the good Lord would help us, surely. And when we found the car we all said, "Praise the Lord." When we got out he said to us, "God bless you." "God bless you and thank you," Joe and I said in unison, like a response in church.

"That dude is a fucking angel."

"He really is one," I said.

"Yeah, that's what I just said. A for-real angel."

There was more than half a pint of Jim Beam in the glove compartment. We sat there with the heater on and the windows steamed up, eating Cheerios and croutons from the bag for feeding ducks and finishing the bottle of whiskey.

"I'll admit it," he said. "Nothing ever tasted so good."

We were quiet all the way home in the rain. He drove. I kept wiping the steam off the windows. I asked him not to tell my kids or Jesse about all the charges or about the cop. It was a disturbing the peace problem, ok? Cool, he said. We didn't speak after that. I didn't feel guilty or ashamed, didn't worry about the trouble I was in or what I was going to do. I thought about Jesse being gone.

I tried to call Cheryl before I went to Jesse's, but she hung up on me, tried again but the machine was on. I was going to drive but worried about parking in their neighborhood. I was worried about walking in their neighborhood too. I guess it says something that I left my Porsche in the office garage, walked the seven or eight blocks to their apartment.

The downstairs door was graffitied plywood behind metal bars. They buzzed me in to a dusty marble foyer, lit from a star-shaped skylight four stories up. It was still a beautiful tile and marble building, with a sweep of stairs, faded mirrors in art deco frames. Someone slept against an urn; figures with their faces averted passed me on the stairs, all vaguely familiar from the courthouse or jail.

By the time I got to their apartment I was out of breath, sickened by smells of urine, cheap wine, stale oil, dust. Carlotta opened the door. "Come in," she smiled. I stepped into their technicolor world that smelled of corn bread and red chili, limes and cilantro and her perfume. The room had high ceilings, tall windows. There were oriental rugs on the polished wood floors. Huge ferns, banana plants, birds of paradise. The only furniture in this room was a bed with red satin sheets. Outside in the late sun was the golden dome of the Abyssinian Baptist Church, a grove of tall old palm trees, the curve of the BART train. The view was like a vista in Tangiers. She let me absorb this for a minute, then she shook my hand.

"Thank you for helping us, Mr. Cohen. Eventually I'll be able to pay you."

"Don't worry about that. I'm glad to do it," I said, "especially now that I've read the report. It's an obvious distortion."

Carlotta was tall and tanned, in a soft white jersey dress. She looked around thirty, had what my mother used to call bearing. She was even more of a surprise than the apartment, than Jesse, well maybe not Jesse. I could see how the combination of them would be disturbing. I kept staring at her. She was a lovely woman. I don't mean pretty, although she was. Gracious. If we did end up going to trial, she would look terrific in court.

This would turn out to be only my first visit. I came back every Friday after that, walking, no, rushing from my office to their place. It was as if I had taken some drink, like Alice, or was in a Woody Allen movie. Not where the actor climbs down from the screen. I climbed up into it.

That first evening she led me into the other room which had a fine Bokhara carpet, some saddlebags, a table set for three, with flowers and candles. "Angie" was playing on the stereo. These tall windows had bamboo blinds and the slight wind made shadows like banners on the walls.

Jesse called hello from the kitchen, came out to shake my hand. He was in jeans and a white T-shirt. They both glowed with color, had been at the estuary all day.

"How do you like our place? I painted it. Check out the kitchen. Baby-shit yellow, nice, no?"

"It is fantastic, this apartment!"

"And you like her. I knew you would." He handed me a gin and tonic.

"How did you...?"

"I asked your secretary. I'm the cook tonight. You probably have questions to ask Maggie while I finish up."

She led me to the "terrace," a space outside the windows, above the fire escape, big enough for two milk crates. I did have dozens of questions. The report said she claimed to be a teacher. She told me about losing her job at a Lutheran high school, about being evicted. She was frank. She said the neighbors had been complaining for a long time, because there were so many of them living there, because of loud music. This had just been the last straw. She was glad her ex-husband took the three youngest to Mexico.

"I'm completely mixed up, messed up, right now," she said. It was hard to believe her because of her beautiful calm voice.

She briefly told me what happened at the airport, taking more blame for it than Jesse had given her. "As far as the charges, I am guilty of them, except the marijuana, they planted that. But the way they *describe* it is sick. Like Joe *did* kiss us both, but from friendship. I don't have any sex ring with young boys. What was sick and wrong was how the cop was beating Jesse, and how others stood there watching it. Any normal person would have done what I did. Although, thank God, the cop didn't die."

I asked her what she was going to do after the trial. She looked panicked, whispered what Jesse had told me in the office, that they had decided not to deal with it until the trial.

"But I can get it together. Get myself together then." She said she spoke Spanish, thought about applying at hospitals for jobs, or as a court translator. She had worked for almost a year on a trial in New Mexico, had good references. I knew the case, and the judge and lawyer she had worked with. Famous case... an addict who shot a narc five times in the back and got off with manslaughter. We talked about that brilliant defense for a while, and I told her where to write about court translating.

Jesse came out with some guacamole and chips, a fresh drink for me, beers for them. She slid to the ground and he sat. She leaned back against his knees. He held her throat with one fine long-fingered hand, drank his beer with the other.

I will never forget it, the way he held her throat. The two of them were never flirtatious or coy, never made erotic or even demonstrative gestures, but their closeness was electric. He held her throat. It wasn't a possessive gesture; they were fused.

"Of course, Maggie can get a dozen jobs. And she can find a house and her kids can all come home. Thing is they are better off without her. Sure they miss her and she misses them. She was a good mother. She raised them right, gave them character and values, a sense of who they are. They are confident and honest. They laugh a lot. Now they are with their Daddy who is very rich. He can send them to Andover and Harvard, where he went. Rest of the time they can sail and fish and scuba dive. If they come back to her, I'll have to leave. And if I leave, she'll drink. She won't be able to stop and that will be a terrible thing."

"What will you do if you leave?"

"Me? Die."

The setting sun was in her brilliant blue eyes. Tears filled her eyes, caught in the lashes and didn't fall, reflected the green palms so that it looked like she was wearing turquoise goggles.

"Don't cry, Maggie," he said. He tilted her head back and drank the tears.

"How could you tell she was crying?" I asked.

"He always knows," she said. "At night, in the dark when I'm facing away from him, I can smile and he'll say, 'What's so funny?'"

"She's the same. She can be out cold. Snoring. And I'll grin. Her eyes will pop open and she'll be smiling back at me."

We had dinner then. A fantastic meal. We talked about everything but the trial. I can't remember how I got started on stories about my Russian grandmother, dozens of stories about her. I hadn't laughed so hard in years. Taught them the word *shonda*. What a *shonda!*

Carlotta cleared the table. The candles were halfway down. She came back with coffee and flan. As we were finishing, she said, "Jon, may I call you counselor?"

"God, no," Jesse said. "That sounds like junior high. He'll ask me where my anger comes from. Let's call him Barrister. Barrister, have you given some thought to this lady's plight?"

"I have, my good man. Let me get my briefcase and I'll show you just where we stand."

I said yes to a cognac. They both were drinking whiskey and water now. I was excited. I wanted to be matter-of-fact, but I was too pleased. I went through the document and compared it to a three-page list of untrue, misleading, libelous or slanderous statements from the report. "Lewd," "wanton behavior," "lascivious manner," "threatening," "menacing," "armed and dangerous." Pages of statements which could prejudice a judge and jury against my client, which in fact had given me a distorted idea of her even after talking with Jesse.

I had a copy from the airport security saying that she and her clothing and bag had been thoroughly searched and no drugs or weapons had been found.

"The best part, though, is that you were right, Jesse. Both these guys have long lists of serious violations. Suspensions for improper use of force, beating suspects. Two separate investigations for killing unarmed suspects. Many, many complaints of brutality, excessive force, false arrest and manufacturing evidence. And this is only after a few days research! We do know that both these cops have had serious suspensions, were demoted, sent from beats in the city to South San Francisco. We will insist upon Internal Affairs investigations of the arresting officers, threaten to sue the San Francisco Police Department.

"So, let's not just threaten them, let's do it," Jesse said.

I would get to learn that drink gave him courage but it made her more fragile. She shook her head. "I couldn't go through with it."

"Bad idea, Jesse," I said. "But it is a good way to handle the case."

The court date wasn't until the end of June. Although my aides continued to get more evidence against the policemen, there wasn't much we needed to discuss. If the case wasn't dismissed, then we'd have to postpone the trial and, well, pray. But I still went over to the Telegraph apartment every Friday. It made my wife Cheryl furious and jealous. Except for handball games, this was the first time I ever went anywhere without her. She didn't understand why she couldn't come too. And I couldn't explain, not even to myself. Once she even accused me of having an affair.

It was like an affair. It was unpredictable and exciting. Fridays I would wait all day until I could go over there. I was in love with all of them. Sometimes Jesse, Joe, and Carlotta's son Ben and I would play poker or pool. Jesse taught me to be a good poker player, and a good pool player. It made me feel childishly cool to go with them into downtown pool halls and not be afraid. Joe's mere presence made us all safe anywhere.

"He's like having a pit bull, only cheaper to feed," Jesse said.

"He's good for other things," Ben says. "He can open bottles with his teeth. He's the best laugher there is." That was true. He rarely spoke, but caught humor immediately.

Sometimes we walked with Ben in downtown Oakland while he took photographs. Carlotta got us to make frames with our hands, look at things as if through a lens. I told Ben it had changed my way of seeing.

What Joe liked to to was to sneak into photographs. When the contacts were printed, there he'd be sitting on a stoop with some winos or looking lost in a doorway, arguing with a Chinese butcher about a duck.

One Friday, Ben brought a Minolta, told me he'd sell it to me for fifty dollars. Sure. I was delighted. Later I noticed that he gave the money to Joe, which made me wonder.

"Play with it before you get any film. Just walk around at first, looking through it. Half the time I don't have any film in my camera."

The first photographs I took were at a store only a few blocks from my office. It sells one shoe for a dollar each. One side of the room has piles of old left shoes, the right side has right shoes. Old men. Poor young men. The old shoe seller in a rocking chair putting the money in a Quaker Oats box.

That first roll of film made me happier than anything in a long time, even a good trial. When I showed them the prints, they all high-fived me. Carlotta hugged me.

Ben and I went out together several times, early in the morning, in Chinatown, the warehouse district. It was a good way to get to know someone. I'd be focusing on little kids in school uniforms, he'd be taking an old man's hands. I told him I felt uncomfortable taking people, that it seemed intrusive, rude.

"Mom and Jesse helped me with this. They always talk to everybody, and people talk back. If I can't get a picture without the person seeing me now I'll just talk to them, come right out and ask, 'Do you mind if I take your picture?' Most of the time they say, 'Of course I mind, asshole.' But sometimes they don't mind."

A few times we talked about Carlotta and Jesse. Since they all got along so well, I was surprised by his anger.

"Well, sure I'm mad. Part of it is childish. They're so tight I feel left out and jealous, like I lost my mother and my best friend. But another part of me thinks it's good. I never saw either one of them happy before. But they're feeding each other's destructive side, the part that hates themselves. He hasn't played, she hasn't written since they moved to Telegraph. They're going through his money like water, drinking it mostly."

"I never get the feeling that they are drunk," I said.

"That's because you've never seen them sober. And they don't really start drinking until we've gone. Then they careen around town, chasing fire trucks, doing God knows what. Once they got into the US Mail depot and were shot at. At least they're nice drunks. They are incredibly sweet to each other. She never was mean to us kids, never hit us. She loves us. That's why I can't understand why she's not getting my brothers back."

Another time, on Telegraph, he showed me the words to a song Jesse had written. It was fine. Mature, ironic, tender. Reminded me of Dylan, Tom Waits and Johnny Cash mixed together. Ben also handed me an *Atlantic Monthly* with a story of hers in it. I had read the story a few months before, had thought it was great. "You two wrote these fine things?" They both shrugged.

What Ben said had made sense, but I didn't see any self-hatred or destructiveness. Being with them seemed to bring out a positive side of me, a corny side.

Carlotta and I were alone on the terrace. I asked her why being there made me feel so good. "Is it simply because they are all young?"

She laughed. "None of them are young. Ben was never young. I was never young. You probably were an old child too, and you like us because you can act out. It is heaven to play, isn't it? You like coming here because the rest of your life vanishes. You never mention your wife, so there must be troubles there. Your job must be troubles. Jesse gives everybody permission to be themselves and to think about themselves. That it's OK to be selfish.

"Being with Jesse is a sort of a meditation. Like sitting zazen, or being in a sensory deprivation tank. The past and future disappear. Problems and decisions disappear. Time disappears and the present acquires an exquisite color and exists within a frame of only now this second, exactly like the frames we make with our hands."

I saw she was drunk, but still I knew what she meant, knew she was right.

For a while, Jesse and Maggie slept every night on a different roof downtown. I couldn't imagine why they did this, so they took me to one. First we found the old metal fire escape, and Jesse jumped high up and pulled it down. Once we were up the stairs and onto the ladder, he pulled the stairs up after us. Then we climbed, high. It was eerie and magical looking out onto the estuary, the bay. There was still a faint pink sunset beyond the Golden Gate Bridge. Downtown Oakland was silent and deserted. "On weekends, it's just like *On the Beach* down here," Jesse said.

I was awed by the silence, by the sense of being the only ones there, the city beneath us, the sky all around. I was not sure where we were until Jesse called me over to a far ledge. "Look." I looked, and then I got it. It was my office, on the fifteenth floor of the Leyman building, a few floors above us. Only a few windows away was Brillig's. The small tortoise-shaded light was on. Brillig sat at his big desk with his jacket and tie off, his feet on a hassock. He was reading. Montaigne probably, because the book was bound in leather and he was smiling.

"This isn't a nice thing to do," Carlotta said. "Let's go."

"Usually you love to look at people in windows."

"Yes, but if you know who they are it is not imagining but spying."

Going back down the fire escape I thought that this typical argument was why I liked them. Their arguments were never petty.

Once I arrived when Joe and Jesse were still out fishing. Ben was there. Maggie had been crying. She handed me a letter from her fifteen-year-old Nathan. A sweet letter, telling her what they all were doing, saying that they wanted to come home.

"So, what do you think?" I asked Ben when she went to wash her face.

"I wish they'd get rid of the idea that it's Jesse or the kids. If she got a job and a house, stopped drinking, if he'd come by once in a while, they'd see it could be okay. It *could* be okay. Trouble is they're both scared that if the other one sobers up, they'll leave."

"Will she stop drinking if he leaves?"

"God no. I hate to think about that."

Ben and Joe went to a ball game that night. Joe always referred to them as the "fuckin' A's."

"*Midnight Cowboy*'s on TV. Want to come watch it?" Jesse asked. I said, sure, I loved that film. I thought they meant to go to a bar, forgetting about his age. No, they meant the Greyhound Bus Station, where we sat in adjoining seats, each with a little TV set we put quarters in. During the commercials Carlotta got more quarters, popcorn. Afterwards we went to a Chinese restaurant. But it was closing. "Yes, we always arrive when it's closing. That's when they order takeout pizza." How they had originally found this out I can't imagine. They introduced me to the waiter and we gave him money. Then we sat around a big table with the waiters and chefs and dishwashers, eating pizzas and drinking cokes. The lights were off; we ate by candlelight. They were all speaking Chinese, nodding to us as they passed around different kinds of pizzas. I felt somehow that I was in a real Chinese restaurant.

The next night Cheryl and I were meeting friends for dinner in Jack London Square. It was a balmy night, the top was down on the Porsche. We had had a good day, made love, lazed around in bed. As we got near the restaurant, Cheryl and I were laughing, in a good mood. We got stopped by one of the freight trains that invariably crawled through the Square. This one went on and on. I heard a shout.

"Counselor! Jon! Hey, barrister!" Jesse and Carlotta were waving to me from a boxcar, blowing kisses.

"Don't tell me," Cheryl said. "That must be Peter Pan and his ma." She said, "Jon's personal Bonnie and Clyde."

"Shut up."

I had never said that to her before. She stared straight ahead, as if she hadn't heard me. We went to the elegant restaurant with our elegant, articulate liberal friends. The food was excellent, the wines perfect. We talked about films and politics and law. Cheryl was charming; I was witty. Something terrible had happened between us.

Cheryl and I are divorced now. I think our marriage began to end because of those Friday nights, not because she began having an affair. She was furious because I never took her to meet them. I'm not sure why I didn't want to, whether I was afraid she would dislike them, or they would dislike her. Something else... some part of me that I was ashamed to let her see.

Jesse and Carlotta had already forgotten the boxcar when I next saw them.

"Maggie's hopeless. We could learn how to do it. We could travel all over the USA. But every time we start clickety clacking along, she gets hysterical. We've only got as far as Richmond and Fremont."

"No, once to Stockton. Far. It's terrifying, Jon. Although lovely too, and you do feel free, like it's your own personal train. Problem is, nothing scares Jesse. What if we ended up in North Dakota in a blizzard and they locked us in? There we'd be. Frozen."

"Maggie, you can't be worrying so much. Look what you do to yourself! Got your shorts in a knot about some snowstorm in South Dakota."

"North Dakota."

"Jon, tell her not to worry so much."

"Everything is going to work out, Carlotta," I said. But I was frightened too.

We checked out the watchman at the marina. At seven-thirty he was always at the other end of the piers. We'd toss our gear over and then climb the fence, down by the water where it wasn't wired for an alarm. It took us a few times before we found our perfect boat, "La Cigale." A beautiful big sailboat with a teak deck. Low in the water. We'd spread out our sleeping bag, turn the radio on low, eat sandwiches and drink beer. Sip whiskey later. It was cool and smelled like the ocean. A few times the fog lifted and we saw stars. The best part was when the huge Japanese ships filled with cars came up the estuary. Like moving skyscrapers, all lit up. Ghost ships gliding past not making a sound. The waves they made were so big they were silent, rolling, not splashing. There were never more than one or two figures on any of the decks. Men alone, smoking, looking out at the city with no expression at all.

Mexican tankers were just the opposite. We could hear the music, smell the smoky engines before we saw the rusty ships. The whole crew would be hanging off the sides, waving to girls on terraces of restaurants. The sailors were all laughing or smoking or eating. I couldn't help it, once I called out *Bienvenidos!* to them, and the watchman heard me. He came over and shined his flashlight at us.

"I seen you two here a coupla times. Figured you weren't hurtin' nobody, and weren't stealing, but you could get me in a mess of trouble."

Jesse motioned for him to come down. He even said, "Welcome aboard." We gave him a sandwich and a beer and told him if we got caught, we'd be sure to show there was no way he would have seen us. His name was Solly. He came every night then, for dinner at eight, and then he'd go on his rounds. He'd wake us early in the morning, before light, just as the birds were starting to whirr above the water.

Sweet spring nights. We made love, drank, talked. What did we talk about so much? Sometimes we'd talk all night long. Once we talked about the bad things from when we were little. Even acted them out with each other. It was sexy, scary. We never did it again. Our conversations were about people, mostly, the ones we met walking round town. Solly. I loved hearing him and Jesse tell about farm work. Solly was from Grundy Center, Iowa, had been stationed at Treasure Island when he was in the Navy.

Jesse never read books, but words people said made him happy. A black lady who told us she was as old as salt and pepper. Solly saying he up and left his wife when she started gettin' darty eyed and scissor billed.

Jesse made everybody feel important. He wasn't kind. Kind is a word like charity; it implies an effort. Like that bumper sticker about random acts of kindness. It should mean how someone always is, not an act he chooses to do. Jesse had a compassionate curiosity about everyone. All my life I have felt that I didn't really exist at all. He saw me. I. He saw who I was. In spite of all the dangerous things we did, being with him was the only time I was ever safe.

The dumbest dangerous thing we did was swim out to the island in the middle of Lake Merritt. We put all our gear, change of clothes, food, whiskey, cigarettes in plastic and swam out to it. Farther than it looks. The water was really cold, stinking foul dirty, and we stank too even when we changed clothes.

The park is beautiful during the day, rolling hills and old oak trees, the rose garden. At night it throbbed with fear and meanness. Horrible sounds came magnified to us across the water. Angry fucking and fighting, bottles breaking. People retching and screaming. Women getting slapped. The police and grunts, blows. The now familiar sound of police flashlights. Lap lap the waves against our little wooded island, but we shivered and drank until it quieted down enough for us to dare swim for shore. The water must have been really polluted, we were both sick for days.

Ben showed up one afternoon. I was alone. Joe and Jesse had gone to play pool. Ben grabbed me by the hair and took me to the bathroom.

"Look at your drunk self! Who are you? What about my brothers? Dad and his girl are on cocaine. Maybe with you they'd die in a car wreck or you'd burn the house down, but at least they wouldn't think drinking was glamorous. They need you. I need you. I need not to hate you." He was sobbing.

All I could do was what I had done a million times before. Say over and over, "I'm sorry."

But when I told Jesse we had to stop, he said ok. Why not smoking too while we were at it. We told the guys we were going backpacking near Big Sur. We drove down the hairpin Highway One above the water. There was a moon and the foam of the ocean was neon-white. Jesse drove with the lights off, which was terrifying and the start of our fighting. After we got there and up in the woods it began to rain. It rained and rained and we fought more, something about ramen noodles. It was cold but we both had bad shakes on top of that. We only lasted one night. We drove home and got drunk, tapered off before trying again.

This time was better. We went to Point Reyes. It was clear and warm. We watched the ocean for hours, quiet. We hiked in the woods, ran on the beach, told each other how great pomegranates tasted. We had been there about three days when we were awakened by weird grunts. Thrashing toward us in the foggy woods were these creatures, like aliens with oblong heads, making guttural sounds, weird laughs. They walked stiff-legged and with a rocking gait. "Good morning. Sorry to disturb you," a man said. The group turned out to be severely retarded teenagers. Their elongated heads were actually rolled-up sleeping bags on top of their packs. "Christ, I need a smoke," Jesse said. It was good to get home to Telegraph. We still didn't drink.

"Amazing how much time drinking took up, no, Maggie?"

We went to movies. Saw *Badlands* three times. Neither of us could sleep. We made love day and night, as if we were furious at each other, sliding off the silk sheets onto the floor, sweating and spent.

One night Jesse came into the bathroom when I was reading a letter from Nathan. He said they had to come home. Jesse and I fought all night. Really fought, hitting and kicking and scratching until we ended up sobbing in a heap. We ended up getting really drunk for days, the craziest we ever got. Finally I was so poisoned with alcohol that a drink didn't work, didn't make me stop shaking. I was terrified, panicked. I believed that I was not capable of stopping, of ever taking care of myself, much less my children.

We were crazy, made each other crazier. We decided neither of us was fit to live. He'd never make it as a musician, had already blown it. I had failed as a mother. We were hopeless alcoholics. We couldn't live together. Neither one of us was fit for this world. So we would just die. It is awkward to write this. It sounds so selfish and melodramatic. When we said it, it was a horrible bleak truth.

In the morning we got in the car, headed for San Clemente. I'd arrive at my parents' house on Wednesday. On Thursday I'd go to the beach and swim out to sea. This way it would be an accident and my parents could deal with my body. Jesse would drive back and hang himself on Friday, so Jon could find him.

We had to taper off drinking just to make the trip. We called Jon, Joe and Ben, to let them know we were going away, would see them next Friday. We took a slow trip down. It was a wonderful trip. Swimming in the ocean. Carmel and Hearst's Castle. Newport Beach.

Newport Beach was so great. The motel lady knocked on our door and said to me, "I forgot to give your husband the towels."

We were watching "Big Valley" when Jesse said, "What do you think? Shall we get married or kill ourselves?"

We were close to my parents' house when we got into a ridiculous fight. He wanted to see Richard Nixon's house before he dropped me off. I said that I didn't want one of the last acts in my lifetime to be seeing Nixon's house.

"Well, fuck off, get out here then."

I told myself that if he said he loved me I wouldn't get out, but he just said, "Let me see your smile, Maggie." I got out, got my suitcase from the back seat. I couldn't smile. He drove off.

My mother was a witch; she knew everything. I hadn't told them about Jesse. I had told them I had been laid off at school, the kids were in Mexico, that I was job hunting. But I had only been there for an hour when she said, "So, you planning to commit suicide, or what?"

I told them I was depressed about finding a job, that I missed my sons. I had thought a visit with them would be a good idea. But it just made me feel that I was procrastinating. I'd better go back in the morning. They were pretty sympathetic. We all were drinking a lot that evening.

The next morning my father drove me to the John Wayne Airport and bought me a ticket for Oakland. He kept saying that I should be a receptionist in a doctor's office, where I'd get benefits.

I was on the MacArthur bus headed for Telegraph about the time I was supposed to be drowning. I ran the blocks from Fortieth Street home, terrified now that Jesse had died already.

He wasn't home. There were lilac tulips everywhere. In vases and cans and bowls. All over the apartment, the bathroom, the kitchen. On the table was a note, "You can't leave me, Maggie."

He came up behind me, turned me around against the stove.

He held me and pulled up my skirt and pulled down my underpants, entered me and came. We spent the whole morning on
the kitchen floor. Otis Redding and Jimi Hendrix. "When a
Man Loves a Woman." Jesse made us his favorite sandwich.
Chicken on Wonder Bread with mayonnaise. No salt. It's an
awful sandwich. My legs were shaking from making love, my
face sore from smiling

We took a shower and got dressed, spent the night up on our
own roof. We didn't talk. All he said was, "It's much worse now."
I nodded into his chest.

Jon arrived the next night, then Joe and Ben. Ben was pleased
that we weren't drinking. We hadn't decided not to, just hadn't.
Of course they all asked about the tulips.

"Place needed some fucking color," Jesse said.

We decided to get Flint's Barbeque and go to the Berkeley
Marina.

"I wish we could take them to our boat," I said.

"I have a boat," Jon said. "Let's go out on my boat."

His boat was smaller than "La Cigale," but it was still nice.
We went out, using the engine, went all around the bay in the
sunset. It was beautiful, the cities, the bridge, the spray. We
went back to the pier and had dinner on deck. Solly walked past,
looked scared when he saw us. We introduced him to Jon, told
him he had taken us out on the water.

Solly grinned, "Boy, you two must have loved that. A boat
ride!"

Joe and Ben were laughing. They had loved it, being out in
the bay, the smell and freedom of it. They were talking about
getting a boat and living on it. Planning it all out.

"What's the matter with you guys?" Joe asked us. It was true.
The three of us were quiet, just sitting there.

"I'm depressed," Jon said. "I've had this boat for a year, and
this is the third time I've been out on it. Never have sailed the
damn thing. My priorities are all out of whack. My life is a mess."

"I'm..." Jesse shook his head, didn't finish. I knew he was sad for the same reason I was. This was a real boat.

Jesse said he didn't want to go to court. I told Carlotta I would be by for her really early. It was the time of gas rationing, so you never knew how long the lines would be. I picked her up on the corner by Sears. Jesse was with her, looking pale, hungover.

"Hey, man. Don't worry. It'll be fine," I said. He nodded.

She put a scarf over her hair. She was clear-eyed and apparently calm, wearing a dusty-rose dress, patent leather pumps, a little bag.

"Jackie O goes to court! The dress is perfect," I said.

They kissed goodbye.

"I hate that dress," he said. "When you get back I get to burn it." They stood looking at one another.

"Come on, get in the car. You're not going to jail, Carlotta, I promise."

We did have a long wait for gas. We talked about everything but the trial. We talked about Boston. The Grolier Book Shop. Lochober's restaurant. Truro and the dunes. Cheryl and I had met in Provincetown. I told her Cheryl was having an affair. That I didn't know what I felt. About the affair, about our marriage. Carlotta put her hand over mine, on the gearshift.

"I'm so sorry, Jon," she said. "The hardest part is not knowing how you feel. Once you do, well, then, everything will be clear to you. I guess."

"Thanks a lot." I smiled.

Both the policemen were in the courtroom. She sat across from them in the spectator section. I spoke with the prosecutor and the judge and we went to his chambers. The two of them looked hard at her before we went in.

It went like clockwork. I had page after page of documentation about the police, the paperwork from the security check which did not find marijuana. The judge got the idea about the police report even before I really got into it.

"Yes, yes, so what do you propose?"

"We propose to sue the San Francisco Police Department unless all charges are dismissed." He thought about it, but not for long.

"I think it appropriate to dismiss the charges."

The prosecutor had seen it coming, but I could tell he hated facing the policemen.

We got back into the courtroom where the judge said that because of a lawsuit pending against the San Francisco Police Department he felt it appropriate to drop all charges against Carlotta Moran. If the policemen had had flashlights, they would have bludgeoned Carlotta to death right there in the courtroom. She couldn't resist an angelic smile.

I felt let down. It had been so quick. And I had expected her to be happier, more relieved. If the other lawyer had handled the case, she'd be locked up now. I even said this to her, fishing for compliments.

"Hey, how about a little elation, er, gratitude?"

"Jon, forgive me. Of course I'm elated. Of course we're grateful. And I know what you charge. We really owe you thousands and thousands of dollars. More than that was that we got to know you, and you liked us. And we love you now." She gave me a warm hug then, a big smile.

I was ashamed, told her to forget the money, that it had gone beyond a case. We got into the car.

"Jon, I need a drink. We both need breakfast."

I stopped and bought her a half pint of Jim Beam. She took some big gulps before we got to Denny's.

"What a morning. We could be in Cleveland. Look around us." Denny's in Redwood City was like being in the heartland of America.

Let Me See You Smile

I realized that she was trying hard to show me she was happy. She asked me to tell her everything that happened, what I said, what the judge said. On the way home, she asked me about other cases, what were my favorites. I didn't understand what was going on until we were on the Bay Bridge and I saw the tears. When we got off the Bridge, I pulled over and stopped, gave her my handkerchief. She fixed her face in the mirror, looked at me with a rictus of a smile.

"So, I guess the party's over now," I said. I put the car top up just in time. It started to rain hard as we drove on toward Oakland.

"What are you going to do?"

"What do you advise, counselor?"

"Don't be sarcastic, Carlotta. It's not like you."

"I'm very serious. What would you do?"

I shook my head. I thought about her face, reading Nathan's letter. I remembered Jesse holding her throat.

"Is it clear to you? What you are going to do?"

"Yes," she whispered, "it's clear."

He was waiting on the corner by Sears. Soaking wet.

"Stop! There he is!"

She got out. He came over, asked how it went.

"Piece of cake. It was great."

He reached in and shook my hand. "Thank you, Jon."

I turned the corner and pulled over to the curb, watched them walk away in the drenching rain, each of them deliberately stomping in puddles, bumping gently into one another.

Mama

"Mama knew everything," my sister Sally said. "She was a witch. Even now that she's dead I get scared she can see me."

"Me too. If I'm doing something really lame, that's when I worry. The pitiful part is that when I do something right I'll hope she can. 'Hey mama, check it out.' What if the dead just hang out looking at us all, laughing their heads off? God, Sally, that sounds like something *she'd* say. What if I am just like her?"

Our mother wondered what chairs would look like if our knees bent the other way. What if Christ had been electrocuted? Instead of crosses on chains, everybody'd be running around wearing chairs around their necks.

"She told me 'whatever you do, don't breed,'" Sally said. "And if I were dumb enough to ever marry be sure he was rich and adored me. 'Never, ever marry for love. If you love a man you'll want to be with him, please him, do things for him. You'll ask him things like 'Where have you been?' or 'What are you thinking about?' or 'Do you love me?' So he'll beat you up. Or go out for cigarettes and never come back."

"She hated the word 'love.' She said it the way people say the word 'slut.'"

"She hated children. I met her once at an airport when all four of my kids were little. She yelled 'Call them off!' as if they were a pack of dobermans."

"I don't know if she disowned me because I married a Mexican or because he was Catholic."

"She blamed the Catholic church for people having so many babies. She said Popes had started the rumor that love made people happy."

"Love makes you miserable," our mama said. "You soak your pillow crying yourself to sleep, you steam up phone booths with your tears, your sobs make the dog holler, you smoke two cigarettes at once."

"Did Daddy make you miserable?" I asked her.

"Who, him? He couldn't make anybody miserable."

But I used Mama's advice to save my own son's marriage. Coco, his wife, called me, crying away. Ken wanted to move out for a few months. He needed his space. Coco adored him; she was desperate. I found myself giving her advice in Mama's voice. Literally, with her Texan twang, with a sneer. "Jes you give that fool a little old taste of his own medcin." I told her never to ask him back. "Don't call him. Send yourself flowers with mysterious cards. Teach his African Grey Parrot to say 'Hello, Joe!'" I advised her to stock up on men, handsome, debonair men. Pay them if necessary, just to hang out at their place. Take them to Chez Panisse for lunch. Be sure different men were sitting around whenever Ken was likely to show up, to get clothes or visit his bird. Coco kept calling me. Yes she was doing what I told her, but he still hadn't come home. She didn't sound so miserable though.

Finally one day Ken called me. "Yo, Mom, get this... Coco is such a sleaze. I go to get some CDs at our apartment, right? And here is this jock. In a purple Lycra bicycle suit, probably sweaty, lying on my bed, watching Oprah on my TV, feeding *my* bird."

What can I say? Ken and Coco have lived happily ever after. Just recently I was visiting them and the phone rang. Coco answered it, talked for a while, laughing occasionally. When she hung up Ken asked, "Who was that?" Coco smiled, "Oh, just some guy I met at the gym."

Mama

"Mama ruined my favorite movie, *The Song of Bernadette*. I was going to school at St. Joseph's then and planned to be a nun, or, preferably, a saint. You were only about three years old then. I saw that movie three times. Finally she agreed to come with me. She laughed all through it. She said the beautiful lady wasn't the Virgin Mary. 'It's Dorothy Lamour, for God's sake.' For weeks she made fun of the Immaculate Conception. 'Get me a cup of coffee, will you? I can't get up. I'm the Immaculate Conception.' Or, on the phone to her friend Alice Pomeroy, she'd say, 'Hi, it's me, the sweaty conception.' Or, 'Hi, this is the two-second conception.'"

"She was witty. You have to admit it. Like when she'd give panhandlers a nickel and say 'Excuse me, young man, but what are your dreams and aspirations?' Or when a cab driver was surly she'd say 'You seem rather thoughtful and introspective today.'"

"No, even her humor was scary. Through the years her suicide notes, always written to me, were usually jokes. When she slit her wrists she signed it Bloody Mary. When she overdosed she wrote that she had tried a noose but couldn't get the hang of it. Her last letter to me wasn't funny. It said that she knew I would never forgive her. That she could not forgive me for the wreck I had made of my life."

"She never wrote me a suicide note."

"I don't believe it. Sally, you're actually jealous because I got all the suicide notes?"

"Well, yes. I am."

When our father died Sally had flown from Mexico City to California. She went to Mama's house and knocked on the door. Mama looked at her through the window but she wouldn't let her in. She had disowned Sally years and years before.

"I miss Daddy," Sally called to her through the glass. "I am dying of cancer. I need you now, Mama!" Our mother just closed the venetian blinds and ignored the banging banging on her door.

Sally would sob, replaying this scene and other sadder scenes over and over. Finally she was very sick and ready to die. She had stopped worrying about her children. She was serene, so lovely and sweet. Still, once in a while, rage grabbed her, not letting her go, denying her peace.

So every night then I began to tell Sally stories, like telling fairy tales.

I told her funny stories about our mother. How once she tried and tried to open a bag of Granny Goose potato chips, then gave up. "Life is just too damn hard," she said and tossed the bag over her shoulder.

I told her how Mama hadn't spoken to her brother Fortunatus for thirty years. Finally he asked her to lunch at the Top of the Mark, to bury the hatchet. "In his pompous ole head!" Mama said. She got him though. He forced her to have pheasant under glass and when it came she said to the waiter, "Hey, boy, got any ketchup?"

Most of all I told Sally stories about how our mother once was. Before she drank, before she harmed us. Once upon a time.

"Mama is standing at the railing of the ship to Juneau. She's going to meet Ed, her new husband. On her way to a new life. It is 1930. She has left the depression behind, Granpa behind. All the sordid poverty and pain of Texas is gone. The ship is gliding, close to land, on a clear day. She is looking at the navy blue water and the green pines on the shore of this wild clean new country. There are icebergs and gulls.

"The main thing to remember is how tiny she was, only five foot four. She just *seemed* huge to us. So young, nineteen. She was very beautiful, dark and thin. On the deck of the ship she sways against the wind. She is frail. She shivers with cold and excitement. Smoking. The fur collar pulled up around her heart-shaped face, her jet black hair.

"Uncle Guyler and Uncle John had bought Mama that coat for a wedding gift. She was still wearing it six years later, so

I got to know it. Burying my face in the matted nicotine fur. Not while she was wearing it. She couldn't bear to be touched. If you got too close she'd put her hand up as if to ward off a blow.

"On the deck of the ship she feels pretty and grownup. She had made friends on the voyage. She had been witty, charming. The captain flirted with her. He poured her more gin that gave her vertigo and made her laugh out loud when he whispered, 'You're breaking my heart, you dusky beauty!'

"When the ship got into the harbor of Juneau her blue eyes filled with tears. No, I never once saw her cry either. It was sort of like Scarlett in *Gone with the Wind*. She swore to herself. No one is ever going to hurt me again.

"She knew that Ed was a good man, solid and kind. The first time she let him bring her home, to Upson Avenue, she had been ashamed. It was shabby; Uncle John and Granpa were drunk. She was afraid Ed wouldn't ask her out again. But he held her in his arms and said 'I am going to protect you.'

"Alaska was as wonderful as she had dreamed. They went in ski-planes into the wilderness and landed on frozen lakes, skied in the silence and saw elk and polar bears and wolves. They camped in the woods in summer and fished for salmon, saw grizzlies and mountain goats. They made friends; she was in a theatre group and played the medium in *Blithe Spirit*. There were cast parties and potlucks and then Ed said she couldn't be in the theatre any more because she drank too much, acted in a manner that was beneath her. Then I was born. He had to go to Nome for a few months and she was alone with a new baby. When he got back he found her drunk, stumbling around with me in her arms. 'He ripped you from my breast,' she told me. He completely took over my care, fed me from a bottle. An Eskimo woman came in to watch me while he was at work. He told Mama she was weak and bad, like all the Moynihans. He protected her from herself from then on, didn't let her drive or have any money. All she could do was walk to the library and read plays and mysteries and Zane Grey.

"When the war came you were born and we went to live in Texas. Daddy was a lieutenant on an ammunition ship, off of Japan. Mama hated being back home. She was out most of the time, drinking more and more. Mamie stopped working at Granpa's office so that she could take care of you. She moved your crib into her room; she played with you and sang to you and rocked you to sleep. She didn't let anybody near you, not even me.

"It was terrible for me, with Mama, and with Granpa. Or alone, most of the time. I got in trouble at school, ran away from one school, was expelled from two others. Once I didn't speak for six months. Mama called me the Bad Seed. All her rage came down on me. It wasn't until I grew up that I realized that she and Granpa probably didn't even remember what they did. God sends drunks blackouts because if they knew what they had done they would surely die of shame.

"After Daddy got back from the war we lived in Arizona and they were happy together. They planted roses and gave you a puppy called Sam and she was sober. But already she didn't know how to be with you and me. We thought she hated us, but she was only afraid of us. She felt it was we who had abandoned her, that we hated her. She protected herself by mocking us and sneering, by hurting us so we couldn't hurt her first.

"It seemed that moving to Chile would be a dream come true for Mama. She loved elegance and beautiful things, always wished they knew 'the right people.' Daddy had a prestigious job. We were wealthy now, with a lovely house and many servants and there were dinners and parties with all the right people. She went out some at first but she was simply too scared. Her hair was wrong, her clothes were wrong. She bought expensive imitation antique furniture and bad paintings. She was terrified of the servants. She had a few friends that she trusted; ironically enough she played poker with Jesuit priests, but most of the time she stayed in her room. And Daddy kept her there.

"'At first he was my keeper, then he was my jailer,' she said. He thought he was helping her, but year after year he rationed drinks to her and hid her, and never ever got her any help. We never went near her, nobody did. She'd fly into rages, cruel, irrational. We thought nothing we did was good enough for her. And she did hate to see us do well, to grow and accomplish things. We were young and pretty and had a future. Do you see? How hard it was for her, Sally?"

"Yes. It was like that. Poor pitiful Mama. You know, I'm like her now. I get mad at everyone because they are working, living. Sometimes I hate you because you're not dying. Isn't that awful?"

"No, because you can tell me this. And I can tell you I'm glad it's not me that is dying. But Mama never had a soul to tell anything to. That day, on the ship, coming into port, she thought she would. Mama believed Ed would be there always. She thought she was coming home."

"Tell me about her again. On the boat. When she had tears in her eyes."

"OK. She tosses her cigarette into the water. You can hear it hiss, as the waves are calm near the shore. The engines of the boat turn off with a shudder. Silently then, in the sound of the buoys and the gulls and the mournful long whistle of the boat they glide toward the berth in the harbor, banging softly against the tires on the dock. Mama smoothes down her collar and her hair. Smiling, she looks out at the crowd, searching for her husband. She has never before known such happiness."

Sally is crying softly. "Pobrecita. Pobrecita," she says. "If only I could have been able to speak to her. If I had let her know how much I loved her."

Me . . . I have no mercy.

Evening in Paradise

Sometimes years later you look back and say that was the beginning of… or we were so happy then… before… after… Or you think I'll be happy when… once I get… if we… Hernán knew he was happy now. The Oceano hotel was full, his three waiters were working at top speed.

He wasn't the kind of man who worried about the future or dwelt on the past. He shooed the chicle-selling kids out of his bar with no thought of his own orphaned childhood on the streets. Raking the beach, shining shoes.

When he was twelve they had started construction on the Oceano. Hernán ran errands for the owner. He idolized Señor Morales, who wore a white suit and a panama hat. Jowls that matched the bags under his eyes. After Hernán's mother died Señor Morales was the only person to call him by his name. Hernán. Not hey kid, *ándale hijo, véte callejero. Buenos días, Hernán.* As the building progressed Sr. Morales had given him a steady job cleaning up after the workers. When the hotel was finished he hired him to work in the kitchen. A room on the roof to live in.

Other men would have hired experienced employees from other hotels. The chefs and desk clerk at the new Oceano were from Acapulco but all of the other workers were illiterate street urchins like Hernán. They were all proud to have a room, their own real room on the roof. Showers and toilets for the men and women workers. Thirty years later every one of the men still worked at the hotel. The laundresses and maids had all come from mountain towns like Chacala or El Tuito. The women stayed until they married or until they got too homesick. New ones were always fresh young girls from the hills.

Socorro was from Chacala. The first day Hernán had seen her she was standing in her doorway in a white dress, her braids plaited with pink satin ribbon. She hadn't put down her rope-tied bundle of belongings. She was turning the light on and off. He was amazed by her sweetness. They smiled at each other. They were both fifteen and they both fell in love that very moment.

The next day Sr. Morales saw Hernán watching Socorro in the kitchen.

"She's a little beauty, no?"

"Yes," Hernán said. "I'm going to marry her."

He worked double shifts for two years until they could marry and move into a little house near the hotel. By the time their first daughter Claudia was born he was an apprentice bartender. After Amalia was born he was a regular bartender and Socorro stopped working. Their second daughter, Amalia, was having her quinceañera party in two weeks. Sr. Morales was godfather to both girls and was giving the party in the hotel. A bachelor, he seemed to love Socorro and the girls almost as much as Hernán, never tired of describing them to people.

"They are so fine, so beautiful. Delicate and pure and proud and…"

"Smart, strong, hard-working," Hernán would add.

"*Diós mío*…those women have hair… *tan, pero tan brilloso.*"

John Apple was at the bar as usual, looking out at the *malecón* above the beach. Trucks and buses rumbled by on the cobblestones outside. John nursed his beer, muttering.

"Smell those nasty fumes? What a racket. It's all over now, Hernán. No more paradise. The end of our fishy little sleeping village."

Hernán's English was very good but he missed things like John's remark. All he knew was that had been hearing it over and over for years. He ignored the sigh as John pretended again to drain his empty glass. Somebody else could buy him his next drink.

"Not the end," Hernán said. "A new Puerto Vallarta."

Dozens of luxury resorts were going up, the new highway was finished, the big airport just opened. Instead of one flight a week there were five or six international flights a day. Hernán had no regrets about how peaceful the town used to be, when this was the only good bar and he was the only one working in it. He liked having so many waiters to help. He was not even tired now when he got home, could have dinner with Socorro, read the paper, talk awhile.

More and more people were coming in. Hernán sent Memo to the kitchen to get bus boys to help out, to bring some extra chairs. Most of the guests at the hotel were reporters or cast and crew of *The Night of the Iguana*. Most of them were in the bar mingling with the "in" people from town, local Mexicans and Americans. Tourists and honey-mooners looked for Ava and Burton and Liz.

In those days one Mexican movie a week was shown on the plaza. There was no television so the town wasn't impressed by the cast of *The Night of the Iguana*. Everybody knew who Elizabeth Taylor was, though. Her husband Richard Burton was in the movie.

Hernán liked them and he liked the director, John Huston. The old man was always respectful to Socorro and to his daughters. He spoke Spanish to them and lifted his hat when he saw them in town. Socorro had her brother bring in *raicilla* from the mountains near Chacala, moonshine mescal for Sr. Huston.

Hernán kept it in a huge mayonnaise jar under the bar, tried to dole it out slowly, and to cut it as often as possible without Sr. Huston noticing.

Mexican lawyers and bankers were trying out their English on the blonde ingénue, Sue Lyons. Ruby and Alma, two American divorcées, were flirting with cameramen. Both women were very wealthy, owned houses on cliffs above the water. They kept on thinking they'd find romance at the Oceano bar. Usually they met married men on fishing trips or, now, newsmen or cameramen. No man that would ever want to stay around.

Alma was sweet and beautiful until late in the evening when her eyes and mouth turned into bruises and her voice became a sob, like she just wished you'd hit her and leave. Ruby was close to fifty, lifted and dyed and patched together. She was funny and fun but after she drank a lot she got mean and then limp and then Hernán had someone take her home. John Apple went over to sit with them. Alma ordered him a double margarita.

Luis and Victor stood at the entrance long enough to be noticed by everyone. They slid into the bar and sat down where they would be visible. Dark and handsome, they both wore tight white pants, open white shirts. Barefoot, with a bright bracelet on one ankle. White smiles, wet black hair. "*Ratoncitos tiernos.*" Tender little rats whores call the sexy young ones.

Hernán was already working in the Oceano kitchen when he had first known them as children. Begging from tourists, rolling drunks. They had originally come from Culiacán, called each other *Compa*, for *compadre*.

For years Luis and Victor had slept under *petates* in boats at night, hustled all day. Hernán understood them and didn't judge them, not even for stealing. The way they treated women didn't shock him. He judged the women though. One day he had seen Victor approach Amalia on the *malecón*. She was wearing the plaid skirt and white blouse from school, holding her books tightly against her new breasts. Hernán ran out from the bar and raced across the street. "Go home!" he said to Amalia. To Victor he said, "If you speak to either of my daughters again I will kill you."

Hernán poured martinis into chilled glasses, put them on Memo's tray. He left the bar and went over to the young men.

"*Quibo.* Why does it make me so nervous, seeing you two in my bar?"

"*Cálmate, viejo.* We've come to witness two historic events."

"Two? One must be Tony and the other Beto. What's with Beto?"

"He's coming to celebrate with the movie people. He got a part in *The Night of the Iguana.* Real money. *Lana.*"

"*No me digas!* Good for him. So now he's not just a beach boy. What's the part?"

"Playing a beach boy!"

"Watch him mess it up. I already know the other event. Tony's doing it to Ava Gardner."

"That's no event. *Fíjate.* There's the event!"

A magnificent new Chris Craft sprayed into the harbor, rocking the sunset-lit magenta water. Tony stood and waved, let go of the anchor of *La Ava.* A small boy in a rowboat went out to get him.

"*Híjola.* She actually bought it for him?"

"Title's in his name. She was waiting for him last night, naked in a hammock, had it taped to her tit. Guess what he did first."

"Went to see the boat."

The three of them laughed as the beautiful, unsteady Ava came down the stairs, smiling at everyone. She sat alone in a booth, waiting for Tony. Hernán was pleased that although everyone was looking at her and admiring her, nobody bothered her. My customers have manners, he thought.

Hernán went back to the bar, worked quickly to catch up. *Pobrecita.* She is shy. Lonely. He hummed a tune from a Pedro Infante movie. "Rich people cry too."

Hernán watched like everyone else when the lovers kissed hello. Flash bulbs flickered like sparklers throughout the room. The Americans all knew her, the whole town loved Tony. He was about nineteen now. He had streaks of blond in his long hair, amber eyes and an angelic smile. He had always worked on the boats unloading, loading, cadging rides, saving money for his own boat, someday, to take tourists water-skiing.

The stories differed. Some people said it happened in a dice game, others said he paid Diego cash to let him take the boats of movie stars to the set in Mismaloya every day. After about three days of his golden eyes gazing into her green ones she started taking boat rides with him on her breaks, until, Tony said, fortune had smiled upon him. Memo said that Tony was the lowest, a gigolo.

"Look at him," Hernán said. "He's in love. He won't hurt her."

Across the room Luis called out to an older American woman passing by the bar.

"Madam, please join us. I am Luis and this is Victor. Help us celebrate my birthday," he said.

"Why, I'd love to." She smiled, surprised. She ordered drinks, paid the waiter with a fistful of bills. She was laughing, pleased by their attention, took out all her purchases to show them.

Luis had grown out of beach-boying. He had a tiny dress shop that was the current rage. He sold colonial paintings and pre-columbian art. No one knew where he got them or who made them. He taught yoga to American women, the same ones who bought all his dresses in every color. It was hard to tell if Luis loved women or hated them. He made them feel good. He got money from all of them one way or another.

Memo asked Hernán if the women paid him to have sex with them. *Quién sabe?* He suspected that Luis took them out, brought them home and robbed them when they passed out. The women would be too embarrassed to tell. Hernán felt no compassion for the women. They asked for it. Traveling alone, drinking, giving themselves to the first *callejeros* they met.

Beto came in with Audrey, a hippy girl of about fifteen. Silken blonde hair, the face of a goddess. Newsmen were popping flashes and the blonde actress grew sullen. Audrey moved like honey. She had the blind eyes of a statue.

Victor came up to the bar to talk to someone. Hernán asked him what Audrey was on.

"Seconal, Tuinal, something like that"

"You don't sell to her, do you?"

"No. Anybody can get sleepers at the pharmacy. They keep her nice and quiet."

Beto was sitting with the crew. They were toasting him, trying to speak Spanish. He smiled and drank. Beto always wore the stupid expression of someone on a bus that just got woken up.

Sr. Huston motioned to Hernán for a *raicilla*. Hernán took the drink over himself, curious to know why the director was talking to Audrey so angrily. Sr. Huston thanked Hernán, sent regards to his family. Then he told Hernán that Audrey was the daughter of a dear friend, a great stage actress. Audrey had run away from home last year.

"Imagine how her mother feels. Audrey was younger than both your daughters when she disappeared."

Audrey pleaded with Sr. Huston not to tell where she was.

"Beto loves me. Finally somebody loves just me. And now Beto has a job. We can get an apartment."

"What drug are you on?"

"I'm sleepy, you silly. We're having a baby!"

She rose, kissed the old man. "Please," she said and went to sit a little behind Beto, singing softly to herself. Sr. Huston stood, stiffly, knocking over his chair. He stood over Beto, began to speak, then shook his head and strode out of the bar. He crossed the street to the *malecón*, where he sat smoking, looking at the water.

Hernán noticed that the newsmen and women and the movie crew all knew Victor; many stopped to talk with him. Victor went to the men's room often, before or after an American went in. He was the main marijuana connection in town, and had a few discreet heroin customers. This was different. No one went out afterwards for a stroll down the beach.

Hernán had heard that it had come to Acapulco. Well, now Puerto Vallarta has its own cocaine, he thought.

Sam Newman pulled up in a taxi, waved to Hernán as he went through the courtyard to register and have his bags sent up. He went over to Tony and Ava Gardner, hugged Tony and kissed Ava's hand. He stopped at tables along his way to the bar, shaking hands, kissing the women he knew, checking out the new ones, who all visibly cheered up. He was a handsome, easy-going American, married to a wealthy older woman who kept him on a loose rein. They lived down the coast in Yelapa. Sam came to town every few weeks for supplies and a rest. Living in paradise wore him out, he said. Grinning, he sat on a bar stool, handed Hernán a bag of Juan Cruz's coffee.

"Thanks, Sam. Socorro was missing her coffee." Hernán mixed him a double Bacardi and Tehuacán. "You come over on the *Paladín*?"

"Yes, unfortunately. Packed with tourists. And John Langley. Guess what he said."

"We're all in the same boat."

"He always says that. He's got a new one. We passed the movie set and this lady grabbed his arm. 'Sir, is that Mismaloya?' Langley removed her hand from his arm and said in that English snob way of his: 'Mr. Maloya to you, madam.' So, besides, Tony's boat, what's happening?"

Hernán told him about Beto's movie career and about Audrey being a runaway and pregnant and on drugs. He invited Sam to Amalia's *quinceañera* party. Of course Sam would be there, he said. Hernán was pleased.

"Sr. Huston is coming too. He is a great man, a man of dignity."

"It's cool that you know that. I mean without knowing that he really *is* a great man. A famous man."

Alma came up, kissed Sam on the lips. John Apple moved back to the bar and Sam bought him a double margarita.

Luis and the American woman were leaving in a cab. Victor was sitting with some reporters. Hernán didn't know what to do about Victor. He would never have him arrested, but he didn't want him dealing in the Oceano. He would ask Socorro tonight. She always knew exactly what to do.

"Sam, take me over to meet Ava Gardner, please," Alma said. "I want to invite her to stay at my house." She and Sam went and joined the enamored couple. On the way over Sam stopped to talk to Victor. They nodded to one another, looking down while they spoke.

Sr. Huston came back inside and sat in "his" large booth. Richard and Liz arrived. Wherever they went it was as if a grenade had been thrown through the window. Flashes exploded, people moaned and screamed, cried out, "Aah! Aah!" Chairs scraped and fell over, glass shattered. Running footsteps, running.

The couple smiled all around and waved, like for a curtain call, then sat with Sr. Huston in the booth. Liz blew a kiss to Hernán. He was already fixing a tray with a double margarita for her, *agua de Tehuacán* for Burton, who wasn't drinking. A *raicilla* cut with plain tequila for the director. Some guacamole and salsa, the way she liked it with plenty of garlic. She was cussing away. Hernán liked her; she was warm and bawdy. She and Burton had big booming laughs, were simply in it, each other, the place, life.

Little by little the bar emptied as people went to dress for dinner. They left walking or in one of the dozens of cabs outside the hotel. Victor went on foot with five or six men, heading north, to the "bad" part of town. Sam and Alma took off in her Jeep with Tony and Ava.

Ruby, Beto and Audrey were all fast asleep. John Apple offered to take them home in Ruby's car. Hernán knew John was thinking of her liquor cabinet and refrigerator. At least he was still in shape to drive. Memo and Raúl helped them out to the car.

Left in the bar were two old men, drinking Madero brandy in big snifters. They set up a chess board and began to play. A young honeymoon couple came in from a walk on the *malecón*, asked for wine coolers.

Hernán wiped down his bar, straightened and replaced bottles. Memo was already asleep, sitting up, as if at attention, on a chair by the kitchen. Hernán looked out at the sea and the palm trees, listening to Liz and Burton and John Huston. They were arguing, laughing, quoting lines from the movie, or other movies, maybe. When he took them fresh drinks Liz asked him if they were making too much noise.

"No, no," Hernán said, "It is wonderful to hear people talk about their work when they love what they do. You are very fortunate."

He sat down behind the bar with his feet up on a stool. Raúl brought him *café con leche* and *pan dulces*. He dunked the pastries in the coffee while he read the paper. There would be some nice quiet hours now. Maybe later some people would have nightcaps before they went to bed. Then he'd walk home, not far, where Socorro would be waiting for him. They would have dinner together and talk about their days and their nights, their daughters. He'd tell her all the gossip. They would argue. She always defended the women. She felt sorry for Alma and Ruby with no one to protect them. He would tell her about Victor and the drugs. Even Sam had seemed to be talking about drugs with him. Socorro would rub Hernán's back when they got into bed. They would laugh about something.

"God, I am fortunate." He said it out loud. He was embarrassed, looked around. Nobody had heard him. He smiled and said, "I am very fortunate!"

Evening in Paradise

"Hernán, are you lonesome? Over there talking to yourself?" Elizabeth Taylor called to him.

"I miss my wife. It's four more hours until I see her!"

They asked him to recommend a restaurant. He told them to go to the Italian place behind the church. Tourists never go, they think it's crazy to eat Italian food in Mexico. It is quiet and good.

They left and then the honeymooners and chess players went upstairs. Raúl slept opposite Memo outside the kitchen door. They looked like decorations, giant tourist puppets, in their black *boleros* and red sashes and moustaches.

Hernán was just about to fall asleep himself when a taxi door slammed. Luis got out with the American woman. She was falling-down drunk. Pancho went to help him get her upstairs and to her room. Luis didn't come back down.

Several minutes later there was the slam of another taxi door, a woman yelling "You dickhead!" and then Ava Gardner came in wearing only one high-heeled shoe so her walk made a hiccup sound through the courtyard and up the stairs. The same taxi door slammed again and Hernán was surprised to see Sam, with no shoes and no shirt. He had an enormous black eye, a cut and swollen lip.

"Which is her room?" "Top of stairs, second, ocean side." Sam went upstairs, changed his mind and came back down, his hand out for the drink Hernán held out for him. He spoke as if he had novocaine in his mouth, his lip was so swollen.

"Hernán. You can't tell a soul. My reputation will be in shreds. You see a disgraced man before you. Totally humiliated. I insulted her! Oh, God."

Another taxi, another slam. Tony came running in, tears streaming down his cheeks. He flew up the stairs and banged on her door. "*Mi vida! Mi sueño!*" Other doors opened all around. "Hush up, you fool! Shaddup! Shaddup!"

Tony came downstairs. He embraced Sam, apologized and shook his hand. He cried in little gasps, like a child.

"Sam, go talk to her. You can explain. I don't speak English. Tell her how it was too dark. Explain to her, please!"

"I don't know, Tony. She's really mad at me. Come on. You just go on in there and kiss her, let her see those alligator tears."

Hernán interrupted. "I don't know what went on. But I'll bet the lady won't even remember tomorrow what terrible thing happened tonight. Don't remind her!"

"Good thinking. Our man, Hernán." Sam went upstairs with Tony, opened Ava's door with a credit card, and gently pushed Tony into the room. He waited a little while but Tony didn't come out.

Sam stood in the cobblestone courtyard, holding up his card, talking to an invisible camera:

"Hi, there! I'm Sam Newman...world traveler, bon vivant, man-about-town. I wouldn't go anywhere without my American Express card."

"Sam, *qué haces?*"

"Nothing. Look, Hernán...You have to swear."

"On my mother's grave. Come on, tell me all about it."

"Well...Oh, God. So we get to Alma's and she tells the cook to make us dinner. We're out on her terrace, drinking more. Music playing. Tony doesn't have a head for alcohol, usually he never drinks. And I had barely started. But those two women were wasted. It was dark and we were all sort of lying around on those waterbed couches she has when Alma takes Tony by the hand and, well, she drags him into her bedroom. Ava is just looking at the stars, I'm panicking and then she notices they are gone, sits up like a shot, hauls me off with her to find them. Well, they're on Alma's bed, naked, balling away. I thought Ava might hit them with a blunt instrument but no she just smiles and leads me back to the terrace. Oh, Lord how have I failed? I am a disgrace. Sick. Right there in front of God and everybody Ava Gardner herself steps out of her dress and lies back on the sofa. Oh Lord, help me. My friend, that woman is magnificent. She is the color of butterscotch pudding, all over. Her breasts are heaven here on earth. Her legs, man she is the fuckin' Duchess of Alba! No. She is the Barefoot Contessa! So I tear off my clothes and lie down with her. And there she is. Ava, warm, in the flesh, looking into my eyes with those green ones I KNOW. My dick disappeared. It went to Tijuana, my balls took off for Ohio. And this Countess, this Goddess, she did everything possible. It was hopeless. I was dying of shame. I apologized and oh fuck like an IDIOT I said, 'Gee, I'm sorry. It's that I've been madly in love with you ever since I was a little kid!' She's the one who hit me in the lip. Then Tony shows up and really starts beating the shit out of me. Just then the damn cook comes in, turns on the light and says, 'Dinner is served.' I gave the cook some money and asked her to go find me a taxi, put my pants on and ran outside. The cook came back with a cab. I got in, then Ava got in after me. Tony was running down the street behind us, but she wouldn't let the guy stop. Ava Gardner. I could shoot myself."

Tony ran lightly down the steps and up to the bar.

"She forgives me, she loves me. She is sleeping now."

"Shall we go back for dinner?" Sam grinned. Tony was offended. Then after a while he said he was, in fact, dying of hunger. Memo had been awake, taking everything in. He said he was hungry too, they should go in the kitchen and fix breakfast.

Victor arrived alone, sat at a far table in the now dim light. Raúl took him hot chocolate and *pan dulces*. Victor never drank or took drugs. Hernán believed he must be very rich by now. Raúl told Victor that Luis was still upstairs. "I'll wait," he said.

Memo came out of the kitchen just as a few people came in for after-dinner drinks. Tony went over to wait for Luis with Victor. Tony had chocolate too and Hernán sent him over some aspirins. Tony didn't mention the evening to Victor, just talked about his new boat.

Sam came to the bar and ordered a Kahlua with brandy. He held his head between his hands. Hernán handed him the drink and said, "You need aspirin, too."

Luis came downstairs, carrying one of the woman's shopping bags. The three friends spoke in whispers, laughing like teen-aged boys. They left, loped effortlessly past the open windows of the bar, their laughter trailing back with the sound of the waves, easy and innocent.

"What was that clicking sound. *Maracas*?"

"Teeth. Luis took the woman's false teeth."

Hernán picked up Sam's empty glass, carefully wiped the circle where it had been.

"It's time for me to go home. Want some ice for that lip?"

"No, it's OK. Thanks. Goodnight, Hernán"

"Good night, Sam. *Hasta mañana.*"

Carmen

Outside every drugstore in town there were dozens of old cars with kids fighting in the back seat. I would see their mothers inside Payless and Walgreen's and Lee's, but we didn't greet each other. Even women I knew…we acted like we didn't. We waited in line while the others bought Terpin-Hydrate with codeine cough syrup and signed for it in a large awkward ledger. Sometimes we wrote our right names, sometimes made the names up. I could tell that, like me, they didn't know which was worse to do. Sometimes I'd see the same women at four or five drugstores a day. Other wives or mothers of addicts. The pharmacists shared our complicity, never acting like they knew us from before. Except once a young one at Fourth Street Drugs called me back to the counter. I was terrified. I thought he was going to report me. He was really shy and blushed when he apologized for interfering in my affairs. He said he knew I was pregnant and he was worried about me buying so much cough syrup. It had a high alcohol content, he said, and it could be easy for me to become an alcoholic without realizing it. I didn't say that it wasn't for me. I said thanks, but I began to cry as I turned and ran out of the store, crying because I wanted Noodles to be clean when the baby came. "How come you're crying, Mama? Mama's crying!" Willie and Vincent were jumping around the back seat. "Sit down!" I reached around and whacked Willie on the head. "Sit down." I'm crying because I'm tired and you guys won't be still."

There had been a big bust in town and a bigger one in Culi-
acón, so there was no heroin in Albuquerque. Noodles at first
had told me he would taper off on the cough syrup and stay
clean, so he'd be clean when the baby came in two months.
I knew he couldn't. He'd never been so strung out before and
now he had hurt his back at a construction job. At least he had
disability.

He was on his knees, talking, had crawled to get the phone.
I know, I know, I've been to the meetings. I'm sick too, an
enabler, a co-addict. All I can say is I felt love, pity, tenderness
for him. He was so thin, so sick. I would do anything for him
not to hurt this way. I knelt down and put my arms around him.
He hung up the phone.

"Fuck, Mona, they've busted Beto," he said. He kissed me and
held me, called the kids over and hugged them. "Hey, you guys,
give your old man a hand, be my crutches to the bathroom."
When the boys left I went in and shut the door. He was shaking
so bad I had to pour the cough syrup into his mouth. The smell
made me retch. His sweat, his shit, the whole trailer smelled of
rotten oranges from the syrup.

I fixed dinner for the boys and they watched "Man from
U.N.C.L.E." on TV. All the kids in school wore levis and T-shirts
except Willie. In third grade, and he wore black pants and a white
shirt. His hair was combed like the blond guy on TV. The boys
had bunk beds in a tiny room, Noodles and I slept in the other
bedroom. I already had a bassinet at the foot of our bed, diapers
and baby clothes in every spare nook. We owned two acres in
Corrales, near the clear ditch, in a grove of cottonwoods. At first
we had plans to start building our adobe house, plant vegetables, but just after we got the land Noodles got strung out again.
Most of the time he was still working construction, but nothing
had happened about the house and now winter was coming.

I made a cup of cocoa and went out on the step. "Noodles,
come see!" But he didn't answer. I heard the twist of another

syrup cap. There was a gaudy splendid sunset. The vast Sandia mountains were a deep pink, the rocks on the foothills red. Yellow cottonwoods blazed on the river-bank. A peach-colored moon was already rising. What's the matter with me? I was crying again. I hate to see anything lovely by myself. Then he was there, kissing my neck and putting his arms around me.

"You know they are called the Sandias because they are shaped like watermelons." "No," I said, "it's because of the color!" We had that argument on our first date, have repeated it a hundred times. He laughed and kissed me, sweet. He was fine now. That's the lousy thing about drugs, I thought. They work. We sat there watching nighthawks sweep across the field.

"Noodles, don't have any more terps. I'll stash the rest of the bottles, give it to you just when you get sick. OK?"

"OK." He wasn't hearing me. "Beto was going to score in Juarez, from La Nacha. Mel is down there. He'll test it. He can't bring it. He can't cross the border. I need you to go. You are the perfect person to do it. You're Anglo, pregnant, sweet-looking. You look like a nice lady."

I am a nice lady, I thought.

"You'll fly to El Paso, take a cab over the border and then fly back. No problem."

I remembered waiting in the car outside the building where La Nacha lived, being afraid in that neighborhood.

"I'm the worst person to go. I can't leave the kids. I can't go to jail, Noodles."

"You won't go to jail. That's the point. Connie'll keep the kids. She knows you have family in El Paso. There could be an emergency. The kids would love to go to Connie's."

"What if narcs stop me, ask me what I'm doing there?"

"We still have Laura's ID. It looks like you, maybe not so pretty but you're both gueras with blue eyes. You'll have a ratty piece of paper with 'Lupe Vega' scrawled on it and an address next door to Nacha's. Say you're looking for your maid, she hasn't shown, she owes you money, something like that. Just act dumb, have them help you look for her."

I finally agreed to go. He said Mel would be there and to watch him try it out. "You'll know if it's good." Yes, I knew the look of a good rush. "Whatever you do, don't leave Mel alone in the room. You leave alone, though, not even with Mel. Have your own cab come back for you in an hour. Don't let them call you a cab."

I got ready to go, called Connie and told her my Uncle Gabe had died in El Paso, could she keep the kids for the night, maybe another day. Noodles gave me a thick envelope with money in it, taped closed. I packed a bag for the boys. They were happy to go. Connie's six kids were like cousins. When I took them to the door Connie shooed them inside, came out onto the porch and hugged me. Her black hair was up in tin rollers, like a kabuki headdress. She wore cutoffs and a T-shirt, looked about fourteen.

"You don't ever have to lie to me, Mona," she said.

"Did you ever do this?"

"Yeah, lots of times. Not after I had children. You won't do it again, I'll bet. Take care. I'll pray for you."

It was still hot in El Paso. I walked across the sinking soft tarmac from the plane, smelling the dirt and sage I remembered from childhood. I told the cab driver to take me to the bridge, but first drive around the alligator pond.

"Alligators? Them old alligators died off years ago. Still want to see the plaza?"

"Sure," I said. I leaned back and watched the neighborhoods flash by. There were changes but as a kid I had skated over this whole city so many times that it seemed I knew every old house and tree. The baby was kicking and stretching. "You like my old hometown?"

"What's that?" the cab driver asked.

"Sorry, I was talking to my baby."

He laughed. "Did he answer?"

I crossed the bridge. I was still happy just with the smells of woodfires and caliche dirt, chili and the whiff of sulfur from the smelter. My friend Hope and I used to love to give smart answers when the border guards asked our nationality. Transylvanian, Mozambican.

"USA," I said. Nobody seemed to notice me. Just in case, I didn't take any of the cabs by the border but walked some more blocks. I ate some *dulce de membrillo*. Even as a kid I didn't like it, but liked the idea that it came in a little balsa box and you used the lid for a spoon. I looked at all the silver jewelry and shell ashtrays and Don Quijotes until I made myself get into a cab and hand him the piece of paper with Lupe's name and the wrong address. "*Cuanto*?"

"Twenty dollars"

"Ten."

"*Bueno*." Then I could no longer pretend I wasn't scared. He drove fast for a long time. I recognized the deserted street and the stucco building. He stopped a few doors down. In broken Spanish I asked him to be back in an hour. For twenty dollars. "OK. *Una hora*."

It was hard climbing the stairs to the fourth floor. I was big with the baby and my legs were swollen and sore. I caught my breath in sobs at each landing. My knees and hands were shaking. I knocked on the door of #43. Mel opened it and I stumbled in.

"Hey, sweetheart, what's happening?"

"Water, please." I sat on a dirty vinyl sofa. He brought me a Diet Coke, wiped the top with his shirt, smiled. He was dirty, handsome, moved like a cheetah. A legend by now, escaping from jails, jumping bond. Armed and dangerous. He brought me a chair to put my feet up on, rubbed my ankles.

"Where is La Nacha?" The woman was never referred to just as Nacha. "The Nacha," whatever that meant. She came in, dressed in a black man's suit and a white shirt. She sat at a chair behind a desk. I couldn't tell if she was a male transvestite or a woman trying to look like a man. She was dark, almost black, with a Mayan face, red-black lipstick and nail polish, dark glasses. Her hair was short, slick. She held a stubby hand out to Mel without looking at me. I handed him the money. I saw her count the money.

That's when I got afraid, really afraid. I had thought I was getting drugs for Noodles. All I cared about was him not being sick. I had thought there was maybe a big wad of tens, twenties in the packet. There were thousands of dollars in La Nacha's hand. He hadn't just sent me to get shit for him. I was making a big, dangerous score. If they caught me it would be as a dealer not a user. Who would take care of the boys? I hated Noodles.

Mel saw that I was shaking. I think I even gagged. He fished around in his pockets, came up with a blue pill. I shook my head. The baby.

"Oh, for Christ's sake. It's just a valium. You'll mess that baby up worse if you don't take it. Take it. Get it together! You hear me?"

I nodded. His scorn shook me. I was calm even before the pill worked.

"Noodles told you I was going to test the shit. If it's good I'll say so and you just take the balloon and leave. You know where to put it?" I knew but would never do that. What if it broke and got to the baby?

He was a devil, could read my mind. "If you don't put it there I will. It's not going to break. Your baby is all wrapped up in a drug-proof bag, safe against every evil of the outside world. Once he's born, sugar, hey, that's another story."

Mel watched as La Nacha weighed the packet and nodded as she handed it to him. She had never looked at me. I watched Mel shoot up. Put cottons and water into a spoon, sprinkle a pinch of brown heroin into it, cook it. Tie up, hit a vein in his hand, blood backing up then plunge and the tie falling off as his face instantly stretched back. He was in a wind tunnel. Ghosts were flying him into another world. I had to pee, I had to throw up. "Where's the bathroom?" La Nacha motioned to the door. I found the bathroom down the hall by the smell. When I got back I remembered that I wasn't supposed to leave Mel alone. He was smiling. He handed me the condom, rolled up into a ball.

"Here you go, precious, you have a good trip. Go on now, put it away like a good girl." I turned around and acted like I was shoving it inside myself but it was just inside my too-tight underpants. Outside, in the dark of the hall I moved it to my bra.

I took the steps slowly, like a drunk. It was dark, filthy.

At the second landing I heard the door open downstairs, noises from the street. Two young boys ran up the stairs. "*Fíjate no más!*" One of them pinned me to the wall, the other got my purse. Nothing was in it but loose bills, makeup. Everything else was in a pocket inside my jacket. He hit me.

"Let's fuck her," the other one said.

"How? You need a dick four feet long."

"Turn her around, *bato.*"

Just as he hit me again a door opened and an old man came running down the stairs with a knife. The boys turned and ran back outside. "Are you well?" the man asked in English.

I nodded. I asked him to go with me. "I hope there is a taxi outside."

"You wait here. If it's there I'll have him use the horn three times."

Your mother did teach you to be a lady, I thought when I wondered about the etiquette. Should I offer him money? I didn't.

His toothless smile was sweet as he opened the taxi door for me.

"*Adiós.*"

I was nauseous on the little twin-engine plane to Albuquerque. I smelled like sweat and the couch and the pee-stained wall. I asked for an extra sandwich and nuts and milk.

"Eatin' for two now!" the Texan across from me grinned.

I drove from the airport home. I'd get the boys after I had a shower. As I drove down the dirt road toward our trailer I could see Noodles in his pea jacket, pacing and smoking outside.

He looked desperate, didn't even come to greet me. I followed him inside.

He sat at the edge of the bed. On the table his outfit was ready and waiting. "Let me see it." I handed him the balloon. He opened the cupboard above the bed and put it on the tiny scale. He turned and slapped me hard across the face. He had never hit me before. I sat there, numb, next to him. "You left Mel alone with it. Didn't you. Didn't you."

"There is enough there to have put me away for a long time," I said.

"I told you not to leave him. What am I going to do now?"

"Call the police," I said, and he slapped me again. This one I didn't even feel. I got a strong contraction. Braxton-Hicks, I thought to myself. Whoever was Braxton-Hicks? I sat there, sweating, stinking of Juarez and watched him pour the contents of the rubber into a film canister. He shook some onto the cottons in his spoon. I knew with a sick certainty that always if there were a choice between me and the boys or drugs, he'd go for the drugs.

Hot water gushed down my legs onto the carpet. "Noodles! My water is breaking! I have to go to the hospital." But by then he had fixed. The spoon made a clink onto the table, his rubber tube fell from his arm. He leaned back against the pillow. "At least it's good shit," he whispered. I got another contraction. Strong. I tore off the filthy dress and sponged myself, put on a white *huipil*. Another contraction. I called 911. Noodles had nodded out. Should I leave him a note? Maybe he'd call the hospital when he woke. No. He would not think of me at all.

First thing he'd do, he'd shoot up what was left in the cottons, have another little taste. I tasted copper in my mouth. I slapped his face but he didn't move.

I opened the can of heroin, holding it with a Kleenex. I poured a large amount into the spoon. I added a little water, then closed his beautiful hand around the can. There was another bad contraction. Blood and mucus were sliding down my legs. I put a sweater on, got my Medi-cal card and went outside to wait for the ambulance.

They took me straight to the delivery room. "The baby's coming!" I said. The nurse took my medical card, asked questions, phone, husband's name, how many live births, what was my due date.

She examined me. "You're totally dilated, the head is right here."

Pains were coming one after another. She ran to get a doctor. While she was gone the baby was born, a little girl. Carmen. I leaned down and picked her up. I laid her, warm and steaming, on my stomach. We were alone in the quiet room. Then they came and wheeled us careening into the big lights. Somebody cut the cord and I heard the baby cry. An even worse pain as the placenta came out and then they were putting a mask over my face. "What are you doing? She is born!"

"The doctor is coming. You need an episiotomy." They tied my hands down.

"Where is my baby? Where is she?" The nurse left the room. I was strapped to the sides of the bed. A doctor came in. "Please untie me." He did and was so gentle I became frightened. "What is it?"

"She was born too early," he said, "weighed only a few pounds. She didn't live. I'm sorry." He patted my arm, awkwardly, like patting a pillow. He was looking at my chart. "Is this your home number? Shall I call your husband?"

"No," I said. "Nobody's home."

Romance

after Chekhov

Snowflakes fell as Morris and Sylvia kissed on the steps. He unlocked the two locks to the entrance of his Riverside Drive apartment. They went inside, shaking themselves like wet dogs, laughing, kissing again on each landing as they climbed the stairs to the fourth floor. Two more locks then and at last they were inside and naked and making love on the slippery rug inside the door.

"Don't leave. I can't bear for you to leave again," Morris whispered. She nodded into his hairy chest.

"There's such little time. It hurts too much to say goodbye." She was crying, but then she smiled.

"My ear is full of tears!"

He kissed her ear, licking the salty tears. "My darling!" he said. "When you live with me you'll never have tears in your ears. I swear."

Don't laugh. This is how people talk when they are in love. Morris and Sylvia were very much in love.

Morris was a professor at NYU. Sylvia was a speech therapist in San Francisco. Each of them was divorced, each had an eight-year-old child. Morris had a son, Seth, and Sylvia a daughter, Sarah. Each of them had an ex-spouse who had joint custody of the child. Neither ex-spouse would allow their child to leave the state. You could call it a Nineties kind of romance. Back in the Sixties people got divorced, the mother got the children, never got the child support and never heard from the father again. People are better parents now. Morris and Sylvia were good parents. Neither of them, no matter how much they loved the other, would do anything to upset their children, and would never consider leaving them.

It was painful because they missed each other badly, because it was so wonderful when they were together. They belonged with each other and that was that. All their money was spent on cross-country plane tickets, and on daily phone calls.

Morris's sister, Shirley, and Sylvia's best friend, Cassandra tried to talk the lovers into breaking up.

"Morris, you know I think she is marvelous," his sister said. "Absolutely stunning, too."

Cassandra said, "Sylvia, you know I adore him."

"But," they both said, "it's simply not going to work. End it and get on with your life. You'll meet someone here, who will love you just as much. Maybe have more money. Anybody would adore your child, and you, of course. Get your life back to normal and stop this constant longing and suffering."

"No," Morris said to his sister. "There is no one in this world I could love more than Sylvia. She is the most beautiful, intelligent woman I've ever known. She's brave, she's witty. She's so strong. Why, she's a...pioneer!"

"No," Sylvia said to Cassandra. "There is no other man as wonderful as Morris. He is intact and self-confident. He is brilliant, talented. He listens to me and talks to me. He's a...Why, he's my hero."

Indeed as the affair stretched into a second year the two seemed more in love than ever. They had long conversations every night about their children's problems and successes, about politics and books and movies and life. They gossiped about family and friends. They spoke about their passion and longing, which only increased as time went by.

Romance

During each of their five or six visits a year they never lapsed into comfortable silences as people do once the honeymoon is over. There was so little time. Five days, a week. They had too many places to go, friends each wanted the other to meet. They had a million things to talk about. They either agreed or disagreed completely. Even disagreeing was wonderful as they both loved to fight. And sex. They couldn't get enough of each other. Between talking and making love, neither slept more than three hours a night.

Morris still lay on top of her on the thin rug. There was a draft from under the door and the floor was cold. They would go take a long hot shower, where they were bound to make love again. He laughed, "I'm still holding onto the keys."

Sylvia sighed. "You know what I wish? I wish I had keys to your apartment. Can I have my own keys?"

"That's silly. I'm always here when you are. I don't want you out of my sight for a minute. Why would you want keys? God. I have a hundred keys. I'd like to throw all mine away."

"Because then at home I could look at them and they'd be the keys to your place in New York. I'd feel connected, committed. I don't know why but it would make our relationship seem less... precarious."

"Our relationship is not precarious. It is the one thing in my life I am totally sure of," he said, solemnly.

The next few days he had the care of Seth. The three of them had fun. They went to the planetarium and the Bronx Zoo, rode the tour boat around Manhattan. Seth and Sylvia were comfortable friends by now. They all played Parcheesi and Monopoly, watched *The Black Stallion*. When he left, Seth hugged Sylvia warmly. "Come back soon, Tiger Lily."

"Tiger Lily?" she asked.

"I heard my Dad call you that on the phone."

"That's true. It was once when he sent me a bouquet of tiger lilies."

"Oh, God," Morris said later. "I hate the thought of him telling *her* that I called you 'Tiger Lily.' Or that I sent you flowers. I never sent anyone flowers until I met you."

"Really. How terrible. You poor thing."

"I suppose men have always sent you flowers, all your life."

"Yes," she smiled, not really lying.

The last day was always the worst. They would commiserate about all the work they had to make up. The classes he had missed, the appointments she had canceled. He had to have a serious talk with his publisher, she had an important conference the next afternoon at four, then pick up Sarah.

"Let me help you," she said. "Or, no, you work.... I'll read the paper. Come on, let's get up and you get to work."

"No. Don't move. I don't ever want to let you out of my arms." He kissed her throat. She moaned.

That night they had dinner in a Thai restaurant. They didn't get a cab home but walked uptown for miles in the clear cold night, their footsteps crunching in unison on fresh snow. Her hand held his inside his pocket.

When they got to the door he started to open the locks.

"Wait," he said. He fished inside his jacket, handed her a set of keys.

"These are your keys. Go on, you open the door."

"Oh, thanks! You dear!" she cried. Her heart was filled with tenderness for him.

They woke at six, exhausted and cold and sore and sad. He made coffee while she showered and packed. She had insisted that he not go with her to the airport. He had work to do, besides it was too painful. She would take a cab. He gave her forty dollars.

"Thanks," she said. "I haven't a cent. Thank heavens Cassandra is meeting me."

They had a bagel and orange juice while they waited for the taxi. They ate in silence; they were miserable. They both wished the cab would hurry. It was that awful period after you have said "goodbye" and "I love you" a hundred times and now wanted it over with.

Morris took her bags downstairs and handed them to the driver, a smiling swarthy man in a red turban. Morris was still in his bathrobe so he blew her a kiss from the doorway.

Once in the cab Sylvia was crying so hard she didn't notice the traffic or where they were going. She couldn't understand, and didn't care, what the driver was saying to her. She was very unhappy. She looked in her purse for more Kleenex, felt the keys Morris had given her and began weeping freshly.

When the cab had driven out of sight Morris leaned his head against the cold frosted glass of the door. "Goodbye, my sweet sweet Sylvia," he said.

He turned and ran, panting, up the three flights of stairs. He showered and dressed, made fresh coffee. He took a mug to his desk, placed a large stack of students' manuscripts in front of him, sharpened three pencils and began to work. He glanced from time to time at the clock. At nine he could call his publisher, at ten his agent.

Morris read carefully, chuckling or cursing, writing rapidly in margins in his firm clear hand. But the unread stack was still high when he called the publisher.

Unexpected bad news. They didn't like the new proposal, didn't want to give him an advance. Never mind the advance, he thought, although he minded it a great deal. This would be a fine book, ten times better than his last one. What fools! He had been so sure they would like it. The disappointment felt like a physical blow.

Morris suddenly was weak with worry. He was very much in debt. Money for Seth's expenses, credit card debts for plane tickets, phone bills. He was late with the outrageous child support payment. Oh, God.

He drank some more coffee, had another bagel, this one with apricot jam. He had skipped his office hours yesterday because Sylvia was there, had six appointments this afternoon. Then dinner with Milo. Very pressing things to discuss with Milo about restructuring the department. Where were the notes he had made? Oh, no, I couldn't have left them at my office. He searched frantically through his briefcase, found the notes and went back to reading the students' work. He desperately needed a nap. Was he too old for Sylvia?

The phone rang. Better not answer it. Very wise decision. The nasal whine of his ex-wife Zelda on the answering machine.

"Morris, dear, I'm sure you're busy shtupping Ms. Tiger Lily, or perhaps out shopping. Just want to remind you that your son's tuition and music are both overdue and I need money to feed and clothe him."

Ten o'clock. Russell may be in by now. He direct-dialed his agent. "Yes. I'll hold." He held, continuing to read and sip coffee.

When Sylvia came in, Morris was talking loudly, pacing around the apartment with the phone cord trailing after him.

"...possibly make that kind of concession...no, not at all... it would be counter to the basic premise of the thing. Surely you..." He was listening, then, red-faced, but finally noticed Sylvia and heard her saying, "Morris. Morris!" Frowning, he waved at her to be quiet, turned away and spoke angrily into the phone.

"I'm counting on you to reason with him. Hey, hold on a minute." He looked at Sylvia. "What are you doing here?"

"I missed the plane."

"You couldn't miss the plane." To the phone he said, "I'll call you back."

"Morris, I need sixty dollars for the taxi."

"You can't need sixty dollars. It's thirty-five, forty with a tip."

"It fifty-five dollar. Five dollar no big tip. Need more tip. Big bags," said the man in the doorway who looked just like the other cab driver, but it was only because he too wore a red turban.

"For Christ's sake."

He went to his wallet but there was only forty. Maybe in my jacket. Yes. He paid the driver who said, "This is lousy tip. Wait all this long time."

"How in Christ's sake did you miss the plane? You left two hours early!"

"Don't scream at me, Morris. I didn't do it on purpose. There was a problem on the expressway. The driver got lost in Yonkers..."

"Great title."

"I tried to call you but your phone was busy busy, then I called the wrong number and didn't even have another quarter to my name. So, foolishly, I came here. I am very lucky that I don't have to buy another ticket."

"So there'll be another cab ride. A hundred and fifty dollars in one day on taxis! How could it cost you fifty-five dollars to get from the airport?"

"He didn't know where Riverside Drive was, that's why. I cannot believe you can be standing there haggling about money at a time like this. I missed my conference. I won't be picking up Sarah. He'd love full custody of her. He'll say this shows how irresponsible I am."

"You *are* irresponsible! You have no concept of money. How can you not have more than a quarter on you?"

"Because all my money goes on visiting you! And, believe me, Sarah and I don't go to plays or restaurants like you do. We live simply. In a tenement. I'm dressed in rags!"

"You have a lovely apartment. And I wouldn't call Ralph Lauren or Ann Klein rags. Poor little match girl!"

"Don't patronize me, you asshole!"

"I cannot believe you would use such an expression."

"Perhaps I have never had the occasion before. Look, what do you suggest I do? I have no money. I can't get a flight until midnight. Meanwhile I have to call home. Don't worry. I'll use my card."

Morris caught her hand, pulled her into his arms. "Darling, this is our first fight! Forgive me. I've had a lousy morning, have so much work to do..."

She was sobbing. "I really needed to be at that meeting. And Sarah was upset about me leaving in the first place, and now you act like I'm the last person you want to see."

"Don't cry, please don't cry. You know what the problem really is? We're both worn out. How about you go have a bath and a nap. We'll have a late lunch before I go to my appointments."

"Your appointments?"

"Yes. I have to go. I didn't go to class or my office for three days. I simply have to go today. And I have to see Milo for dinner."

"I see. May I please use your phone?"

"Sure. Go ahead."

But just then the phone rang. It was Russell, his agent.

"Oh, hi. Hang on a minute." Morris took the phone into the bedroom and closed the door. She couldn't believe it. They had always shared everything. She saw the place with half a bagel and apricot jam. He never ate jam.

She listened, realized he was off the phone. He was sitting on the edge of the bed as she sat down. She began to dial, not noticing how miserable he was.

"I'd think you would at least ask about my book," he said.

She hung up the phone and thought about it. "What I'm asking myself is why you waited until I left to find out about the book."

"I don't know. Maybe because I was afraid it would be bad news, and didn't want to spoil your visit."

"You didn't want my visit to compete with your life. I'm so foolish. I thought we shared everything. Excuse me. I have calls to make."

Morris forced himself to get to work on the student papers. When she had finished calling she came into the room where he was working. She stood, hoping he would turn around but he didn't.

Finally, hours later, he finished working and went into the bedroom. She lay on the bed, asleep, covered with his robe. He kissed her cheek, but she didn't stir.

When she did wake up he was gone. There was fifty dollars on the desk and a note. "Had to meet with students. Didn't want to wake you. Back at five. I love you, M."

It was snowing. She stared out the window. The phone rang. She let it ring, listened to the messages.

"Morris, dear. Why don't you answer my calls? Please, tear yourself away from Ms. Anorexia or Tiger Lily or whomever. I need child support money immediately." Crash.

"Hi, darling. It's Amy. Milo says you two are meeting to revamp. I have ideas too, so I'll drop by Enrico's tonight in time for lots of brandy. Ciao."

Although he was nearly faint with fatigue, Morris took the stairs three at a time when he got home from school.

"Sylvie?"

No answer. She wasn't there. A note was scrawled in pencil, beneath the house keys. "I will never see you again."

In Mexico they say that the baby's true baptism occurs when he first falls off the bed. The romance between Morris and Sylvia began on that snowy day in Manhattan.

Silence

I started out quiet, living in mountain mining towns, moving too often to make a friend. I'd find me a tree or a room in an old deserted mill, to sit in silence.

My mother was usually reading or sleeping so I spoke mostly with my father. As soon as he got in the door or when he took me up into the mountains or down dark into the mines, I was talking nonstop.

Then he went overseas and we were in El Paso, Texas, where I went to Vilas school. In third grade I read well but I didn't even know addition. Heavy brace on my crooked back. I was tall but still childlike. A changeling in this city, as if I'd been reared in the woods by mountain goats. I kept peeing in my pants, splashing until I refused to go to school or even speak to the principal.

My mother's old high school teacher got me in as a scholarship student at the exclusive Radford School for Girls, two bus rides across El Paso. I still had all of the above problems but now I was also dressed like a ragamuffin. I lived in the slums and there was something particularly unacceptable about my hair.

I haven't talked much about this school. I don't mind telling people awful things if I can make them funny. It was never funny. Once at recess I took a drink from a garden hose and the teacher grabbed it from me, told me I was common.

But the library. Every day we got to spend an hour in it, free to look at any book, at every book, to sit down and read, or go

83

through the card catalogue. When there were fifteen minutes left the librarian let us know, so we could check out a book. The librarian was so, don't laugh, soft-spoken. Not just quiet but nice. She'd tell you, "This is where biographies are," and then explain what a biography was.

"Here are reference books. If there is ever anything you want to know, you just ask me and we'll find the answer in a book."

This was a wonderful thing to hear and I believed her.

Then Miss Brick's purse got stolen from beneath her desk. She said that it must have been me who took it. I was sent to Lucinda de Leftwitch Templin's office. Lucinda de said she knew I didn't come from privileged homes like most of her girls, and that this might be difficult for me sometimes. She understood, she said, but really she was saying, "Where's the purse?"

I left. Didn't even go back to get the bus money or lunch in my cubby. Took off across town, all the long way, all the long day. My mother met me on the porch with a switch. They had called to say I had stolen the purse and then run away. She didn't even ask me if I stole it. "Little thief, humiliating me," whack, "brat, ungrateful," whack. Lucinda de called her the next day to tell her a janitor had stolen the purse but my mother didn't even apologize to me. She just said, "Bitch," after she hung up.

That's how I ended up in St. Joseph's, which I loved. But those kids hated me too for all of the above reasons but now worse for new reasons, one being that Sister Cecilia always called on me and I got Stars and Saint pictures and was the pet! pet! until I stopped raising my hand.

Uncle John took off for Nacogdoches which left me alone with my mother and Grandpa. Uncle John always used to eat with me, or drink while I ate. He talked to me while I helped him repair furniture, took me to movies and let me hold his slimy glass eye. It was terrible when he was gone. Grandpa and Mamie (my grandma) were at his dentist office all day and then when they got home Mamie kept my little sister safe away in the kitchen or in Mamie's room. My mother was out, being a gray lady at the Army hospital or playing bridge. Grandpa was out at the Elks or who knows. The house was scary and empty without John and I'd have to hide from Grandpa and Mama when either of them was drunk. Home was bad and school was bad.

I decided not to talk. I just sort of gave it up. It lasted so long Sister Cecilia tried to pray with me in the cloak room. She meant well and was just touching me in sympathy, praying. I got scared and pushed her and she fell down and I got expelled.

That's when I met Hope.

School was almost over so I would stay home and go back to Vilas in the fall. I still wasn't talking, even when my mother poured a whole pitcher of iced tea over my head or twisted as she pinched me so the pinches looked like stars, the big dipper, little dipper, the lyre up and down my arms.

I played jacks on the concrete above the steps, wishing that the Syrian kid next door would ask me over. She played on their concrete porch. She was small and thin but seemed old. Not grown up or mature but like an old woman-child. Long shiny black hair with bangs hanging down over her eyes. In order to see she had to tip her head back. She looked like a baby baboon. In a nice way, I mean. A little face and huge black eyes. All of the six Haddad kids looked emaciated but the adults were huge, two or three hundred pounds.

I knew she noticed me too because if I was doing cherries in the basket so was she. Or shooting stars, except she didn't ever drop a jack, even with twelves. For weeks our balls and jacks made a nice bop bop crash bop bop crash rhythm until finally she did come over to the fence. She must have heard my mother yelling at me because she said,

"You talk yet?"

I shook my head.

"Good. Talking to me won't count."

I hopped the fence. That night I was so happy that I had a friend that when I went to bed I called out, "Good night!"

We had played jacks for hours that day and then she taught me mumbletypeg. Dangerous games with a knife. Triple flips into the grass, and the scariest was one hand flat on the ground, stabbing between each finger. Faster faster faster blood. I don't think we spoke at all. We rarely did, all summer long. All I remember are her first and last words.

I have never had a friend again like Hope, my onliest true friend. I gradually became a part of the Haddad family. I believe that if this had not happened I would have grown up to be not just neurotic, alcoholic and insecure, but seriously disturbed. Wacko.

The six children and the father spoke English. The mother, Grandma and five or six other old women spoke only Arabic. Looking back, it seems like I went through sort of an orientation. The children watched as I learned to run, really run, to vault the fence, not climb it. I became expert with the knife, tops and marbles. I learned cuss words and gestures in English, Spanish and Arabic. For the Grandma I washed dishes, watered, raked the sand in the backyard, beat rugs with a woven-cane beater, helped the old women roll out bread on the Ping-Pong tables in the basement. Lazy afternoons washing bloody menstrual rags in a tub in the backyard with Hope and Shahala, her older sister. This seemed not disgusting but magic, like a mysterious rite. In the mornings I stood in line with the other girls to get my ears washed and my hair braided, to get *kibbe* on fresh hot bread. The women hollered at me, "*Hjaddadinah!*" Kissed me and slapped me as if I belonged there. Mr. Haddad let me and Hope sit on couches and drive around town in the bed of his Haddad's Beautiful Furniture truck.

I learned to steal. Pomegranates and figs from blind old Cuca's yard, Blue Waltz perfume, Tangee lipstick from Kress's, licorice and sodas from the Sunshine Grocery. Stores delivered then and one day the Sunshine delivery boy was bringing groceries to both our houses just as Hope and I were getting home, eating banana Popsicles. Our mothers were both outside.

"Your kids stole them Popsicles!" he said.

My mother slapped me whack whack. "Get inside, you criminal lying cheating brat!" But Mrs. Haddad said, "You lousy liar! *Hjaddajdinah! Tlajhama!* Don't you talk bad about my kids! I'm not going to your store no more!"

And she never did, taking a bus all the way to Mesa to shop, knowing full well that Hope had stolen the Popsicle. This made sense to me. I didn't just want my mother to believe me when I was innocent, which she never did, but to stand up for me when I was guilty.

When we got skates Hope and I covered El Paso, skated over the whole town. We went to movies, letting the other in by the fire exit door. *The Spanish Main, Till the End of Time.* Chopin bleeding all over the piano keys. We saw *Mildred Pierce* six times and *The Beast with Five Fingers* ten.

The best time we had was the cards. Anytime we could, we hung out around her brother Sammy, who was seventeen. He and his friends were handsome and tough and wild. I have told you about Sammy and the cards. We sold chances for musical vanity boxes. We brought him the money and he gave us a cut. That's how we got the skates.

We sold chances everywhere. Hotels and the train station, the USO, Juarez. But even neighborhoods were magic. You walk down a street, past houses and yards and sometimes in the evening you can see people eating or sitting around and it's a lovely glimpse of how people live. Hope and I went inside hundreds of houses. Seven years old, both funny-looking in different ways, people liked us and were kind to us. "Come in. Have some lemonade." We saw four Siamese cats who used the real toilet and even flushed it. We saw parrots and one five-hundred-pound person who had not been out of the house for twenty years. But even more we liked all the pretty things: paintings and china shepherdesses, mirrors, cuckoo clocks and grandfather clocks, quilts and rugs of many colors. We liked sitting in Mexican kitchens full of canaries, drinking real orange juice and eating *pan dulces*. Hope was so smart, she learned Spanish just from listening around the neighborhood, so she could talk to the old women.

We glowed when Sammy praised us, hugged us. He made us bologna sandwiches and let us sit near them on the grass. We told them all about the people we met. Rich ones, poor ones, Chinese ones, Black ones until the conductor made us leave the colored waiting room at the station. Only one bad person, the man with the dogs. He didn't do anything or say anything bad, just scared us to death with his pale smirky face.

When Sammy bought the old car, Hope figured it out right away. That nobody was going to get any vanity box.

She leapt in a fury over the fence into my yard, howling, hair flying like an Indian warrior in the movies. She opened her knife and made big gashes in our index fingers, held them dripping together.

"I will never ever speak to Sammy again," she said. "Say it!"

"I will never ever speak to Sammy again," I said.

I exaggerate a lot and I get fiction and reality mixed up, but I don't actually ever lie. I wasn't lying when I made that vow. I knew he had used us, lied to us and cheated all those people. I was never going to speak to him.

A few weeks later I was climbing the hill up Upson, near the hospital. Hot. (See, I'm trying to justify what happened. It was always hot.) Sammy pulled up in the old blue open car, the car Hope and I had worked to pay for. It is true too that coming from mountain towns and except for some taxis I had rarely been in a car.

"Come for a ride."

Some words drive me crazy. Lately every newspaper article

has a benchmark or a watershed or an icon in it. At least one of these applies to that moment in my life.

I was a little girl; I don't believe it was an actual sexual attraction. But I was awed by his physical beauty, his magnetism. Whatever the excuse...Well, so okay, there is no excuse for what I did. I spoke to him. I got into the car.

It was wonderful, riding in the open car. The wind cooled us off as we sped around the Plaza, past the Wigwam theater, the Del Norte, the Popular Dry Goods Company, then up Mesa toward Upson. I was going to ask him to let me out a few blocks before home just as I saw Hope in a fig tree on the vacant lot where Upson and Randolph came together.

Hope screamed. Sat up in the tree shaking her fist at me, cursing in Syrian. Maybe everything that has happened to me since was a result of this curse. Makes sense.

I got out of the car, sick at heart, shaking, climbed the stairs to our house like an old person, fell onto the porch swing.

I knew that it was the end of my friendship and I knew I was wrong.

Each day was endless. Hope walked past me as if I was invisible, played on the other side of the fence as if our yard did not exist. She and her sisters spoke only Syrian now. Loud if they were outside. I understood a lot of the bad things they said. Hope played jacks alone on the porch for hours, wailing Arabic songs, beautiful; her harsh plaintive voice made me weep for missing her.

Except for Sammy, none of the Haddads would speak to me. Her mother spat at me and shook her fist. Sammy would call to me from the car, away from our house. Tell me he was sorry. He tried to be nice, saying he knew that she was really still my friend and please don't be sad. That he understood why I couldn't talk to him, to please forgive him. I turned away so I couldn't see him when he spoke.

I have never been so lonely in my life. Benchmark lonely. The days were endless, the sound of her ball relentless hour after hour on the concrete, the swish of her knife into the grass, glint of the blade.

There weren't any other children in our neighborhood. For weeks we played alone. She perfected knife tricks on their grass. I colored and read, lying on the porch swing.

She left for good just before school started. Sammy and her father carried her bed and bed table and a chair down to the huge furniture truck. Hope climbed in back, sat up in the bed so she could see out. She didn't look at me. She looked tiny in the huge truck. I watched until she disappeared. Sammy called to me from the fence, told me that she had gone to Odessa, Texas to live with some relatives. I say Odessa, Texas because once someone said, "This is Olga; she's from Odessa." And I thought, so? Turned out it was in Russia. I thought the only Odessa was where Hope went.

School started and it wasn't so bad. I didn't care about being always alone or laughed at. My back brace was getting too small and my back hurt. Good, I thought, it's what I deserve.

Uncle John came back. Five minutes in the door he said to my mother, "Her brace is too small!"

I was so glad to see him. He fixed me a bowl of puffed wheat with milk, about six spoons of sugar and at least three tablespoons of vanilla. He sat across from me at the kitchen table, drinking bourbon while I ate. I told him about my friend Hope, about everything. I even told him about the school troubles. I had almost forgotten them. He grunted or said, "hot damn!" while I talked and he understood everything, especially about Hope.

He never said things like, "Don't worry, it will all work out." In fact, once Mamie said, "Things could be worse."

"Worse? he said. "Things could be a heckuva lot better!" He

was an alcoholic too, but drink just made him sweeter, not like them. Or he'd take off, to Mexico or Nacogdoches or Carlsbad, to jail sometimes, I realize now.

He was handsome, dark like Grandpa, with only one blue eye since Grandpa shot out the other one. His glass eye was green. I know that it is true that Grandpa shot him, but how it happened has about ten different versions. When Uncle John was home he slept in the shed out back, near where he had made my room on the back porch.

Uncle John wore a cowboy hat and boots and was like a brave movie cowboy part of the time, at others just a pitiful crying bum.

"Sick again," Mamie would sigh about them.

"Drunk, Mamie," I'd say.

I tried to hide when Grandpa was drunk because he would catch me and rock me. He was doing it once in the big rocker, holding me tight, the chair bouncing off the ground inches from the red hot stove, his thing jabbing jabbing my behind. He was singing, "Old Tin Pan with a Hole in the Bottom." Loud. Panting and grunting. Only a few feet away Mamie sat, reading the Bible while I screamed, "Mamie! Help me!" Uncle John showed up, drunk and dusty. He grabbed me away from Grandpa, pulled the old man up by his shirt. He said he'd kill him with his bare hands next time. Then he slammed shut Mamie's Bible.

"Read it over, Ma. You got it wrong, the part about turning the other cheek. That don't mean when somebody hurts a child."

She was crying, said he'd like to break her heart.

While I was finishing the cereal he asked me if Grandpa had been bothering me. I said no. I told him that he had done it to Sally, once, that I saw.

"Little Sally? What did you do?"

"Nothing." I had done nothing. I had watched with a mixture of feelings: fear, sex, jealousy, anger. John came around, pulled up a chair and shook me, hard. He was furious.

"That was rotten! You hear me? Where was Mamie?"

"Watering. Sally had been asleep, but she woke up."

"When I'm gone you're the only one here with any sense. You have to protect her. Do you hear me?"

I nodded, ashamed. But I was more ashamed of how I had felt when it happened. He figured it out somehow. He always understood all the things you didn't even get straight in your head, much less say.

"You think Sally has it pretty good. You're jealous of her because Mamie pays her so much attention. So even if this was a bad thing he was doing at least it used to be your bad thing, right? Honey, sure you're jealous of her. She's treated swell. But remember how mad you got at Mamie? How you begged her to help you? Answer me!"

"I remember."

"Well, you were as bad as Mamie. Worse! Silence can be wicked, plumb wicked. Anything else you done wrong, sides from betraying your sister and a friend?"

"I stole. Candy and..."

"I mean hurting people."

"No."

He said he was going to stick around awhile, get me straightened out, get his Antique Repair Shop going before winter.

I worked for him weekends and after school in the shed and the backyard. Sanding, sanding or rubbing wood with a rag soaked in linseed oil and turpentine. His friends Tino and Sam came sometimes to help him with caning, reupholstering, refinishing. If my mother or Grandpa came home they left the back way, because Tino was Mexican and Sam was colored. Mamie liked them, though. and always brought out brownies or oatmeal cookies if she was there.

Once Tino brought a Mexican woman, Mecha, almost a girl, really pretty, with rings and earrings, painted eyelids and long nails, a shiny green dress. She didn't speak English but pantomimed could she help me paint a kitchen stool. I nodded, sure. Uncle John told me to hurry up, paint fast before the paint ran out, and I guess Tino told Mecha the same thing in Spanish. We were furiously slapping the brushes around the rungs and up the legs, fast as we could while the three men held their sides, laughing at us. The two of us figured it out at about the same time, and we both began laughing too. Mamie came out to see what the fuss was. She called Uncle John over to her. She was really mad about the woman, said it was wicked to have her here. John nodded and scratched his head. When Mamie went in, he came over and after a while said, "Well, let's call it a day."

While we cleaned the brushes, he explained that the woman was a whore, that Mamie figured that out by the way she was dressed and painted. He ended up explaining a lot of things that had bothered me. I understood more about my parents and Grandpa and movies and dogs. He forgot to tell me that whores charged money, so I was still confused about whores.

"Mecha was nice. I hate Mamie," I said.

"Don't say that word! Anyhow you don't hate her. You're mad because she doesn't like you. She sees you out wandering the streets, hanging out with Syrians and Uncle John. She figures you're a lost cause, a born Magruder. You want her to love you, that's all. Anytime you think you hate somebody, what you do is pray for them. Try it, you'll see. And while you're busy praying for her, you might try helping her once in a while. Give her some kinda reason to like a surly brat like you."

On weekends sometimes he'd take me to the dog track in Juarez, or to gambling games around town. I loved the races and was good at picking winners. The only time I liked going to card games was when he played with railroad men, in a caboose at the train yards. I climbed the ladder to the roof and watched all the trains coming in and going out, switching, coupling. It got to be that most of the card games were in the back of Chinese laundries. I'd sit in the front reading for hours while somewhere in back he played poker. The heat and the smell of cleaning solvent mixed with singed wool and sweat was nauseating. A few times he left out the back way and forgot me, so that only when the laundryman came to close up did he find me asleep in the chair. I'd have to go home, far, in the dark, and most of the time nobody would be there. Mamie took Sally to choir practice and to the Eastern Star and to make bandages for servicemen.

About once a month we'd go to a barber shop. A different one each time. He'd ask for a shave and a haircut. I'd sit on a chair reading *Argosy* while the barber cut his hair, just waiting for the shave part. Uncle John would be tilted way back in the chair and just as the barber was finishing the shave he'd ask, "Say, do you happen to have any eyedrops?" which they always did. The barber would stand over him and put drops in his eyes. The green glass eye would start spinning around and the barber would scream bloody murder. Then everybody'd laugh.

If only I had understood him half as much as he always understood me, I could have found out how he hurt, why he worked so hard to get laughs. He did make everybody laugh. We ate in cafés all over Juarez and El Paso that were like people's houses. Just a lot of tables in one room of a regular house, with good food. Everybody knew him and the waitresses always laughed when he asked if it was warmed-over coffee.

"Oh, no!"

"Well, how'd you get it so hot?"

I could usually tell just how drunk he was and if it was a lot I'd make some excuse and walk or ride the trolley home. One day though, I had been sleeping in the cab of the truck, woke after he got in and started off. We were on Rim Road going faster faster. He had a bottle between his thighs, was driving with his elbows as he counted the money he held in a fan over the steering wheel.

"Slow down!"

"I'm in the money, honey!"

Silence

"Slow down! Hold on to the wheel!"

The truck thumped, shuddered high up and then thumped down. Money flew all over the cab. I looked out the back window. A little boy was standing in the street, his arm bleeding. A collie was lying next to him, really bloody, trying to get up.

"Stop. Stop the truck. We have to go back. Uncle John!"

"I can't!"

"Slow down. You have to turn around!" I was sobbing hysterically.

At home he reached across and opened my door. "You go on in."

I don't know if I stopped speaking to him. He never came home. Not that night, not for days, weeks, months. I prayed for him.

The war ended and my father came home. We moved to South America.

Uncle John ended up on skid row in Los Angeles, a really hopeless wino. Then he met Dora, who played trumpet in the Salvation Army band. She had him go into the shelter and have some soup and she talked to him. She said later that he made her laugh. They fell in love and were married and he never drank again. When I was older I went to visit them in Los Angeles. She was working as a riveter at Lockheed and he had an Antique Repair Shop in his garage. They were maybe the sweetest two people I ever knew, sweet together, I mean. We went to Forest Lawn and the La Brea tarpits and the Grotto restaurant. Mostly I helped Uncle John in the shop, sanding furniture, polishing with the turpentine and linseed oil rag. We talked about life, told jokes. Neither of us ever mentioned El Paso. Of course by this time I had realized all the reasons why he couldn't stop the truck, because by this time I was an alcoholic.

A Love Affair

It was hard to tend to the front and back offices alone. I had to change dressings, take temperatures and blood pressures and still try to greet new patients and answer the phones. A big nuisance because to do an EKG or assist in a wound stitching or a Pap smear I'd have to tell the answering service to take calls. The waiting room would be full, with people feeling neglected, and I'd hear the phones ringing ringing.

Most of Dr. B's patients were very old. Often the women who got Pap smears were obese, with difficult access, so it took even longer.

I think there was a law that said I had to be present when he was with a female patient. I used to think this was an outdated precaution. Not at all. Amazing how many of those old ladies were in love with him.

I would hand him the scapula and, later, the long stick. After he had the scrapings from the cervix he would smear them on the glass slide I held, which I would then spray with a protective film. I would cover the slide with another one, put it in a box and label it for the lab.

My main job was to get the women's legs high up into the stirrups and their buttocks moved down to the end of the table where they would be even with his eyes. Then I draped a sheet over their knees and was supposed to help the women relax. Chat and make jokes until he came in. That was easy, the chatting part. I knew the patients and they were all pretty nice.

The hard part was when he came in. He was a painfully shy man, with a serious tremor of his hands that occasionally manifested itself. Always when he signed checks or did Pap smears.

He squatted on a stool, eyes level with their vagina, with a light on his forehead. I handed him the (warmed) scapula and, after a few minutes, with the patient gasping and sweating, the long cotton-tipped stick. He held it, waving it like a baton, as he disappeared beneath the sheet, toward the woman. At last his hand emerged with the stick, now a dizzy metronome aimed at my waiting slide. I still drank in those days, so my hand, holding the slide, shook visibly as it tried to meet his. But in a nervous up and down tremble. His was back and forth. Slap, at last. This procedure took so long that he often missed important phone calls, and of course the people in the waiting room got very impatient. Once Mr. Larraby even knocked on the door and Dr. B. was so startled he dropped the stick. We had to start all over. He agreed then to hire a part-time receptionist.

If I ever look for another job, I'll ask for an enormous salary. If anyone works for as little as Ruth and I did, something is very suspicious.

Ruth had never had a job and she didn't need a job, which was suspicious enough. She was doing this for fun.

This was so fascinating to me that I asked her to lunch after the interview. Tuna melts at the Pill Hill Café. I liked her right off the bat. She was unlike anybody I had ever met.

Ruth was fifty, married for thirty years to her childhood sweetheart, an accountant. They had two children and three cats. Her hobbies, on the job application, were "cats." So Dr. B. always asked her how her cats were. My hobbies were "reading," so he'd say to me, "On the shores of Itchee Goomee" or "Nevermore quoth the raven."

Every time there was a new patient he would write a few

sentences on the back of the chart. Something he could use for conversation when he entered the exam room. "Thinks Texas is God's country." "Has two toy poodles." "Has five hundred dollar a day heroin habit." So when he went in to see them he'd say things like, "Good morning! Been up to God's country lately?" or "You're out of luck if you think you can get drugs from me."

Over lunch Ruth told me that she had started to feel old and in a rut so she had joined a support group. The Merry Pranksters, or M.P., which really stood for Meno Pause. Ruth always said this like it was two words. The group was dedicated to putting more zip into women's lives. They focused on different members at a time. The last one had been Hannah. The group convinced her to go to Weight Watchers, to Rancho del Sol spa, take bossa nova lessons and then to get liposuction and a face lift. She looked wonderful but was in two new groups now. One for women who had face lifts but were still depressed and another for "Women Who Love Too Much." Ruth sighed, "Hannah's always been the kind of woman who has affairs with stevedores."

Stevedores! Ruth used some surprising words, like "heretofore" and "hulabaloo." Said things like she missed having "That Time of the Month." It always was such a warm and cozy time.

The M.P. group had Ruth take flower arranging, join a theater group, a Trivial Pursuit club and get a job. She was supposed to have a love affair but she hadn't thought about that yet. She already had zip in her life. She loved flower arranging, and now they were working on making bouquets with weeds and grasses. She had a bit part, non-singing, in *Oklahoma*.

I liked having Ruth in the office. We joked a lot with the patients and talked about them as if they were our relatives. She even thought filing was fun, singing, "Abcdefg hi jk lmnop lmnopqrst uvwxyZ!" until I'd say, "Stop, let *me* file."

It was easier now when I was with patients. But, in fact, she did very little work. She studied her pursuit cards and called her friends a lot, especially Hannah, who was having an affair with the dance instructor.

On lunch hour I'd go with Ruth to collect weed bouquets, scrambling hot and sweaty up the freeway embankment for Queen Anne's lace and tobacco weed. Rocks in our shoes. She seemed like an ordinary pretty middle-aged Jewish lady but there was a wildness and freedom about her. Her shout when she spied a pink rocket flower in the alley behind the hospital.

She and her husband had grown up together. Their families were very close, some of the few Jews in a small Iowa town. She couldn't remember when everybody didn't expect her and Ephraim to marry. They fell in love for real in high school. She studied home economics in college and waited for him to graduate in business and accounting. Of course they had saved themselves for marriage. They moved into his family home and cared for his invalid mother. She had come with them to Oakland, was still living with them, eighty-six years old now.

I never heard Ruth complain, not about the sick old lady or her children or Ephraim. I was always complaining about my kids or my ex-husband or a daughter-in-law and especially about Dr. B. He had me open all his packages in case there were bombs in them. If a bee or a wasp came in, he went outside until I killed it. These are just the silly things. He was mean. Especially mean to Ruth, saying things like, "This is what I get for hiring the handicapped?" He called her "Dyslexia," because she transposed phone numbers. She did that a lot. About every other day he told me to fire her. I'd tell him we couldn't. There was no cause. She really helped me and the patients liked her. She cheered the place up.

"I can't stand cheeriness," he said. "Makes me want to slap the grin off her face."

She continued to be nice to him. She thought he was like Heathcliff or Mr. Rochester in *Jane Eyre,* only little. "Yeah, real little," I said. But Ruth never heard negative remarks. She believed that someone, at some time, must have broken Dr. B.'s heart. She brought him kugel and ruguleh and hamentaschen, was always thinking of excuses to go into his office. I hadn't figured out that she had chosen him to be the love affair until he came into my office and closed the door.

"You have to fire her! She is actually flirting with me! It is unseemly."

"Well, strange as it may seem, she finds you wildly attractive. I still need her. It's hard to find someone easy to work with. Be patient. Please, sir." The "sir" did it, as usual.

"All right," he sighed.

She was good for me, put zip in my life. Instead of spending my lunch hour brooding and smoking in the alley I'd get dirty and have fun picking bouquets with her. I even started cooking, using some of the hundreds of recipes she xeroxed all day. Baked pearl onions with a dash of brown sugar. She brought in clothes from Schmatta used clothing store and I bought them. A few times when Ephraim was too tired I went with her to the opera.

She was wonderful to go to the opera with, because at intermission she didn't just stand around looking bored like everybody does. She'd lead me around the main foyer so we could admire the clothes and jewels. I wept with her at *La Traviata*. Our favorite scene was the old woman's aria in *The Queen of Spades*.

One day Ruth asked Dr. B. to go to the opera with her. "No! What an inappropriate request!" he said.

"That asshole," I said when he went out the door. All she said was that doctors were just too busy to have love affairs so she guessed it would have to be Julius.

Julius was a retired dentist who had been in the cast of *Oklahoma*. He was a widower and he was fat. She said fat was good, fat was warm and comfortable.

I asked her if it was because Ephraim was not so interested in sex anymore. "*Au contraire!*" she said. "It's the first thing he thinks of every morning and the last at night. And if he's home in the day he chases me around then too. Really..."

I saw Julius at Ephraim's mother's funeral at the Chapel of the Valley. The old woman had died quietly in her sleep.

Ruth and her family were on the steps of the funeral home. Two lovely children, handsome, gracious, comforting their parents, Ruth and Ephraim. Ephraim was darkly handsome. Lean, brooding, soulful. Now *he* looked like Heathcliff. His sad and dreamy eyes smiled into mine. "Thank you for your kindness to my wife."

"There he is!" Ruth whispered, pointing at red-faced Julius. Gold chains, a too-tight single-breasted blue suit. He must have been chewing Clorets gum, his teeth were green.

"You're crazy!" I whispered back to her.

Ruth had picked the Chapel of the Valley because the undertakers were our favorites. Dr. B.'s patients died often so almost every day some mortician came to get him to sign the death certificate. In black ink, the law required, but Dr. B. persisted in signing them with a blue pen, so the morticians had to drink coffee and hang around until he came back and signed them in black.

I waited in the rear of the chapel, wondering where to sit. Many Hadassah women had come; it was crowded. One of the chapel's morticians appeared next to me. "How lovely you look in gray, Lily," he said. The other one, with a boutonniere, came up the aisle and said in a low mournful voice, "How good of you to come, dear. Do let me find you a nice seat." I followed the two men down the aisle, feeling rather smug, like being known in a restaurant.

It was a beautiful service. The rabbi read the part in the Bible about the good wife being more precious than rubies. Nobody would have thought that about the old woman, I don't think. But I believed the eulogy was about Ruth and so did Ephraim and Julius, the way they were both gazing at her.

A Love Affair

On Monday I tried to reason with her. "You are a woman who has everything. Health, looks, humor. A house in the hills. A cleaning woman. A garbage compactor. Wonderful children. And Ephraim! He is handsome, brilliant, rich. He obviously adores you!"

I told her the group was steering her in the wrong direction. She shouldn't do anything to upset Ephraim. Thank her lucky stars. The M.P. were just jealous. They probably had alcoholic husbands, football-watching husbands, impotent or unfaithful ones. Their children carried beepers, were pierced, bulimic, drugged, tattooed.

"I think you're embarrassed to be so happy, are going to do this so you can share with the M.P.s. I understand. When I was eleven an aunt gave me a diary. All I wrote in it was: 'Went to school Did homework.' So I started to do bad things in order to have something to write in it"

"It's not going to be a serious affair," she said. "It's just to pep things up."

"How about me having an affair with Ephraim? That would pep me up. You'd be jealous and fall madly in love with him again."

She smiled. An innocent smile, like a child's.

"Ephraim would never do that. He loves me."

I thought she had dropped the affair idea until one Friday she brought in a newspaper.

"I'm going out with Julius tonight. But I'm telling Ephraim that I'm going out with you. Have you seen any of these movies, to tell me about them?"

I told her all about *Ran,* especially when the woman pulls out the dagger, and when the fool weeps. The blue banners in the trees, the red banners in the trees, the white banners in the trees. I was really getting into it, but she said, "Stop!" and asked where we would go after the movie. I took us, them, to Café Roma in Berkeley.

She and Julius went out every Friday. Their romance was good for me. Usually I got home from work, read novels and drank 100 proof vodka until I fell asleep, day in day out. During the Love Affair I began to actually go to string quartets, movies, to hear Ishiguro or Leslie Scaloppino while Ruth and Julius went to the Hungry Tiger and the Rusty Scupper.

They went out for almost two months before they did You Know What. This event was going to occur in Big Sur, on a three-day trip. What to tell Ephraim?

"Oh, that's easy," I said. "You and I will go to a Zen retreat. No phones! Nothing to tell because we're just going to be silent and meditate. We'll sit in the hot springs under the stars. In the lotus position on cliffs overlooking the ocean. Endless waves. Endless."

It was annoying not to be able to go out freely those days, to screen my phone calls. But it worked. Ephraim took the children out to dinner, fed the cats, watered the plants and missed her. Very very much.

On the Monday after the trip there were three big bouquets of roses in the office. One card said, "To my cherished wife with love." Another was from "Your secret admirer," and one card said, "She Walks in Beauty." Ruth confessed that she had sent that last one to herself. She adored roses. She had hinted to both men that she loved roses, but never dreamt they'd actually send any.

"Get rid of the funeral arrangements right now," Dr. B. said, on his way to the hospital. Earlier he had asked me again to fire her and again I had refused. Why did he dislike her so?

"I told you. She's too cheerful."

"I usually feel the same way about cheerful people. But hers is genuine."

"Christ. That's really depressing."

"Please, give her a chance. Anyway, I have a feeling she's going to be miserable soon."

"I hope so."

Ephraim stopped by to take Ruth to coffee. She had done nothing all morning, had been on the phone to Hannah. I could tell the main reason he had come was to see how she liked the roses. He was very upset about the other ones. She told him one was from a patient called Anna Fedaz, but then just giggled about the secret admirer. Poor guy. I watched jealousy hit him smack in the face, in the heart. Left hook to the gut.

He asked me how I had liked the retreat. I hate to lie, really can't stand lying. Not for moral reasons. It's so hard, figuring it out. Remembering what you have said.

"Well, it was a lovely place. Ruth is very serene and seemed to adapt perfectly to the atmosphere there. I find it hard to meditate. I just worry, or go back over every mistake I ever made in my whole life. But it was, er, centering. Serene. You and Ruth run along now. Have a nice lunch!"

Later I got the scoop. Big Sur had been *the* adventure of Ruth's life. She knew she wouldn't be able to tell the M.P.s about doing You Know What. Oral S. for the first time! Well, yes, she had done Oral S. to Ephraim, but never had it done to *her*. "And M A R . . . I know it has a 'J' in it somewhere."

"Marijuana?"

"Hush! Well, mostly it made me cough and get nervous. Yes, that was very nice, Oral S. But the way he kept asking, 'Are you ready?' made me imagine we were going somewhere and ruined the mood."

They were going to Mendocino in two weeks. The story was that she and I were going to a writers' workshop and book fair in Petaluma. Robert Haas was to be the writer-in-residence.

One night in the middle of the week, she called and asked if she could come over. Like a fool I expected her, didn't understand that it was a cover, that she had gone to meet Julius. So when Ephraim phoned I could honestly sound cross because she still hadn't arrived, was even crosser the next time. "I'll have her call you the minute she gets here." After a while he called again, this time furious because she was home now and said I had not given her the message.

The next day I told her I wouldn't do this for her anymore. She said that was fine, that they were starting play practice on Monday.

"You and I are in a flower-arranging class on Fridays, at Laney. That's it."

"Well, that's the last one. You've been so lucky he hasn't asked any specifics."

"Of course he wouldn't. He trusts me. But my conscience is clear now. Julius and I don't do You Know What anymore."

"Then what *do* you do? Why go to all this secrecy and trouble to *not* do You Know What?"

"We found out that neither one of us is a swinger type. I like You Know What with Ephraim much more, and Julius isn't that interested. I like the sneaking around part. He likes buying me presents and cooking for me. My favorite thing is to knock on a motel door in Richmond or somewhere and then he opens the door and I rush in. My heart beating away."

"So what do you do then?"

"We play Trivial Pursuit, watch videos. Sometimes we sing. Duets, like 'Bali Hai' or 'Oh, What a Beautiful Morning.' We go for midnight walks in the rain!"

"Walk in the rain on your own time!" Dr. B. shouted. We hadn't noticed him come in.

He was serious. He stood there while she packed up all her *Bon Appetit* magazines and Trivial Pursuit cards and her knitting. He told me to write her a check for two weeks pay, plus what we owed her.

After Dr. B. left she called Julius, told him to meet her at Denny's right away.

"My career is ruined!" she sobbed.

She hugged me goodbye and left. I moved out to her desk, where I could see the waiting room.

Ephraim came in the door. He walked slowly toward me and shook my hand. "Lily," he said, in his deep enveloping voice. He told me that Ruth was supposed to have met him at the Pill Hill Café for lunch, but she never showed up. I told him that Dr. B. had fired her, for no reason. She probably had completely forgotten lunch, had gone home. Or shopping, maybe.

Ephraim continued to stand there.

"She can find much better jobs. I'm the office manager, and of course I'll give her a good recommendation. I'll really miss her."

He stood there, looking at me.

"And she will miss you." He leaned in the little window above my desk.

"This is for the best, my dear. I want you to know that I understand. Believe me, I feel for you."

"What?"

"There are many things I don't share with her as you do. Literature, Buddhism, the opera. Ruth is a very easy woman to love."

"What are you saying?"

He held my hand then, looked deep into my eyes as his soft brown ones filled with tears.

"I miss my wife. Please, Lily. Let her go."

Tears began to slide down my cheeks. I felt really sad. Our hands were a warm wet little pile on the ledge.

"Don't worry," I said. "Ruth loves only you, Ephraim."

The Wives

Anytime Laura thought about Decca, she saw her as if in a stage set. She had met Decca when she and Max were still married, many years before Laura married him. The house on High Street, in Albuquerque. Beau had taken her. Through the wide-open door into a kitchen with dirty pots and pans, dishes and cats, open jars, plates of runny fudge, uncapped bottles, cartons of takeout Chinese, through a bedroom, bumping into piles of clothes, shoes, stacks of magazines and newspapers, mesh sweater dryers, tires. Dimly lit center stage a bay window with frayed saffron nicotine-stained shades. Decca and Max sat in leather chairs, facing a miniature TV on a stool. The table between them held an enormous ashtray full of cigarette butts, a magazine with a knife and a pile of marijuana, a bottle of rum and Decca's glass. Max wore a black velour bathrobe, Decca a red silk kimono, her dark hair loose and long. They were stunning to look at. Stunning. Their presence hit you physically, like a blow.

Decca didn't speak but Max did. His thick-lashed heavy-lidded stoned dark eyes looked deep into Laura's. He rasped, "Hey, Beau, what's happening?" Laura couldn't remember anything after that. Maybe Beau asked to borrow the car or some money. He was staying with them, on his way to New York. Beau was a saxophone player she had met by chance, walking her baby in his stroller on Elm Street.

Decca. How come aristocratic Englishwomen and upper class American women all have names like Pookie and Muffin? Have they kept the names their nannies called them? There is a news reporter on NBC called Cokie. No way is Cokie from a nice family in Ohio. She is from a fine old wealthy family. Philadelphia? Virginia? Decca was a B—, one of the best Boston families. She had been a debutante, studied at Wellesley, was partly disinherited when she eloped with Max, who was Jewish. Years later, Laura too had been disinherited when her family heard of her own elopement with Max, but they relented when they realized how wealthy he was.

Decca called around eleven that night. Laura's sons were asleep. She left them a note and Decca's number in case one of them woke up, said she'd be back soon.

The reason it always seems like a stage set, she told herself, is because Decca never locks her doors and never gets up to answer the doorbell or a knock. So you just go in and find her *in situ*, stage right, in a dim light. At some point, before she sat down and started drinking, she had lit a piñon fire, candles in niches and kerosene lanterns whose soft lights catch now in her cascading silken hair. She wears an elaborately embroidered green kimono over a still lovely body. Only close up can you see that she is over forty, that drink has made her skin puffy, her eyes red.

It is a large room in an old adobe house. The fire reflects in the red tile floor. On the white walls are Howard Schleeter paintings, a Diebenkorn, a Franz Kline, some fine old carved Santos. Underwear dangles from a John Chamberlain sculpture. Over the baby's crib in a corner hangs a real Calder mobile. If you looked you could see fine Santo Domingo and Acoma pots. Old Navajo rugs are hidden beneath stacks of *Nations, New Republics, I.F. Stone Newsletters, New York Times, Le Monde, Art News, Mad Magazines,* pizza cartons, Baca's takeout cartons. The mink-covered bed is piled with clothes, toys, diapers, cats.

The Wives

Empty straw-covered jugs of Bacardi lie on their sides around the room, occasionally spinning when cats bat at them. A row of full jugs stands next to Decca's chair, another by the bed.

Decca was the only female alcoholic Laura knew that didn't hide her liquor. Laura didn't admit to herself yet that she drank, but she hid her bottles. So her sons wouldn't pour them out, so she wouldn't see them, face them.

If Decca was always set on stage, in that great chair, her hair in the lamplight shining, Laura was particularly good at entrances. She stands, elegant and casual in the doorway, wearing a floor-length Italian suede coat, in profile as she surveys the room. She is in her early thirties, her prettiness deceptively fresh and young.

"What the fuck are you doing here?" Decca says.

"You called me. Three times, actually. Come quick, you said."

"'I did?" Decca pours some more rum. She feels around under her chair and comes up with another glass, wipes it out with her kimono.

"I called you?" She pours a big drink for Laura, who sits in a chair on the other side of the table. Laura lights one of Decca's Delicados, coughs, takes a drink.

"I know it was you, Decca. Nobody else calls me 'Bucket Butt' or 'Fat-assed sap.'"

"Must have been me," Decca laughs.

"You said to come right away. That it was urgent."

"How come you took so long then? Christ, I'm operating in total blackout now. You still on the sauce? Well, yeah, that's obvious."

She pours them both more rum. Each of them drinks. Decca laughs.

"Well, you learned how to drink, anyway. I remember when you two were first married. I offered you a martini and you said, 'No thanks. Alcohol gives me vertigo.'"

"It still does."

"Weird how both his wives ended up lushes."

"Weirder still we didn't end up junkies."

"I did," Decca says. "For six months. I got into drinking trying to get off of heroin."

"Did using make you closer to him?"

"No. But it made me not care." Decca reaches over to an elaborate stereo system, changes the Coltrane tape to Miles Davis. *Kind of Blue.* "So our Max is in jail. Max won't handle jail in Mexico."

"I know. He likes his pillowcases ironed."

"God, you're a ditz. Is that your assessment of the situation?"

"Yeah. I mean if he's like that about pillowcases, imagine how hard everything else will be. Anyway, I came to tell you that Art is taking care of it. He's sending down money to get him out."

Decca groans. "Christ, it's all coming back to me. Guess how the money is getting there? With Camille! Beau was on the plane with her to Mexico City. He called me from the airport. That's why I called you. Max is going to marry Camille!"

"Oh, dear."

Decca pours them both more rum.

"Oh, dear? You're so lady-like it makes me sick. You'll probably send them crystal. You're smoking two cigarettes."

"You sent *us* crystal. Baccarat glasses."

"I did? Must have been a joke. Anyway, Camille told Max they're going to Acapulco for their honeymoon. Just like you did."

"Acapulco?" Laura stands up, takes off her coat and throws it on the bed. Two cats jump off. Laura is wearing black silk pajamas and slippers. She is weaving, either from emotion or so much rum. She sits.

"Acapulco?" She says this sadly.

"I knew that would get you. Probably to the same suite at the Mirador. The scent of bougainvillea and hibiscus wafting into their room."

"Those flowers don't smell. Nardos would be wafting." Laura holds her head in her hands, thinking.

"Stripes. Stripes from the sun through the wooden shutters." Decca laughs, opens a new jug of rum and pours.

"No, Mirador is too quiet and old for Camille. He'll take her to some jive beach motel with a bar in the swimming pool, the stools underwater, umbrellas in the coconut drink. They'll drive around town in a pink jeep with fringe on it. Admit it, Laura. This pisses you off. A dumb file clerk. Tawdry little tart!"

"Come on, Decca. She's not so bad. She's young. The same age as each of us were when we married him. She's not exactly dumb."

This fool is genuinely kind, Decca thought. She must have been so kind to him.

"Camille *is* dumb. God, but so were you. I knew you loved him, though, and would give him sons. They are beautiful, Laura."

"Aren't they?"

I am dumb, Laura thought, and Decca is brilliant. He must have missed Decca a lot.

"I wanted a baby so badly," Decca says. "We tried for years. Years. And fought over it, because I was so obsessed, each of us blaming the other. I could have killed that ob/gyn Rita when she had his baby."

"You know she researched all over town and picked him. She didn't want a lover, just a baby. Sappho. What a name, no?"

"Weird. Weirder is years after we're divorced and I'm forty years old, I get pregnant. One night, one damn night, no maybe ten blooming minutes in mosquito-infested San Blas I fuck an Australian plumber. Bingo."

"Is that why you named your baby Melbourne? Poor kid. Why not Perth? Perth is pretty." Unsteadily, Laura gets up and goes to look at the child. She smiles and covers him.

"He's so big. Wonderful ginger hair. How is he doing?"

"He's great. He's a pretty damn great kid. Starting to talk."

Decca stands, stumbles slightly as she crosses the room to check on the child and then goes to the bathroom. Laura finishes her drink, starts to stand and go home.

"I'll be going now," she says to Decca when she comes back.

"Sit down. Have another drink." She pours. They are drinking from ludicrously small tea cups considering how often they are refilled.

"You don't seem to grasp the seriousness of this situation. Now, I'm fine, set for life. I got a huge divorce settlement plus I have family money. What about any inheritance for your children? This woman will wipe him out. You were a fool not to get child support. Blithering fool."

"Yeah. I thought I could support us. I had never had a job before. His habit was eight hundred dollars a day and he was always wrecking cars. So I just got money for their college funds. You want to know the honest truth? I didn't think he could possibly live much longer."

Decca laughs, slapping her knee. "I knew you didn't! What's her name, she didn't wany any child support either. Old lawyer Trebb called me after your divorce came through. He wanted to know why it was that all three of us women had gigantic life insurance policies from Max."

Decca sighs, lights up a fat joint that had been lying on the table. It sputters and crackles; little flames make three big holes in her lovely kimono. One right in the middle of the Italy-shaped rum stain. She beats on them, coughing, until the fires are out, passes the joint to Laura. When Laura inhales, she too creates a little shower of sparks that burn holes in her silk top.

"At least he taught me how to de-seed weed," she says, talking funny through the smoke.

"So," Decca continues. "he'll be clean when he gets out. Alive and well in Acapulco. I gave him the best years of my life and now look. He's alive and well in Acapulco with a car-hop." Decca's speech is slurred now, her nose running as she wails, "The best years of my life!"

"Hell, Decca, I gave him the *worst* years of my life!"

The two women find this hysterically funny, slap at each other, hold their sides, stomp their feet and knock over the ashtray, laughing so hard. Laura starts to take a drink but spills it down the front of her pajamas.

"Seriously, Decca," Laura says. "This may be a really good thing. I hope they're happy. He can show her the world. She will adore him, take care of him."

"Take him to the cleaners. Is she a floozy or what? Tacky car-hop."

"You're dating yourself. She's more of a Clinique salesgirl, I'd say. You know she was once Miss Redondo Beach?"

"You have style, B.B. A subtle, lady-like bitch. You'll act simply delighted for the nuptial pair. Probably throw rice at them. So tell me now, how does it *really* feel, thinking of them in Acapulco? Imagine. Sunset now. The sun is making a green dot and vanishing. 'Cuando Calienta el Sol' is playing. Lots of throbbing saxophone, maracas. No, the music is playing. 'Piel Canela' now but they're still in bed. She's asleep, tired after sun and water-skiing. Steamy sweaty sex. He lies full against her back. He grazes the back of her neck with his lips, leans, chews on her ear, breathing."

Laura spills some of a freshly poured drink down her shirt-front. "He did that to you?" Decca passes her a towel to dry herself with.

"Bucket-Butt, you think you've got the only ear lobe in the world?" She grins, enjoying this now. "Then he'd brush your breast with the palm of his hand, right? You'd groan and turn toward him. Then he'd catch your head in..."

"Stop it!"

They're both depressed now. They smoke and drink with the

elaborately careful slow motion of the very drunk. Cats come near them, weaving but they both absentmindedly kick them away.

"At least there weren't any before me," Decca said.

"Elinor. She still calls him, middle of the night. Cries a lot."

"She doesn't count. She was his student at Brandeis. One rainy intense weekend at Truro. Her family called the dean. End of romance and teaching career."

"Sarah?"

"You mean Sarah? His sister Sarah? You're not so dumb, B.B. Sarah is our biggest rival of all. I never said it out loud though. Do you think they ever actually made love?"

"No, of course not. But they are so close. Fiercely close. I don't think anybody could adore him like she does."

"I was jealous of her. God, I was jealous of her."

"Decca. Listen! Oh, wait a minute. I've got to pee." Laura stands, totters, reels across the room into the bathroom. Decca hears her fall, the crack of head against porcelain.

"You okay?"

"Yeah."

Laura returns, crawling on all fours to her chair.

"Life is fraught with peril," she giggles. There is already a big blue goose bump on her forehead.

"Listen, Decca. There is nothing to worry about. He'll never marry Camille. Maybe he said that to get her down there. But he won't. I'll bet you a billion dollars. And you know why?"

"Yep. I've got it. Sister Sarah! She'll never get past old Sarah."

Decca had been tying her hair up with an elastic, high on top of her head so it looked like a crooked palm tree. Laura's hair had come loose from her chignon, so a hunk just flops out of one side of her head. They sit smiling stupidly at one another in their burned wet clothes.

"That's right. Sarah really likes you and me. You know why?"

"Because we are well-bred."

"Because we are ladies." They toast each other with a fresh drink, laughing uproariously, kicking the floor.

"It's true," Decca says. "Although perhaps at this moment we're not quite at our best. So, tell me, were you jealous of Sarah too?"

"No," Laura says. "I never had a real family. She helped me feel part of one. Still does, and she loves the boys. No, I was jealous of the dope dealers. Juni, Beto, Willy, Nacho."

"Yeah, all the pretty punks."

"They always found us. A year and a half clean. Beto found us in Chiapas, at the foot of the church on the hill. San Cristobal. Streaks of rain on his mirror sunglasses."

"You ever know Frankie?"

"I knew Frankie. He was the sickest."

"I saw his dog die, once when he got busted. He even had his toy poodle strung out on junk."

"I once stabbed a connection, in Yelapa. I didn't even hurt him, really. But I felt the blade go in, saw him bleed."

Decca is crying now. Sad sobs, like a child's. She puts on Charlie Parker with Strings. "April in Paris."

"Max and I were in Paris in April. Rained the whole damn time. We were both pretty lucky, Laura, and drugs ruined it all. I mean for a short time we had everything a woman could want. Well, I knew him in his golden years. Italy and France and Spain. Mallorca. Everything he did turned to gold. He could write, play saxophone, fight bulls, race cars." She pours them more rum.

Laura can't express herself. "I knew him when, when he was..."

"You almost said happy, didn't you. He was never happy."

"Yes, he was. We were. No one ever was so happy as we were."

Decca sighs, "That might be true. I thought it, seeing you all together. But it wasn't enough for him."

"Once we were in Harlem. Max and a musician friend went into the bathroom to fix. The man's wife looked at me, across the kitchen table, and she said, 'There our men go, to the lady in the lake.' Maybe we were wrong, Decca. Hubris or something, wanting to mean too much to him. Maybe this girl, what's her name? Maybe she'll just be there."

Decca had been talking to herself. Aloud she said, "No one could ever ever mean so much to me. Have you met any man who can touch him? His mind? His wit?"

"No. And none of them are so kind or sweet, like how he cries at music, kisses his sons goodnight."

Both women are sobbing now, blowing their noses. "I get really lonesome. I try to meet men," Laura says. "I even joined the ACLU."

"You what?"

"I even went to the Sundowner for Happy Hour. But all the men just got on my nerves."

"That's it. Other men *jar* after Max. They say 'you know' too much or repeat the same stories, laugh too loud. Max never bored, Max never jarred."

"I went out with this pediatrician. A sweet guy who wears bow ties, flies kites. The perfect man. Loves children, healthy, handsome, rich. He jogs, drinks rosé wine coolers." The women roll their eyes. "OK, so I have it all set up. The children are asleep. I'm in white chiffon. We're at the table on the terrace. Candles. Stan Getz and Astrud Gilberto Bossa Nova. Lobster. Stars. Then Max shows up, drives up on the lawn in a Lamborghini. Wearing a white suit. He gives us a little wave, goes in to see the kids, says something idiotic like he loves to look at them when they're sleeping. I lost it. Smashed the rosé wine cooler pitcher on the bricks, threw the plates of lobster, smash, smash, salad plates, smash. Told the guy to hit the road."

"Which he did, right?"

"Right."

"See, Laura, Max would never have left. He'd have said something like, 'Honey, you need some loving,' or he'd start throwing plates and dishes too until you were both laughing."

"Yeah. Actually he sort of did when he came out. He smashed some glasses and a vase of freesia but he rescued the lobster and we ate it. Sandy. He just grinned and said, 'That pediatrician is hardly an improvement.'"

"There's never been a man like him. He never farted or belched."

"Yes, he did, Decca. A lot."

"Well, it never got on my nerves. You just came over to upset me. Go home!"

"Last time you told me to go home you were in my house."

"I did? Hell, I'll go home then."

Laura gets up to leave. She lurches toward the bed to get her coat, stands there, getting her bearings. Decca comes up behind her, embraces her, touches her neck with her lips. Laura holds her breath, doesn't move. Sonny Rollins is playing "In Your Own Sweet Way." Decca leans, kisses Laura on the ear.

"Then he brushes your nipple with the palm of his hand."

She does this to Laura. "Then you turn to him and he holds your head in both hands and kisses you on the mouth." But Laura doesn't move.

"Lie down, Laura."

Laura stumbles, slides down onto the mink-covered bed. Decca blows out the lantern and lies down too. But the women are facing away from each other. Each is waiting for the other to touch her the way Max did. There is a long silence. Laura weeps, softly, but Decca laughs out loud, whacks Laura on the buttock.

"Good night, you fat-assed sap."

In just a short time, Decca is asleep. Laura leaves quietly, arrives home and showers, dresses before her children wake up.

Sometimes in Summer

Hope and I were both seven. I don't think we knew what month it was or even what day it was unless it was Sunday. Summer had already been so hot and long with every day just like the other that we didn't remember that it had rained the year before. We asked Uncle John to fry an egg on the sidewalk again, so at least we remembered that.

Hope's family had come over from Syria. It wasn't likely that they would sit around and talk about weather in Texas in the summertime. Or explain how the days are longer in summer, but then they start getting shorter. My family didn't talk to each other at all. Uncle John and I ate together sometimes. My grandma Mamie ate in the kitchen with my little sister Sally. My mother and Grandpa, if they ever ate, ate in their own rooms, or out somewhere.

Sometimes everybody would be in the living room. To listen to Jack Benny or Bob Hope or Fibber McGee and Molly. But even then nobody talked. Each laughed alone and stared at the green eye on the radio the way people stare at the television now.

What I mean is there was no way Hope or I would have heard about summer solstice, or how it always rained in El Paso in the summer. No one at my house ever talked about stars, probably didn't even know that in summer there were sometimes meteor showers in the northern sky.

Heavy rains overflowed the arroyos and the drainage ditches, destroyed houses in Smeltertown and carried away chickens and cars.

When the lightning and thunder came we reacted in primitive terror. Crouched on Hope's front porch, covered in blankets, listening to the cracks and rumbles with awe and fatalism. We couldn't not watch, though, huddled shivering and made each other look when the arrows lit up all along the Rio Grande and cracked into the cross of Mount Cristo Rey, zigzagged into the smelter smoke-stack crack crack. Boom. At the same time the trolley on Mundy Street shorted out in a cascade of sparks and all the passengers came running out just as it began to rain.

It rained and rained. It rained all night. The phones went out and the lights went out. My mother didn't come home and Uncle John didn't come home. Mamie started a fire in the wood stove and when Grandpa got home he called her an idiot. The electricity is out, fool, not the gas, But she shook her head. We understood perfectly. Nothing was to be trusted.

We slept on cots on Hope's porch. We did sleep although we both swore we were up all night watching the sheets of rain come down like a big glass brick window.

We had breakfast in both houses. Mamie made biscuits and gravy; at Hope's house we had *kibbe* and Syrian bread. Her grandma braided our hair into tight French braids so that the rest of the morning our eyes slanted back as if we were Asian. We spent the morning spinning around in the rain and then shivering drying off and going back out. Both of our grandmothers came to watch as their gardens washed completely away, down the walls, out into the street. Red caliche clay water quickly rose above the sidewalks and up to the fifth step of the concrete stairways of our houses. We jumped into the water which was warm and thick like cocoa and carried us along for blocks, fast, our pigtails floating. We'd get out, run back in the cold rain, back past our houses all the way up the block and then jump back into the river of the street and become swept away some more over and over.

The silence gave this flood a particularly eerie magic. The trolleys couldn't run and for days there were no cars. Hope and I were the only children on the block. She had six brothers and sisters, but they were bigger, either had to help in the furniture store or were just gone somewhere always. Upson Avenue was mostly retired smelter workers or Mexican widows who spoke little English, went to mass at Holy Family in the morning and the evening.

Hope and I had the street all to ourselves. For skating and hopscotch and jacks. Early in the morning or in the evening the old women would water their plants but the rest of the time they all stayed inside with the windows and blinds shut tight to keep out the terrible Texan heat but most of all the caliche red dust and the smoke from smelter.

Every night they burned at the smelter. We would sit outside where the stars would be shining and then the flames would shoot out of the stack, followed by massive sick convulsions of black smoke that darkened the sky and veiled everything around us. It was quite lovely really, the billows and undulations in the sky, but it would sting our eyes and the smell of sulfur was so strong we would even gag. Hope always did but she was just pretending. To give you an idea of how scary it was every night, when the newsreel of the first atom bomb was shown at the Plaza theater some Mexican joker hollered, *"Mira,* the *esmelter!"*

There was a break in the rains and that's when the second thing happened. Our grandmothers shoveled the sand away and swept their sidewalks. Mamie was a terrible housekeeper. She always used to have colored help, that's why, my mother said.

"And you had Daddy!"

She didn't think that was funny. "I'm not going to waste my time cleaning this roach-infested dump."

But Mamie took trouble with the yard, sweeping the steps and sidewalk, watering her little garden. Sometimes she'd be right on the other side of the fence from Mrs. Abraham but they ignored one another completely. Mamie did not trust foreigners and Hope's grandmother hated Americans. She liked me because I made her laugh. One day all the children were lined up at the stove and she was giving them *kibbe* on fresh hot bread. I just got in line and she served me before she realized it. That's how I got my hair brushed and braided every morning too. The first time she pretended she didn't notice, told me in Syrian to hold still, hit me on the head with the brush.

There was a vacant lot next to the Haddad house. In summer it was overgrown with weeds, bad thistles so you wouldn't even want to walk through it. In fall and winter you could see that the lot was carpeted with broken glass. Blue, brown, green. Mostly from Hope's brother and his friends shooting BB guns at bottles but also just throwaways. Hope and I looked for bottles to turn in for refund, and the old women took bottles to the Sunshine Market in their faded Mexican baskets. But in those days most people would drink a soda and then just toss the bottle anywhere. Beer bottles would fly out from cars all the time making little explosions.

I understand now that it had to do with the sun setting so late, after we had both eaten dinner. We were back outside, squatting on the sidewalk playing jacks. For only a few days, from our position low on the ground, we could see beneath the weeds on the lot at the very moment when the sun lit the mosaic carpet of glass. At an angle, shining through the glass like a cathedral window. This magical display only lasted a few minutes, only happened for two days. "Look!" she said the first time. We sat there, frozen. I had the jacks clasped tightly in a sweaty palm. She held the golf ball up in the air, like the statue of Liberty. We watched the kaleidoscope of color spread out before us dazzling then soft and blurry then it vanished. The next day it happened again, but the day after that the sun just quietly turned to dusk.

Sometime soon after the glass or maybe it was before, they burned early at the smelter. Of course they burned at the same time. Nine P.M. but we didn't realize that.

In the afternoon we had been sitting on my steps, taking off our skates when the big car pulled up. A shiny black Lincoln. A man sat in the driver's seat wearing a hat. He made the window near us go down. "Electric windows," Hope said. He asked who lived in the house. "Don't tell him," Hope said, but I told him, "Dr. Moynahan."

"Is he home?"

"No. Nobody's home but my mother."

"Is that Mary Moynahan?"

"Mary Smith. My father is a lieutenant in the war. We're here for the duration," I said.

The man got out of the car. He wore a suit with a vest and a watch chain, had a stiff white shirt. He gave each of us a silver dollar. We had no idea what they were. He told us they were dollars.

"Will they take them for money in a store?" Hope asked.

He said yes. He went up the stairs and knocked on the door. When there was no answer he turned the metal crank that rang a raspy bell. After a while the door opened. My mother said angry things that we couldn't hear and then she slammed the door.

When he came back down he gave each of us two more silver dollars.

"I apologize. I should have introduced myself. I'm F.B. Moynahan, your uncle."

"I'm Lu. This is Hope."

He asked then where Mamie was. I told him she was at First Texan Baptist, across from the library downtown. "Thank you," he said and drove off. We both put our dollars in our socks. Just in time, because my mother was running down the steps, her hair in pin curls.

"That was your uncle Fortunatus, the snake. Don't you dare tell a soul he came. Do you hear me?" I nodded. She whacked me on the shoulder and the back.

"Don't say a single word to Mamie. He broke her heart when he left. Left them all to starve. She'll get all upset. Not a word. Understand?" I nodded again.

"Answer me!"

"I won't say a word."

She gave me another whack for good measure and went back upstairs.

Later everyone was at home, in their own rooms as usual. The house had four bedrooms to the left of a long hall, a bathroom at the end, with the kitchen dining and living room on the other side. The hall was always dark. Pitch black at night, blood red from the stained-glass transom during the day. I used to be terrified of going to the bathroom until Uncle John taught me to start at the front door, whisper over and over to myself, "God will take care of me. God will take care of me," and run like hell. That day I tiptoed because in the front bedroom my mother was telling Uncle John that Fortie had come. Uncle John said he wished he'd been there so he could have shot him. I stopped then outside the door to Mamie's room. She was singing Sally to sleep. So sweet. "Way down in Missoura when my mammy sung to me." When I came out of the bathroom Uncle John was in Grandpa's room. I listened there as Grandpa told Uncle John that Fortunatus had tried to come inside the Elks' club. Grandpa had sent word for him to leave or else he'd call the police. They talked some more but I couldn't hear. Just bourbon gurgling into glasses.

Finally Uncle John came into the kitchen. I had iced tea while he drank. He put mint in his glass so Mamie would think he was drinking tea too. He told me that Uncle Fortunatus had left home years and years before, just when they really needed him. Both John and Grandpa were drinking badly and couldn't work. Uncle Tyler and Fortunatus were supporting the family until Fortunatus went to California in the middle of the night. Left a note that said he'd had enough of Moynahan trash. He didn't ever send any money or even a letter, didn't come home when Mamie almost died. Now he was president of some railroad. "Best not to mention seeing him," Uncle John told me.

Everybody was in the living room for Jack Benny. Sally was still asleep. Mamie sat on her little chair, with the Bible open as usual. But she wasn't reading it. She was looking down at it and there was a look of happiness on her old face. I understood that Uncle Fortunatus had found her and had talked with her. When she looked up, I smiled. She smiled back at me and looked back down. My mother was standing in the doorway, smoking. This smiling made her nervous and she began to make all these Shh! signs and faces at me behind Mamie's back. I just looked at her with a blank stare like I had no idea what she was talking about. Grandpa was listening to the radio and laughing at Jack Benny. He was already drunk. Rocking hard in his leather rocking chair and tearing the newspaper into little strips, burning it up in the big red ashtray. Uncle John was drinking and smoking in the dining room doorway, taking it all in. He was ignoring my mother's signs to him to get me out of there. I figured he could see that Mamie was smiling too. My mother was making Shoo! signs at me to leave. I acted like I didn't notice and sang along with the Fitch commercial. "If your head scratches, don't itch it! Fitch it! Use your head! Save your hair! Use Fitch shampoo!" She was looking at me so mean I couldn't stand it, so I took one of the silver dollars out of my sock.

"He, look what I got, Grandpa!"

He stopped rocking. "Where'd you get that? You and them A-rabs steal that money?"

"No. It was a present!"

My mother was slapping me. "Rotten little brat!" She dragged me out of the room and threw me out the front door. I remember it as her carrying me by the neck like a cat, but I was very big already so that can't be true.

The minute I was outside, Hope hollered to come quick. "They're burning early!" That's what I mean about us thinking it was early. It just hadn't gotten dark.

Massive billows and swirls of black smoke were rising from the smokestack high into the air tumbling and cascading with a terrible speed unfurling in billows over our neighborhood as if it were night now with foggy wisps creeping over the roofs and down alleys. The smoke thinned and danced and spread further over the whole downtown. Neither of us could move. Tears flowed from our eyes because of the foul sting and stink of the sulfur fumes. But as the smoke dissipated over the rest of the town it too was backlit like the glass had been by the sun and now even smoke turned into colors. Lovely blues and greens and the iridescent violet and acid green of gasoline in puddles. A flare of yellow and a rusty red but then mostly a soft mossy green that reflected in our faces. Hope said, "Yucko, your eyes turned all those colors." I lied and said hers did too but her eyes were black as ever. My pale eyes do change color so they probably did turn in the spirals of the smoke.

We never chattered like most little girls. We didn't even talk much. I know we didn't say a word about the terrible beauty of the smoke or of the glowing glass.

Suddenly it was dark and late. We both went inside. Uncle John was asleep on the porch swing. Our house was hot and smelled of cigarettes and sulfur and bourbon. I crawled into bed next to my mother and fell asleep. It seemed like the middle of the night when Uncle John shook me awake and took me outside. Wake your pal Hope, he whispered. I threw a rock at her screen and in seconds she was outside with us. He led us to the grass and told us to lie down. Close your eyes. Closed? Yes. Yes. OK, open your eyes and look toward Randolph Street up in the sky. We opened our eyes to the clear Texas sky. Stars. The sky was filled with stars and it was as if there were so many that some were just jumping off the edge of it, tumbling and spilling into the night. Dozens, hundreds, millions of shooting stars until finally a wisp of cloud covered them and softly more clouds covered the sky above us.

"Sweet dreams," he whispered when he sent us back to bed.

By morning it was raining again. It rained and flooded all week until finally we got tired of getting cold and muddy and we ended up spending our dollars going to movies. The day Hope and I got home from *The Spanish Main* my father had come back safe from the war. Very soon we went to live in Arizona so I don't know what happened in Texas the summer after that one.

Mijito

I want to go home. When *mijito* Jesus falls asleep I think about home, my mamacita and my brothers and sisters. I try to remember all the trees and all the people in the village. I try to remember me because I was different then, before *tantas cosas que han pasado*. I had no idea. I didn't know television or *drogas* or fear. I have been afraid since the minute I left the trip and the van and the men and running and even when Manolo met me I got more afraid because he wasn't the same. I knew he loved me and when he held me it was like by the river, but he was changed, with fear in his gentle eyes. All of the United States was scary coming to Oakland. Cars in front of us, behind us, cars going the other way cars cars cars for sale and stores and stores and more cars. Even in our little room in Oakland where I'd wait for him the room was full of noise not just the television but cars and buses and sirens and helicopters, men fighting and shooting and people yelling. The *mayates* frighten me and they stand in groups all down the street so I was afraid to go outside. Manolo was so strange I was afraid he didn't want to marry me but he said, "Don't be crazy, I love you *mi vida*." I was happy but then he said, "Anyway you need to be legal so you can get welfare and food stamps." We got married right away and that same day he took me to the welfare. I was sad. I wanted to maybe go to a park or have some wine a little *luna de miel* party.

We lived in the Flamingo Motel on MacArthur. I was lonely. He was gone most of the time. He got mad at me for being so scared but he forgot how different it was here. We didn't have inside bathrooms or lights at home. Even the television frightened me; it seemed so real. I wished we had a little house or room that I could make pretty and where I could cook for him. He would come with Kentucky Fry or Taco Bell or hamburgers. We ate breakfast every day in a little café and that was nice like in Mexico.

One day there was a banging on the door. I didn't want to open it. The man said he was Ramón, Manolo's uncle. He said Manolo was in jail. He was going to take me to talk to him. He made me pack up all my things and get in the car. I kept asking him, "Why? What happened? What did he do?"

"*No me jodes! Callate!*" he told me. "*Mira,* I don't know. He'll tell you. All I know is you'll be staying with us until he goes to court."

We went into a big building and then in an elevator to the top floor. I had never been in an elevator. He talked to some police and then one took me through a door to a chair in front of a window. He pointed to a phone. Manolo came and sat down on the other side. He was thin and unshaven and his eyes were full of fear. He was shaking and pale. All he was wearing was some orange nightclothes. We sat there, looking at each other. He picked up a phone and pointed to me to pick up mine. It was my first telephone call. It didn't sound like him but I could see him talking. I was so afraid. I can't remember everything, except that he said he loved me and he was sorry. He said he would let Ramón know when he'd go to court. He hoped he'd come home to me then. But if he didn't, to wait for him, my husband. Ramón and Lupe were *buena gente*. they would take care of me until he got out. They needed to take me to the welfare to change my address. "Don't forget. I'm sorry," he said in English. I had to think how you said it in Spanish. *Lo siento.* I feel it.

Mijito

If only I had known. I should have told him I'd love him and wait for him always, that I loved him with all of my heart. I should have told him about our baby. But I was so worried and too frightened to talk into the phone so I just looked at him until the two policemen took him away.

In the car I asked Ramón what had happened, where did they take him? I kept asking him until he stopped his car and said how did he know, to shut up. My check and food stamps would go to them for feeding me and I'd need to take care of their kids. As soon as I could I had to get my own place and move out. I told him I was three months pregnant and he said, "Fuck a duck." That's the first English I said out loud. "Fuck a duck."

Dr. Fritz should be here soon, so at least I can get some of these patients into rooms. He should have been here two hours ago, but as usual he added another surgery. He knows he has office hours Wednesdays. The waiting room is packed, babies screaming, children fighting. Karma and I'll be lucky to get out of here by seven. She's the office supervisor, what a job. The place is steamy and hot, reeking of dirty diapers and sweat, wet clothes. It's raining of course and most of these mothers have taken long bus rides to get here.

When I go out there I sort of cross my eyes, and when I call the patient's name I smile at the mother or grandmother or foster care mom but I look at a third eye in their forehead. I learned this in Emergency. It's the only way to work here, especially with all the crack babies and AIDS and cancer babies. Or the ones who will never grow up. If you look the parent in the eyes you will share it, confirm it, all the fear and exhaustion and pain. On the other hand once you get to know them, sometimes that's all you can do, look into their eyes with the hope or sorrow you can't express.

The first two are post-ops. I set out gloves and suture removers, gauze and tape, tell the mothers to undress the babies. It won't be long. In the waiting room I call "Jesus Romero."

A teen-age mother walks toward me, her infant wrapped in a rebozo like in Mexico. The girl looks cowed, terrified. "*No Inglés,*" she says.

In Spanish I tell her to take off everything but his diaper, ask her what is the matter.

She says, "*Pobre mijito* he cries and cries all the time, he never stops."

I weigh him, ask her his birth weight. Seven pounds. He is three months old, should be bigger by now.

"Did you take him for his shots?"

Yes, she went to La Clinica a few days ago. They said he has a hernia. She didn't know babies needed shots. They gave him one and told her to come back next month but to come here right away.

Her name is Amelia. She is seventeen, had come from Michoacan to marry her sweetheart but now he is in Soledad prison. She lives with an uncle and aunt. She has no money to go back home. They don't want her here and don't like the baby because he cries all the time.

"Do you breast feed him?"

"Yes, but I don't think my milk is good. He wakes up and cries and cries."

She holds him like a potato sack. The expression on her face says, "Where does this sack go?" It occurs to me that she has nobody to tell her anything at all.

"Do you know to change breasts? Start off each time with a different breast and let him drink a long time, then put him on the other breast for a while. But be sure and change. This way he gets more milk and your breasts make more milk. He may be falling asleep because he's tired, not full. He also is probably crying because of the hernia. The doctor is very good. He'll fix your baby."

Mijito

She seems to feel better. Hard to tell, she has what doctors call a "flat affect."

"I have to go to the other patients. I'll be back when the doctor comes." She nods, resigned. She has that hopeless look you see on battered women. God forgive me, because I am a woman too, but when I see women with that look I want to slap them.

Dr. Fritz has come, is in the first room. No matter how long he makes the mothers wait, no matter how mad Karma and I get, when he is with a child we all forgive him. He is a healer. The best surgeon, he does more surgeries than the others combined. Of course they all say he is obsessive and egomaniacal. They can't say he is not a fine surgeon though. He is famous, actually, was the doctor who risked his life to save the boy after the big earthquake.

The first two patients go quickly. I tell him there is a pre-op with no English in Room Three, that I'd be right in. I clean the rooms and put more patients in. When I get to Room Three he is holding the baby, showing Amelia how to push the hernia in. The baby is smiling at him.

"Have Pat put him on the surgery schedule. Explain the pre-op and fasting carefully. Tell her to call if she can't push it in when it pops out." He hands her back the baby. "*Muy bonito*," he says.

"Ask her how Jesus got the bruises on his arms. The ones you should have made note of." He points to the marks on the underside of the baby's arms.

"I'm sorry," I say to him. When I ask her she looks frightened and surprised. "*No sé.*"

"She doesn't know."

"What do you think?"

"Seems to me that she's . . ."

"I can't believe you're going to say what I think you are. I have calls to return. I'll be in Room One in ten minutes. I'll need some dilators, an 8 and a 10."

He was right. I was going to say that she seemed a victim herself, and yes I know what victims often do. I explain to her how important the surgery is, and the pre-op the day before. To call if the baby was sick or had a bad diaper rash. No milk three hours before the surgery. I get Pat to come set up a date with her and go over the instructions again.

I forget about her then until at least a month has gone by when for some reason it occurs to me she never brought the baby for a post-op. I asked Pat when the surgery was.

"Jesus Romero? That ma is such a retard. No-show for the first surgery. Didn't bother to call. I call her and she says she couldn't get a ride. O-Kay. So I tell her we'll have a same day pre-op, to come in really early for an exam and blood work, but that she has got to come. And hallelulia, she shows. But guess what?"

"She feeds the baby half hour before surgery."

"You got it. Fritz will be out of town so next slot I have is a month away."

It was very bad living with them. I couldn't wait until Manolo and I would be together. I gave them my check and food stamps. They gave me just a little money for things for me. I took care of Tina and Willie, but they didn't speak Spanish, didn't pay me any attention. Lupe hated having me there and Ramón was nice except when he got drunk he was always grabbing me or poking at me from behind. I was more afraid of Lupe than him so when I wasn't working in the house, I just stayed in my little corner in the kitchen.

"What are you doing there for hours and hours?" Lupe asked me.

"Thinking. About Manolo. About my *pueblo*."

"Start thinking about moving out of here."

Ramón had to work on the court day so Lupe took me. She could be nice sometimes. In the court we sat in the front.

Mijito

I almost didn't know him when he came in, handcuffed and with chains tying his legs together. Such a cruel thing to do to Manolo who is a sweet man. He stood under the judge and then the judge said something and two polices took him away. He looked back at me, but I didn't know him with that face of anger. My Manolo. On the way home Lupe said it didn't look good. She didn't understand the charges either but it wasn't just possession of drugs because they would've sent him to Santa Rita. Eight years in Soledad prison is bad.

"Eight years? *Cómo que* eight years!"

"Don't you go lose it now. I'll put you out right here in the street. I'm serious."

Lupe told me I had to go to the Clinica because I was pregnant. I didn't know she meant I should have an *aborto*. "No," I told the lady doctor, "no, I want my baby, *mijito*. His daddy is gone my baby is all I have." She was nice at first but then she got mad said I was just a child I couldn't work how could I care for him? That I was selfish, *porfiada*. "It's a sin," I told her. "I won't do it. I want my baby." She threw her notebook down on the table.

"*Válgame diós.* At least come in for checkups before the baby is born."

She gave me a card with the day and time to come but I never went back. The months went by slow. I kept waiting to hear from Manolo. Willie and Tina just watched the tele and were no trouble. I had the baby at Lupe's house. She helped but Ramón hit her when he got home and hit me too. He said bad enough I showed up. Now a kid too.

I try to keep out of their way. We have our little corner in the kitchen. Little Jesus is beautiful and he looks like Manolo. I got pretty things for him at the Good Will and at Payless. I still don't know what Manolo did to go to jail or when we will hear from him. When I ask Ramón he said, "Kiss Manolo goodbye. See if you can get some work."

I watch Lupe's kids while she works and keep their house clean. I do all the wash in the laundromat downstairs. But I get so tired. Jesus cries and cries *no importa* what I do. Lupe told me I had to take him to the Clinica. The buses scare me. The *mayates* grab at me and scare me. I think they're going to take him from me.

In the Clinica they got mad at me again, said I should have had pre-natal care, that he needed shots and was too small. He was seven pounds I said, my uncle weighed him. "Well, he's only eight now." They gave him a shot, said I had to come back. The doctor said Jesus had a hernia which could be dangerous. He had to see a surgeon. A woman there gave me a map and wrote down the bus and BART train to get to the surgeon's office, told me where to stand even to get the bus and BART back. She called and made me an appointment.

Lupe had taken me, she was outside in the car with the kids when I got in. I told her what they said and then I began to cry. She stopped the car and shook me.

"You're a woman now! Face it. We'll give you some time till Jesus is OK, then you're going to have to figure out your own life. The apartment is too small. Ramón and I are dead tired and your kid cries day and night, or you do, worse. We're sick of it."

"I'm trying to help out," I said.

"Yeah, thanks a lot."

We were all up early the day I took him to the surgeon's. Lupe had to take the kids to day care. It's free and they like it better than staying home with just me so they were happy. But Lupe was mad because she had to drive so far to child care and now Ramón had to take the subway. It was scary, the bus, and then the BART and then another bus. I was too nervous to eat so I was hungry and dizzy from being frightened. But then I saw the big sign like they told me and I knew it was the right place. We had to wait so long. I left home at six in the morning and the doctor didn't see Jesus until three. I was so hungry. They explained everything real clear and the nurse told me about feeding him different to make more milk. The doctor was nice with Jesus and said he was *bonito* but he thought I hurt him, showed her blue spots on his arms. I didn't see the spots before. It's true. I hurt my baby, *mijito*. It was me who made them last night when he cried and cried. I had him under the blankets with me. I held him tight, "Hush hush stop crying, stop it stop it." I never grabbed him like that before. He didn't cry any less or any more.

Two weeks went past. I marked the days on the calendar. I told Lupe I had to go to the pre-op one day and for the surgery the next day.

"No way, José," Lupe said. The car was in the shop. She couldn't take her Willie and Tina to child care. So I didn't go.

Ramón stayed home. He was drinking beer and watching an A's game. The kids were taking a nap and I was feeding Jesus in the kitchen. "Come on in and watch the game, *prima*," he said so I went in. Jesus was still drinking but I had him covered with a blanket. Ramón got up for more beer. He hadn't seemed drunk until he got up but then he was falling around, then he was on the floor by the sofa. He pulled the blanket down and my T-shirt up. "Gimme some of that *chichi*," he said and was sucking on my other breast. I shoved him away and he hit the table but Jesus fell too and the table scratched his shoulder. There was blood running down his little arm. I was washing it with a paper towel and the phone rang.

It was Pat the lady from surgery real mad because I didn't call and didn't go. "I'm sorry," I told her in English.

She said there was a cancellation tomorrow. I could get the pre-op on the same day if I for sure took him real early. Seven in the morning. She was mad at me. She said he could get real sick and die, that if I kept missing surgeries the State could take him away from me. "Do you understand this?"

I said yes, but I didn't believe they could take my baby away from me.

"Are you coming tomorrow?" she asked.

"Yes," I said. I told Ramón that the next day I had to take Jesus for surgery, could he watch Tina and Willie.

"So I suck your tit you think you get something back? Yeah, I'll be here. I'm out of work anyways. Don't get any ideas about telling Lupe nothing. Your ass would be out of here in five minutes. Which would be fine with me, but as long as it's here I mean to get me some."

He took me in the bathroom then, with Jesus in the living room crying on the floor and the kids hitting on the door. He bent me over the sink and banged and banged into me but he was so drunk it didn't last long. He slid to the floor passed out. I went out. I told the kids that he was sick. I was shaking so bad I had to sit down, rocked *mijito* Jesus and watched cartoons with the kids. I didn't know what to do. I said an Ave María but it seemed like there was so much noise everywhere how could a prayer ever get heard?

When Lupe got home he came out. I could tell the way he looked at me he knew he had done something bad but he didn't remember what. He said he was going out. She said terrific.

She opened the refrigerator. "Asshole drank all the beer. Go to the Seven-Eleven, Amelia, will you? Oh Christ, you can't even buy beer. What good are you? Have you even looked for a job or a place?"

I told her I had been watching the kids, how could I go anywhere? I said tomorrow was Jesus' surgery.

"Well, as soon as you can, you get started. They have ads for jobs and houses on billboards in groceries, the pharmacy."

"I can't read."

"They have ads in Spanish."

"I can't read Spanish *tampoco*."

"Fuck a duck."

I said it too. "Fuck a duck." It made her laugh, at least. Oh how I miss my pueblo where the laughter is soft like breezes.

"OK, Amelia. Tomorrow I'll look for you, I'll call around. Do me a favor and watch the kids now. I need a drink. I'll be at the Jalisco."

She must have run into Ramón, they came back together really late. There was only beans and Kool-Aid for the kids and me to eat. No bread, no flour for tortillas. Jesus was fast asleep in our corner in the kitchen but the minute I lay down he started to cry. I fed him. I could tell he was getting more now but after he slept awhile he was crying again. I tried to give him a pacifier but he just pushed it out. I was doing it again holding him so tight whispering, "Hush hush," but then I stopped when I realized that I was hurting him but also I didn't want the doctor to see blue marks. The shoulder was bad enough all scraped and bruised, *pobrecito*. I prayed again to our mother Mary to help me, please to tell me what to do.

It was dark when I left the next morning. I found people who helped me get the right bus and BART and bus. At the hospital they showed me where to go. They took blood from Jesus' arm. A doctor examined him but he didn't speak Spanish. I don't know what he was writing down. I know he wrote about the shoulder because he measured it with his thumb and then wrote. He looked at me with a question. "Childrens push," I said in English and he nodded. They told me the surgery would be at eleven so I had fed him at eight. But hours and hours went by until it was one o'clock. Jesus was screaming. We were in a space with a bed and a chair. I was sitting in the chair but then the bed looked so good I got on it and held him to me. My breasts were dripping with milk. It's like they heard him crying. I couldn't bear it and I thought just a few seconds of milk wouldn't hurt.

Dr. Fritz was yelling at me. I took Jesus off my breast but he shook his head and nodded at me to go on ahead and feed him. A Latina nurse came in then to say they couldn't do the surgery now. She said they had a big waiting list and I had screwed them over twice. "You call Pat, get another date. Go on now, go home. Call her tomorrow. That child needs the surgery, you hear me?"

In my whole life at home nobody ever got mad at me.

When I stood up I must have fainted. The nurse was sitting by me when I woke up.

"I ordered you a big lunch. You must be hungry. Did you eat today?"

"No," I said. She fixed pillows behind me and a table over my lap. She held Jesus while I ate. I ate like an animal. Everything, soup, crackers, salad, juice, milk, meat, potatoes, carrots, bread, salad, pie; it was good.

"You need to eat well every day while you're nursing the baby," she said. "Will you be all right, going home?"

I nodded. Yes. I felt so good, the food was so good.

"Come on, now. Get ready to go. Here are some diapers for him. My shift was over an hour ago and I need to lock up."

Pat has a hard job. Our office of six surgeons is in Children's Hospital in Oakland. Every day each surgeon has a packed schedule. Also every day some get cancelled, others put in their place and several emergencies added as well. One of our doctors is on call every day for the emergency room. All kinds of traumas, chopped-off fingers, aspirated peanuts, gunshot wounds, appendixes, burns, so there can be six or eight surprise surgeries a day.

Almost all of the patients are Medi-Cal and many are illegal aliens and don't even have that, so none of our doctors are in this for the money. It's an exhausting job for the office staff too. I work ten-hour days a lot. The surgeons are all different and for different reasons can be a pain in the butt sometimes. But even though we complain we respect them, are proud of them too, and we get a sense that we help. It is a rewarding job, not like working in a regular office. It has for sure changed the way I see things.

I have always been a cynical person. When I first started working here I thought it was a huge waste of taxpayers' money to do ten, twelve surgeries on crack babies with weird anomalies just so they could be alive and disabled after a year spent in a hospital, then moved from one foster home to another. So many without mothers, much less fathers. Most of the foster parents are really great but some are scary. So many children who are disabled or with brain damage, patients who will never be more than a few years old. Many patients with Down's syndrome. I thought that I could never keep a child like that.

Now I open the door to the waiting room and Toby who is all distorted and shaky, Toby who can't talk, is there. Toby who pees and shits into bags, who eats through a hole in his stomach. Toby comes to hug me, laughing, arms open. It's as if these kids are the result of a glitch God made answering prayers. All those mothers who don't want their children to grow up, who pray that their child will love them forever. Those answered prayers got sent down as Tobys.

For sure Tobys can crack up a marriage or a family, but when they don't it seems to have the reverse effect. It brings out the deepest good and bad feelings and the strengths and dignity that otherwise a man and a woman would never have seen in themselves or the other. It seems to me that each joy is savored more, that commitment has a deeper dimension. I don't think I'm romanticizing either. I study them hard, because I saw those qualities and they surprised me. I've seen several couples divorce. It seemed inevitable. There was the martyr parent or the slacking parent, the blamer, the why-me or the guilty one, the drinker or the crier. I've seen siblings act out from resentment, cause even more havoc and anger and guilt. But much more often I have seen the marriage and the family grow closer, better. Everybody learns to deal, has to help, has to be honest and say it sucks. Everybody has to laugh, everybody has to feel grateful when whatever else the child can't do he can kiss the hand that brushes his hair.

I don't like Diane Arbus. When I was a kid in Texas there were freak shows and even then I hated the way people would point at the freaks and laugh at them. But I was fascinated too. I loved the man with no arms who typed with his toes. But it wasn't the no arms that I liked. It was that he really wrote, all day. He was seriously writing something, liking what he was writing.

I admit it is pretty fascinating when the women bring in Jay for a pre-op with Dr. Rook. Everything is bizarre. They are midgets. They look like sisters, maybe they are, they are very tiny and plump with rosy cheeks and curly hair, turned-up noses and big smiles. They are lovers, stroke one another and kiss and fondle with no embarrassment. They had adopted Jay, a dwarf baby, with multiple, serious problems. Their social worker, who is, well, gigantic, has come with them, to carry him and his little oxygen tank and diaper bag. The mothers each carry a stool, like a milking stool, and sit on the little stools in the exam rooms talking about Jay and how much better he is, he can focus now, recognizes them. Dr. Rook is going to do a gastrostomy on him so he can be fed by a tube through an opening in his stomach.

He is an alert but calm baby, not especially small but with a huge deformed head. The women love to talk about him, willingly tell us how they carry him between them, how they bathe him and care for him. Pretty soon he'd need a helmet when he crawled because their furniture was only a foot or so high. They had named him Jay because it was close to joy, and he brought them so much joy.

I am going out the door to get some paper tape. He is allergic to tape. Look back and see the two mothers on tiptoes looking up at Jay who is on his stomach on the exam table. He is smiling at them, they at him. The social worker and Dr. Rook are smiling at each other.

"That is the sweetest thing I ever saw," I say to Karma.

"Poor things. They're happy now. But he may only have a few more years, if that," she says.

"Worth it. Even if they had today and no more. It's still worth all the pain later. Karma, their tears will be sweet." I surprised myself saying this, but I meant it. I was learning about the labor of love.

Dr. Rook's husband calls her patients River babies, which makes her furious. He said that's what people used to call such babies in Mississippi. He is a surgeon with us too. He somehow manages to get almost all surgeries with real insurance like Blue Cross. Dr. Rook gets most of the disabled or totally non-functioning children, but not just because she is a good surgeon. She listens to the families, cares about them, so she gets a lot of referrals.

Today there is one after another. The children are mostly older and heavy. Dead weight. I have to lift them, then hold them down while she removes the old button and puts in a new one. Most of them can't cry. You can tell it must really hurt but there are just tears falling sideways into their ears and this awful unworldly creaking, like a rusty gate, from deep inside.

The last patient is so cool. Not the patient, but what she does. A pretty red-faced newborn girl with six fingers on each hand. People always joke when babies are born about making sure it has five fingers and five toes. It's more common than I thought. Usually the doctors schedule them for an in-and-out surgery. This baby is only a few days old. Dr. Rook asks me for Xylocaine and a needle and some cat gut. She deadens the area around the finger and then she ties a tight knot at the base of each extra little finger. She gives them some liquid Tylenol in case the baby seems to be hurting later, tells them not to touch it, that pretty soon, like a navel, the finger would turn black and fall off. She said her father had been a doctor in a small town in Alabama, that she had watched him do that.

Once Dr. Kelly had seen a little boy who had six fingers on each hand. His parents really wanted the surgery but the child didn't. He was six or seven years old, a cute kid.

"No! I want them! They're mine! I want to keep them!"

I thought old Dr. Kelly might reason with the boy, but instead he told the parents that it seemed to him the child wanted to continue having this distinction.

"Why not?" he said. The parents couldn't believe he was saying this. He told the parents that if the boy changed his mind then they could do it. Of course, the younger the better.

"I like how he sticks up for his rights. Put her there, son," and he shook the kid's hand. They left, the parents furious, cursing at him, the child grinning.

Will he always feel this way? What if he plays the piano? Will it be too late if or when he changes his mind? Why not six fingers? They are weird anyway and so are toes, hair, ears. I wish we had tails, myself.

I am daydreaming about having a tail or leaves instead of hair, cleaning and restocking the exam rooms for the night when I hear a banging on the door. Dr. Rook had gone and I was the only one there. I unlock the door and let in Amelia and Jesus. She is crying, shivering as she speaks. His hernia is out and she can't push it in.

I get my coat, turn on the alarms and lock the door, walk with her down the block to the Emergency Room. I go in to be sure she gets registered. Dr. McGee is on call. Good.

"Dr. McGee is a sweet old doctor. He'll take care of your Jesus. They'll probably operate on him tonight. Don't forget to call to bring the baby to the office. In about a week. Call us. *Oye,* for God's sake, don't feed him."

It was crowded on the subway and the bus but I wasn't afraid. Jesus was sleeping. It seemed like the Virgin Mary answered me. She told me to take my next Welfare check and go home to Mexico. The *curandera* would take care of my baby and my *mamacita* would know how to stop him from crying. I would feed him bananas and papayas. Not mangos because sometimes mangos give babies stomachaches. I wondered when babies got teeth.

Mijito

Lupe was watching a *telenovela* when I got home. Her kids were asleep in the bedroom.

"Did he get the surgery?"

"No. Something happened."

"Yeah, I'll bet. What dumb thing did you do? Huh?"

I put him down in our corner without waking him up. Lupe came into the kitchen.

"I found a place for you. You can stay there at least until you find your own place. You can get your next check here and then tell Welfare your new address. Do you hear me?"

"Yes. I want my check money. I'm going home."

"You're crazy. First place this month's money is spent. Whatever you have is the last of it. *Estas loca?* It wouldn't get you even halfway to Michoacan. Look, girl, you're here. Find a job in a restaurant, someplace they'll let you stay in the back. Meet some guys, go out, have some fun. You're young, you're pretty, would be if you fixed yourself up. You're as good as single. You're learning English fast. You can't just give up."

"I want to go home."

"Fuck a duck," she said and she went back to the tele.

I was still sitting there when Ramón came in the back door. I guess he didn't see her on the sofa. He started grabbing my breasts and kissing my neck. "Sugar, I want some sugar!"

"*Ya estuvo,*" she said. To Ramón she said, "Go soak your head, you stinking fat pig," and shoved him out of the room. To me she just said, "You're out of here. Get all your shit together. Here's a plastic bag."

I put everything in my *bolsa* and the bag, picked up Jesus.

"Go on, take him and get in the car. I'll bring the things."

It looked just like a boarded-up old store but there was a sign, and a cross over the door. It was dark but she banged on the door. An old Anglo man came out. He shook his head and said something in English but she talked louder, pushed me and Jesus through the door and took off.

He turned on a flashlight. He tried to talk to me but I shook my head. No English. He was probably saying they didn't have enough beds. The room was full of cots with women on them, a few children. It smelled bad, like wine and vomit and pee. Bad, dirty. He brought me some blankets and pointed to a corner, same size as my kitchen corner. "Thank you," I said.

It was horrible. The minute I lay down, Jesus woke up. He wouldn't stop crying. I made sort of a tent to keep the sound in, but some of the women were cussing and saying, "Shaddup shaddup." They were mostly old white wino women but some young black ones who were shoving me and pushing me. One little one was slapping me with tiny hands like quick hornets.

"Stopit!" I screamed. "Stopit! Stopit!"

The man came out with the flashlight and led me through the room into a kitchen and a new corner. "*Mis bolsas!*" I said. He understood and went back in and brought my bags. "I'm sorry," I said in English. Jesus nursed and fell asleep, but I leaned against the wall and waited for morning. I am learning English, I thought. I went over all the English I knew. Court, Kentucky Fry, hamburger, goodbye, greaser, nigger, asshole, ho, Pampers, How much? Fuck a duck, children, hospital, stopit, shaddup, hello, I'm sorry, General Hospital, All My Children, inguinal hernia, pre-op, post-op, Geraldo, food stamps, money, car, crack, pólis, Miami Vice, José Canseco, homeless, real pretty, no way, José, Excuse me, I'm sorry, please, please, stopit, shaddup, shaddup, I'm sorry. Holy Mary mother of God pray for us.

Just before light the man and an old woman came in and started to boil water for oatmeal. She let me help her, pointed to sugar and napkins to put in the middle of the lined-up tables.

We all had oatmeal and milk for breakfast. The women looked really bad off, crazy or drunk some of them. Homeless and dirty. We all waited in line to take a shower, by the time it was Jesus and me the water was cold and just one little towel. Then me and Jesus were homeless too. During the day the space was a nursery for children. We could come back at night for soup and a bed. The man was nice. He let me leave my *bolsa* there so I just took some diapers. I spent the day walking around Eastmont Mall. I went to a park but then I was scared because men came up to me. I walked and walked and the baby was heavy. The second day the little one who had been slapping me showed me or somehow I understood her that you can ride all day on the buses, getting transfers. So I did that because he was too heavy and this way I could sit down and look around or sleep when Jesus did because at night I didn't sleep. One day I saw where La Clinica was. I decided the next day I'd go there and find somebody there to help me. So I felt better.

The next day though, Jesus started to cry in a different way, like barking. I looked at his hernia and it was pooched way out and hard. I got on the bus right away but still it was long, the bus then BART then another bus. I thought the doctor's was closed but the nurse was there, she took us to the hospital. We waited a long time but they finally took him to surgery. They said they'd keep him for the night, put me on a cot next to a little box for him. They gave me a ticket to go and eat in the cafeteria. I got a sandwich and a Coke and ice cream, some cookies and fruit for later but I fell asleep it was so good not to be on the floor. When I woke the nurse was there. Jesus was all clean and wrapped in a blue blanket.

"He's hungry!" she smiled. "We didn't wake you when he got out of surgery. Everything went fine."

"Thank you." Oh, thank God! He was fine! While I fed him I cried and prayed.

"No reason to cry now," she said. She had brought me a tray with coffee and juice and cereal.

Dr. Fritz came in, not the doctor that did the surgery, the first doctor. He looked at Jesus and nodded, smiled at me, looked over his chart. He lifted the baby's shirt. There was still a scrape and a bruise on his shoulder. The nurse asked me about it. I told her it had been the kids were I was staying, that I didn't live there no more.

"He wants you to know that if he sees any more bruises he is going to call CPS. Those are people who might take your baby, or maybe they will just want you to talk to somebody.

I nodded. I wanted to tell her that I needed to talk to somebody.

We have had some busy days. Both Dr. Adeiko and Dr. McGee were on vacation so the other doctors were really busy. Several gypsy patients which always means the whole family, cousins, uncles, everybody comes. It always makes me laugh (not really laugh since he doesn't like any joking or unprofessional behavior), because one thing Dr. Fritz always does when he comes into the room is politely greet the parent, "Good morning." Or if it's both, he'll nod at each and say, "Good morning. Good morning." And with gypsy families I suffer not laughing when he squeezes into the room and says, "Good morning. Good morning. Good morning. Good morning. Good morning," etc. He and Dr. Wilson seem to get a lot of hypospadius babies which is when male babies have holes on the side of their penises, sometimes several so that when they pee it's like a sprinkler. Anyway, one gypsy baby called Rocky Stereo had it but Dr. Fritz fixed it. The whole family, about a dozen adults and some children, had come for the post-op and were all shaking his hand. "Thank you. Thank you. Thank you. Thank you." Worse than his good mornings! It was sweet and funny and I started to say something later, but he glared. He never discusses patients. None of them do, actually. Except Dr. Rook, but only rarely.

I don't even know the original diagnosis for Reina. She is fourteen now. She comes in with her mother, two sisters and a brother. They push her in a huge stroller-wheel-chair her father made. The sisters are twelve and fifteen, the boy is eight, all beautiful children, lively and funny. When I get in the room they have her propped on the exam table. She is naked. Except for the feeding button her body is flawless, satin smooth. Her breasts have grown. You can't see the hoof-like growth she has instead of teeth, her exquisite lips are parted and bright red. Emerald green eyes with long black lashes. Her sisters have given her a shaggy punk cut, a ruby stud in her nose, painted a butterfly tattoo on her thigh. Elena is polishing her toenails while Tony arranges her arms behind her head. He is the strongest, the one who helps me hold her upper torso while her sisters hold her legs. But right now she lies there like Manet's Olympia, breathtakingly pure and lovely. Dr. Rook stops short like I did, just to look at her. "God, she is beautiful," she says.

"When did she start to menstruate?" she asks.

I hadn't noticed the tampax string among the jet black silken hairs. The mother says it is her first time. Without irony she says, "She is a woman now."

She is in danger now, I think.

"OK, hold her down," Dr. Rook says. The mother grabs her waist, the girls her legs, Tony and I hold her arms. She fights violently against us but Dr. Rook at last gets the old button out and puts in a new one.

She was the last patient of the day. I'm cleaning the room, putting fresh paper on the table when Dr. Rook comes back in. She says, "I'm so grateful for my Nicholas."

I smile and say, "And I for my Nicholas." She's talking about her six-month-old baby, I'm talking about my six-year-old grandson.

"Goodnight," we say and then she goes over to the hospital.

I go home and make a sandwich, turn on an A's game. Dave Stewart pitching against Nolan Ryan. It has gone into ten innings when the phone rings. Dr. Fritz. He's at the ER, wants me to come. "What is it?"

"Amelia, remember her? There are people who can speak Spanish, but I want you to talk to her."

Amelia was in the doctor's room at the ER. She had been sedated, stared even more blankly than usual. And the baby? He leads me to a bed behind a curtain.

Jesus is dead. His neck was broken. There are bruises on his arms. The police are on the way, but Dr. Fritz wants me to talk to her calmly first, see if I can find out what happened.

"Amelia? Remember me?"

"*Sí. Cómo no?* How are you? Can I see him, *mijito* Jesus?"

"In a minute. First I need for you to tell me what happened."

It took a while to figure out that she had been riding around on buses in the daytime, spending the nights in a homeless shelter. When she got there tonight two of the younger women took all her money from where she had it pinned inside her clothes. They hit her and kicked her, then left. The man who runs the place didn't understand Spanish and didn't know what she was saying. He kept telling her to be quiet, put his fingers up to his mouth to tell her to be quiet, to keep the baby quiet. Then later the women came back. They were drunk and it was dark and other people were trying to sleep, but Jesus kept crying. Amelia had no money at all now and didn't know what to do. She couldn't think. The two women came. One slapped her and the other one took Jesus, but Amelia grabbed him back. The man came and the women went to lie down. Jesus kept crying.

"I couldn't think about what to do. I shook him to make him be quiet so I could think about what to do."

I held her tiny hands in mine. "Was he crying when you shook him?"

"Yes."

"Then what happened?"

Mijito

"Then he stopped crying."

"Amelia. Do you know that Jesus is dead?"

"Yes, I know. *Lo sé.*" And then in English she said, "Fuck a duck. I'm sorry."

Del Gozo Al Pozo

Every morning Seferino drove Claudia to the post office, to the kiosk on Insugentes for the *Jornada* and to Sanborn's for the *Herald-Tribune*. Amalia, the cook, went to the Super every day but Seferino took Doña Claudia three or four times a week to the market in Coyoacán. When the vendors saw them coming they would smile. The old flower lady and squash lady even laughed out loud. The gringa, Doña Claudia, was very tall, big. She would stride through the market with her bags of vegetables and fruit, with little fat Seferino puffing after her, a gloomy Sancho Panza. He stayed four paces behind, carrying even more bags of oranges, peppers, jicama. On Fridays she always bought flowers. Seferino marched along like a thick-trunked flowering tree, peering through spears of red gladioli, tuberoses, canna lilies.

Seferino interfered with her purchases only when she was coming out badly in the bargain. Usually Claudia did well, even though she refused to haggle. She watched for a while and figured out what the shrewdest shoppers paid for epazote, then she would offer the same. If the price were raised she'd say no. After a few weeks the vendors saw this as a variation on the ritual of bargaining and accepted it, and her, even if they laughed at the sight of her and Seferino.

Seferino unloaded the purchases into the van. The seat behind the driver had been removed so Claudia had to shout to Seferino above the traffic noises from her seat in the far back. After the market Seferino drove her to the Jarocho café. He always said no to her offer of a coffee. He waited, double parked, while she sat on a bench in the sun, drinking a double cappuccino made with coffee from Veracruz, dunking a *pan dulce*. She watched the people walking by, listening to the banter of the regulars in the coffee line.

Workmen sing as they toss wooden crates of empty Coca-Cola bottles down from the balcony. The dozen litre glass bottles rise two or three inches into the air, drop back down into the crate just before the man on the ground catches them. Across the street a young man dances as he paints on a scaffold three stories high, cars run the lights, bicycles miss hitting old women. Everywhere risk and defiance weave through the most mundane daily affairs.

When she got back to the van he always said, "*Panza llena, corazón contenta.*" Then she'd say, "Home, James," and he would smile. He spoke no English but knew it was a joke that meant home to Amores Street, to her sister Sally's apartment.

In the beginning, when Sally wasn't so sick, she would have visitors in the mornings. Claudia would go to museums or to the Zona Rosa or the Benjamin Franklin Library. This library has only American writers which makes you feel very patriotic and proud but the stacks appear to be eerily askew, the A's without Austen, the T's without Trollope.

If Claudia went somewhere, Seferino would take the groceries home and appear for her at a designated time. The car and driver were from Sally's ex-husband, a high-ranking PRI politician, so Seferino could park or doublepark anywhere.

Seferino greeted her each morning with a *dicho*. Today is Monday, even hens don't lay. Today is Tuesday, don't get married or go to sea, etc. Whatever Claudia called out to Seferino he shouted back an answer in aphorism. When he picked her up at the hairdresser, after she dyed her hair, he said, "With your permission, Doña Claudia: hair can lie, teeth can cheat, only wrinkles tell the truth." After a few hours at the Anthropology museum, she remarked, "*Que gozo!* What a delight!" He shrugged and called out, "*Sí, Doña Claudia. Pero, del gozo al pozo!*"

He said this any time things were going well. From pleasure you go to the pits, or, from delight to the cess pool. Maybe this is an old Mayan saying. The sacrificial victims were made deliriously happy with mushrooms and liquor before they got tossed into the well.

Many of his adages proved to be opposite of ones in English. We think the way to hell is paved with good intentions, but in Spanish the intent is all that counts. For us beauty is only skin deep, but in Spanish any beauty is a blessing.

When things were grim, with Sally's cancer or with the PRI's situation or with the children, Seferino always said, "*Pues, Doña Claudia, como yo digo: paciencia y barajar.*" Patience, and shuffle the cards.

It reminded her of one of her mother's jokes. The little kid says, "Daddy, now can I go out to play?" and the father says, "Shut up and deal." She hollered this to Seferino. It didn't translate well, but he laughed.

Before Sally had her chemo treatments at home, Claudia and Seferino would help her down the four flights of stairs and into the van. "*Mira, Señora!*" he kept calling to Sally on the drive to the clinic, to show her trees in bloom or little girls dressed for first communion.

At first, before treatments or X-rays, Seferino and Claudia would take her to a café for a real breakfast and to read all the papers. Sally went along with it for a while. She got mad at the papers and gossiped about the other patrons, teased Seferino about his mistresses. Then she admitted that she was only going to please them. She no longer had any interest in cafés. Sally, who used to spend entire days at the La Vega café arguing politics, lecturing her children, gossiping with the changing cast of characters, listening to Julián the waiter's problems. In the mirror Claudia saw tears in Seferino's eyes.

So then they would just take her to chemo and X-ray, help her back up the stairs, until finally she never went out at all.

Claudia would assist the doctor in Sally's room, laying out the various chemo drugs, starting the IVs, calming Sally. Each time he said this would be the last chemo. Sally would be very sick for weeks and then feel a little better. Then the doctor would call and say he had a new chemo drug that might keep back the tumor in her lungs, stem the cancer in her liver and pancreas. He could keep her alive longer. So months and months passed and she stayed alive and got sicker and sicker, her hope reviving each time he offered another chemo.

Sally was depressed and angry; she hollered at her children and at Claudia. In the evenings she would weep, inconsolably, for hours and hours at a time, stopping only to gag and vomit and rage at Claudia and her daughter Mercedes, for not crying with her, for not sharing her pain.

Her younger children stayed away. When they came home she would accuse them of killing her with their indifference. They began to act out badly, getting really wild, which made Sally even more frantic. Seferino chauffeured young Sergio around at night but more and more often was having to bribe officials to drop charges on him for disturbing the peace, drugs, vandalism. Then he'd have to go off to another police station to pay off Alicia's speeding ticket or an indecent behavior charge.

"Promise me you'll take care of them," Sally would say to Claudia, and Claudia promised she would. Sally believed that Claudia would be there for them. Claudia's conviction that they would indeed be fine reassured her sister. Claudia knew that they too were suffering from their mother's dying, from her pain, from fear, anger, guilt. This long illness had pre-empted five years of their youth.

Del Gozo Al Pozo

Claudia had many talks with them, especially Sergio, who was sixteen, and lived at home. His room reeked of rum, glue, paint thinner, marijuana. His father had remarried, was so busy in the PRI he rarely saw the children. The few times Claudia had tried to talk to him about Sergio's heavy drinking and drug use the father had responded that boys will be boys.

Seferino drove Sergio to and from school and out everywhere at night. He thought of himself as a surrogate father to Sergio. He was scandalized by Alicia, her miniskirts and mohawk, rings in her nose and tattoos. He worried because the press loved Alicia, her scandalous avant-garde dance group, what she wore or didn't. At a state dinner when President Salinas stopped at their table, Alicia had waved a chicken leg at him and said, *"Que pasó?"*

It was bad publicity for the PRI, Seferino said. "The PRI? Get real," said Claudia, in English. In Spanish she sighed, *"Ni modo.* What can one do?"

"One cannot interfere with God's will," Seferino said, "especially when it's raining."

More and more often Claudia and Seferino would have long discussions about the children. They stood in the sun on the sidewalk, before she got into the car. Serious problem. What to do? The talks always ended with Seferino sighing and saying, *"No hay remedio,"* as he opened the door for her.

Claudia was a nurse, had come from California to care for Sally, but mostly just to be with her, talking, talking, laughing. Claudia read to her for hours every day, books in English. They watched *Te Conté,* a Chilean soap opera, completely involved with the melodrama, but also watching for familiar scenes from their childhood, the racetrack, Calle Ahumada, Santa Lucía hill, a view of the Andes.

Sally had wanted Claudia to come get her house in order, to get windows and doorknobs fixed, organize closets and papers, teach the cook how to make new dishes. Claudia cooked on weekends so that the children would come home, so Sally could see them. But mostly for them to get closer to one another, for after Sally was gone.

With Claudia running things, Sally's servants worked much harder than before. They grew fond of Claudia, but she was always Doña Claudia, not dear like Señora Sally.

Before she got cancer, Sally had planned to move to a house in Malinalco, a beautiful town west of Cuernavaca. The house was almost finished, the pool was even filled. Seferino and Andrew the architect went down every week to check on the progress. Claudia bought plants at the nursery in Coyoacán to send to Tomás, the gardener. Guayabana, lemon trees, oranges, avocado. Nopal and maguey, hibiscus and jacaranda. She didn't want to go there without Sally.

For years the letters Sally wrote to her had been about the house. The view, the town, the convent, the blue sky. Claudia and Mercedes tried to convince Sally to go. They would make a bed in the back of the van. Miguel, her ex-husband, even offered a PRI helicopter to go from the apartment roof straight to the grass in front of the house.

"I don't want to see it! Leave me the hell alone!" Sally shouted.

Later she told Claudia that there was no reason to see the house. She would never live there. The pleasure had been in the planning of it, imagining her bedroom that overlooked the garden. She had made elaborate changing plans for the garden, lists of friends to invite down for weekends.

"I am no longer present in my dreams," Sally said. Claudia could understand better then how it felt to be dying.

"I can't daydream about being in Paris or making love with Andrés or going to Malinalco. Any time I think of a place, I am aware that I simply won't ever be there again."

Claudia embraced her sister, "Whatever do you think about?"

"I remember. You've helped me remember hundreds of details from the past. I can imagine the children doing things. Claudia,

I want so much for them! I imagine you. Please go to Malinalco. Think about living there. See what the house needs, what the garden needs. I'd be happy, dreaming about you living there."

Claudia resisted going until Seferino convinced her that someone needed to make lists of what was needed to stock the kitchen, what linens were needed, plants for the trellises around the pool.

"Doña Claudia. Nothing ventured, nothing gained."

She went one day with Andrew the architect who sat next to her on his donut pillow, another pillow for his neck. A mask to cover his eyes during the trip. They were to leave at nine, but Andrew had to make five or six stops, for handles, fixtures, hinges. Seferino raised his eyebrows to Claudia in the rearview mirror.

It was eleven before they were on the *periférico* out of town, past Sedue and suddenly into space and clear blue sky. Mountains beyond them, huge cumulus clouds billowing around their peaks. Forests of deep green pines, fir, miles of pink cosmos, of wild blue sweet pea and purple stock. The landscape was alpine but nopal and maguey mixed with pine and aspen trees. Stone monasteries and Catholic churches in each lovely place where the Mexica had once lived. A white horse gallops in a green meadow, baby lambs play by a mountain stream.

They had lunch in a chalet-like restaurant. Soup of fresh picked mushrooms and broiled just-caught brook trout. There is a bowl of salsa on the table, and hot tortillas in a cloth, but the mushrooms and trout smell like a foreign country, like Montana.

Although he had made a patronizing production about Seferino joining them for lunch, *Claro, hombre,* Andrew talked on and on in English to Claudia about Mexican architects of the fifties. Seferino said nothing, whether keeping his "place" or because he couldn't stand Andrew, Claudia couldn't tell. She said nothing too.

"Good God, it's way past time to go!" Andrew said, accusingly, as if they had kept him waiting. Back in the car he covered his eyes again.

"It is so beautiful, Seferino, how can he bear not to look at it?"

"*Pues*, Doña Claudia, seeing is believing."

"You mean what he doesn't know can't hurt him?"

"You two are like children," Andrew said. "You think that because I can't see you I can't hear you."

Claudia stuck her tongue out at Andrew into the rear view mirror. Seferino laughed.

At the beautiful house there were dozens of workmen building a wall, another dozen leveling a parking area, more planting trees. Guido, the engineer, struck a matador pose on top of a ledge in his suede coat, tight pants and snakeskin boots. He spoke on a portable phone, to a woman, obviously. Seferino waited in the servants' area outside the kitchen while Andrew showed Claudia through the house.

As she entered each room she remembered Sally's letters about the house, long before it was ever on a blueprint.

("Oh, and a kitchen you can sit around in and smell *nardos* from the open windows, look far out onto cows grazing, and a fireplace in the living room because even in summer the mountain nights are cool. Andrés and I can lie in front of it and look up at the stars, through the skylight. No *esmog*!")

In Sally's bedroom Claudia sat, weeping, in the room that was her sister's dream come true.

Andrew was in the bathroom droning on about solar heat. He had much to discuss with Guido. Perhaps Seferino could give her a tour of the village, quite picturesque. They went out the kitchen door.

"Seferino, take the lady for a spin, perhaps to the convent. Exquisite murals, delicate, unique. The bridge also is 16th century, quite fine."

"Flies don't get into your mouth if you keep it shut," Seferino muttered as he opened the van door. On the road into town he looked at her in the mirror. "Doña Claudia, did it make you sad to see the Señora's house?"

"Yes. I can see why she wouldn't want to come. It's not fair. It's horrible.'"

"*Andale*. Go on. Cry."

They stood at the foot of the mountain and temple that rose above the town.

"Doña Claudia, please come back with me soon. You would like the climb up there. The entrance is in the shape of a serpent's jaws."

Claudia shaded her eyes, looking up at the temple, intact, majestic. "It's magical."

"*Exacto!* It was magic, *is*, maybe. In Moctezuma's time this was where sorcerers came to learn their craft. The place was discovered by Malinalxochil, the maguey flower, the beautiful sister of Huitzilpochtli, when she led a dissident band of Mexica from Patzcuaro."

"Seferino, are you making all this up?"

"No, Doña. I'm reading it from that big sign right behind you."

There was a description of the ruin at the beginning of the trail up the hill. It went on to say that Malinalco had rebelled against Cuernavaca and the Spaniards right in the middle of Cortez's attack upon Teotichlan. Since Cuernavaca and the area around Malinalco were the centers for gold, Cortez sent an army led by Andrés de Tapia to overcome the Indians, but most of the Indians took refuge inside the serpent temple.

Seferino and Claudia went to the convent in the village. The murals were lovely, with delicate and fragile designs, just as Andrew had said. There was a small chapel with statues of the twelve apostles. Claudia knelt by the candles in front of the altar, missing her sister already, remembering her funny letter about the apostles. Seferino knelt in the back of the church.

Claudia walked through the cool convent in the late afternoon light, grieving for Sally but smiling to come upon a lovely wall. A deep window framing a perfect scene. Seferino walked paces behind her as usual. His footsteps echoed hers on the silken worn stone.

Seferino opened the van door for her, left for a few minutes. He came back with "*huaraches*," hot cakes of blue corn *maza* with beans inside. There were Coca-Colas in an ice chest in the van.

The village was so quiet she didn't have to raise her voice so he could hear her from the back seat. "Cosmos. Those pink flowers we saw growing wild. More bougainvillea, in different colors for all those pillars around the pool. Against that deep pink-brown of the house and buildings. You must admit Andrew did a wonderful job on the house."

"Señora Sally designed the house. He did just what she said to do."

"We'd better go, no?"

"Yes. You'll see. He'll keep us waiting, then blame us for his being late to tea…"

Claudia didn't go back to Malinalco, even when the house was finished, the lawns put in. Sally was very ill, with continuous oxygen and IVs. Claudia and Mercedes took turns staying awake. Mostly Mercedes stayed up and woke Claudia to give Sally injections, change the IVs. At first there were bedpans and vomit basins, but less and less as she could no longer eat. Claudia hated giving her shots, it seemed she hit bone wherever she put the needle.

Miguel, the minister, Sally's ex-husband, came one morning as Claudia sat in the kitchen on a stool, waiting for water to boil for Sally's bath. As Miguel left he stopped by the kitchen and deftly handed each of the maids, and Claudia, a folded one hundred thousand peso bill.

When he had gone, the maids burst into laughter. "The Señor

gave you a tip! A tip!" Seferino was embarrassed for Claudia, shocked that she would laugh with the maids about it.

"It's OK, Seferino. You must admit I've been working very hard. Of course I look like an employee to him."

She realized that her role had actually changed because she did so much physical work. Except for Seferino, she was no longer Doña, but Claudia, the one who lifted and bathed the señora, changed her diapers and the linens.

Sally could only eat crushed ice now. Claudia put ice in a towel and smashed it in a fury, whap, whap against the wall.

Sally could not live much longer. Claudia and Mercedes went to Goyozo funeral home to make arrangements. It was ghastly. Claudia wished somebody spoke English so she could tell them how extremely unctuous the funeral lady was. She and Mercedes held hands in the back seat but didn't speak. Mercedes called to Seferino, *"Oye,* take us to Sanborn's." They bought nail polish and perfume, French *Vogue, Hola Magazine* and chocolate eclairs, stumbling like drunks through the aisles.

Sally became too ill to leave; Claudia stopped going out in the mornings. She saw Seferino when he arrived to take Sergio to school. One morning he was sitting, dejected, when she came into the kitchen. *"Que pasó?"*

He shook his head. *"Del gozo al pozo."*

Salinas was rearranging his cabinet. The minister would be "campaigning" to be governor of a southern state. The department of ecology was eliminated, replaced by Urban Affairs, headed by Colosio, who would be the next candidate for President.

"So I stay only until the poor Señora dies and then only God knows. I'll be sent to some office to file, or stamp papers. Doña Claudia, I, who was born to drive! My daughter Lydia has already lost her job as secretary."

"Can't she stay on with Colosio?"

"No. He got rid of all the women. Secretaries, telephone operators, cleaning women. He says they always cause trouble."

"For him, maybe. He's so handsome."

"You'll put in a word with the Señor?"

Just as he said that the buzzer rang three times. It meant Miguel, the Señor, was coming up to see Sally. Claudia went in, to take her ice, and tell her Miguel was coming. "I'm so glad," Sally whispered and when Miguel came in, she smiled at him. "Oh, my dear," she said. Claudia left them.

Seferino was sitting in the living room, something he had never done before.

"Did you speak to him?" she asked.

"Yes. I said, 'Señor Licenciado,' since he is no longer minister, 'please consider the fate of me and my daughter. Surely there are positions for us during your campaign.' He told me those jobs had to go to natives from the state. 'But, after all these years, sir?' I said. And imagine what he said to me?"

"What?"

"He said, 'That's life.'"

Sally died soon after that day, quietly. Claudia lifted her to change her sheets and she was light, like bones, like an angel. Mercedes and Claudia lay next to her as slowly she stopped breathing and grew cold.

The next few days were a blur, the long day and night vigil, the rosaries, the mass. Hundreds of people who had loved her. Claudia felt nothing but kept going to the casket to look at her sister. In Mexico they don't embalm bodies, bury them immediately. As the hours went by, Claudia could see her sister's lovely skin begin to discolor and decompose. Grief came to her not with sadness but with the sense of betrayal, of a mockery.

For days then, on Amores Street they sat around, aimless and zombie-like. Since the death had been expected, they were even more taken by surprise.

Three rings. The Señor. He sat with them at the dining room

table. Claudia brought him coffee and water. Everything had been arranged. He had to start campaigning, day and night, in the south. It was time for Claudia to return home. The children would be better off together traveling. They would learn to get along with each other.

Claudia was to leave for Oakland tomorrow, the children for Paris, London and New York day after tomorrow. They would spend the summer traveling, all reservations had been made. The apartment would be remodeled while they were gone.

Mercedes and Claudia went to the Gitana café, had lattes and *pan dulces*. Mercedes would never question a decision of her father's, worried only how to manage Sergio and Alicia in Europe. Claudia worried that mourning, saying goodbye to Sally, would get completely bypassed. Which it was. Not until months later did Mercedes call her in Oakland. "Tia, I want to come up and cry."

That day over coffee, after days and days of no sleep, they confessed that they still didn't realize Sally's death.

"If anything, I feel happy," Claudia said. "Do you know what I mean?"

"Exactly. Me too. I feel like when we've finished a movie or a video and they're striking the sets. I feel good. We took good care of her, no, *Tia*?"

"Yes, we did."

The next day when Seferino and Mercedes went with Claudia to the airport, Mercedes was sullen and angry.

"You promised my mother you would care for us, but you really can't wait to go home. I'll be stuck forever with those brats."

"They'll be OK. You'll see. If not, I'll come back. You're mad because everyone has left you, and now you think I'm leaving you too. But I'll always be with you, *entiendes*?" Mercedes and she embraced, then Claudia hugged Seferino. All. three of them were crying, loud. Mercedes turned and ran through the airport lobby, high heels clattering on the marble floor.

A New Life

"...Can you think of what it would be like to live the rest of one's life in a new way? Oh, to wake up some fine clear morning feeling as if you had started living all over again, as if the past were all forgotten, gone like a puff of smoke."

Uncle Vanya

Please don't suggest anything, like for me to volunteer as a pink lady or to seek psychiatric help.

I told my friend Marla that I was ready to commit suicide. What a mistake. She recently became a psychologist. She tried to get to the root of my hostilities and to make me stay with my anger. I'm not mad at anybody. I can't blame anybody but myself for having been a lousy wife and mother and general failure. I'm sixty years old and still working at a horrible receptionist job.

It is too late to learn anything new. I am incompetent. I can't drive on the freeway or make U-turns without an arrow and if an answering machine answers I get scared and hang up.

I'm just fed up with myself and my entire life. And sure I'm angry that I don't even have a friend I can talk to about killing myself without getting a lecture about how hostile this is.

I bought a how-to book on ways to kill yourself. This is a depressing book. It has a chapter on dumb ways that don't work, like don't pull the toaster into the tub with you. It tells you how to con doctors into stronger and stronger medicines so you can stockpile them until you have enough to make a soup. The author could call it a tea, or an infusion. But soup? *She died from soup.*

To get the right medicine, you have to keep going back and going back to doctors, each time saying, "Nope, still can't sleep."

This means you have insurance and a job that gives you time off to keep going to see doctors. The patience to wait, reading *Smithsonians*. The motivation to persist. If you have patience and motivation, you're obviously not suicidal.

Although the author gets very specific about dosages he says that the main thing is not to forget the plastic bag. Just wrap a plastic bag around your head and fasten it with a rubber band. *She died of plastic bag. She died after a long battle with a plastic bag.*

A nice accidental drowning is the only dignified way. At Lake Temescal, just keep swimming, past the rushes and the redwinged blackbirds and then you're out of sight, out of mind.

It's not that I'm worried about the future that much. I'm curious, still. It's my past that I can't get rid of, that hits me like a big wave when I least expect it.

Grocery shopping, for example. I go up and down the aisles and chat with people in line, joke with the checkers. It's pleasant, really. But some days I'll remember things. Like when Terry and I got in an argument and he soaked me with the hose to spray lettuce with. I have a fit, quietly, missing him. Or the time... Oh lord, I could go on all day. The good parts are as hard to deal with as the bad ones. The point is, they are in the past.

Maybe I'll just walk around my Oakland neighborhood, witness a murder. Testify and then I'll have to get witness protection and they'll send me to Lubbock, Texas with a new identity.

I have two fine sons and three dear grandsons. Jason is a prosecuting attorney in Marin and Miles is an Oakland policeman. Marla says they chose their professions because they grew up without a father, that they have become the authority figures they themselves needed. I suspect it is me they want to arrest and prosecute.

And their wives... If only they had married schizophrenics

or women who were beneath them. I feel so petty complaining because their wives are perfect. And not compulsively perfect, they really are nice women.

Jason's wife Alexis is an architect. Beautiful, witty. Runs eight miles a day, volunteers for charity bazaars, reads to the twins every night even when she gives sit-down dinners for twelve. Miles' wife Amanda is beautiful too, warm and giving. She is a speech therapist, sews all her own clothes, makes bread and weaves. They are all good parents. They do things like climb Mt. Tam with their children, go whale watching and to Lawrence Hall of Science.

I always have Thanksgiving and Christmas at my house, and they include me in other holidays and picnics, surprise me with little presents. They call to say hello or to see if I need anything. I babysit, take books and toys to my grandchildren, who are very dear.

We are joined because we are family. I am the mother, the grandmother. Aside from that, our lives themselves are not connected. We are different generations, have different values and interests.

On the other hand, we all like each other. It's not as if there were any problems. There aren't any, really, except that I am not essential. I carry the titles of mother, grandmother, employee, but, in fact, I am an unnecessary person.

Jason tossed the pages onto the table. "This is a suicide note. Pure and simple."

"No way. She was always writing things like this, just day-dreaming on paper."

"I can't believe she felt this way. She must have been in real clinical depression. I'm telling you, Miles, she's in the lake."

"No way. You know how on birthdays, Christmas, she doesn't just say 'Happy Birthday,' but writes eight pages about what a miracle it was the day you were born and how you were wise and witty when you were two minutes old? If she was killing herself, she would have written a long letter. Two long letters, one to each of us, about how great we are and how sorry she was she didn't have anything to offer and had failed us. Right or not?"

Miles unbuttoned the collar of his uniform. He had just come off duty when Jason called from their mother's apartment. He poured them both coffee. Jason, in an Armani suit, looked silly in the huge wicker chair, like Huey Newton reincarnated, holding his mother's purple umbrella instead of a machine gun.

"So where is she? She's been gone at least five days. She hasn't shown up at work for three. Even if she were going to drown herself she would have called in sick. That's how she was." He found his eyes filling with tears, surprising himself and Miles.

"Hey, how come you're saying *was*? All we know is that she's gone. She could have been taking a walk, fallen down and got amnesia or something. Let's search the place and be sure nothing's missing. If she was just going out what would she have worn?"

"For starters, she would have taken this umbrella. It's been raining for a week."

The brothers looked through the house, in her drawers and closets. Nothing seemed to be gone. There were two dusty suitcases in the hall closet. Jason was looking through her desk when Miles came to the top of the stairs.

"Her leather purse is gone and that black coat. Jason, she's been kidnapped. It must have been from the street since nothing is missing here."

"Kidnapped? Well, maybe. Her checkbook is here, her credit cards and insurance card and driver's license."

"Even if she were going to drown herself she would have driven to the lake. Her car's here."

"If it was for ransom don't you think we would have heard?"

"How should I know? You're the cop. What do we do now? Put out an APB? Put her picture on a milk carton?"

"Ma's picture on a milk carton? Remember when she was chopping onions and she waved that knife at me for drinking from the milk carton?" The brothers laughed.

"Yeah, put her picture and a message. 'Millie Bradford, now missing, says *Use a glass! Don't drink from the carton!*'" Jason stopped laughing abruptly. "Where could she *be*, man?"

"I don't know. I just *feel* she's OK. But we need to get the police in on this."

"You know what this means, don't you? Reporters and volunteers and fliers."

"I can't be on TV. Neither one of us can afford that kind of publicity. Too many nuts out there. We've got to think. I need a drink."

Miles found some cognac. He poured two glasses. He had already figured out what was on Jason's mind.

"You're thinking that some psycho that I busted or that you put away has snatched her."

"It's a possibility. And if we get on TV some other asshole might say, 'Right on, that's the dude that did me. I'll get me his wife, coupla kids.'"

"You're being paranoid."

"It has happened. It could happen. To our families."

"Yeah. But we have to report it. We have to find her."

"I'll get the chief over here."

The brothers called their wives and said they would be late. While they waited for the police chief, Miles made them bacon, lettuce and tomato sandwiches. They ate in silence. Chewing, Miles looked at his brother and his eyes smiled at him. It was the first time in over ten years that the two of them had sat together alone. They felt comfortable, at home. Jason smiled back at him. He and Miles would not have admitted that they felt good at this particular time.

You see it all the time, on "Unsolved Crimes" on TV, how people create whole new identities. So when two things happened at once they seemed to be an omen.

I began going through my papers and throwing everything out except things my boys might want. Letters, souvenirs. I came across Jennie Wilson's birth certificate. Jennie died years ago, but years before that she had stayed with me while she got her passport and ticket for Europe. The birth certificate had stayed behind, forgotten in a drawer. The day I found it I went to the DMV and got a new driver's license.

This actually may have been all I would have needed to do. In an instant I became Jennie Wilson. A person. Not a worker or a mother or a wife or a daughter, just a person, license number N24367. Simply holding the rectangle gave me a sense that I existed. I had become an individual. I was someone who had never lived before.

The feeling was so intense that I realized, I saw clearly, that all my life I had been playing roles created by myself or by others.

How could I stop doing this? What changes could I make in my behavior to keep this wonderful sense of uniqueness?

I called in sick the next day. I turned off the phone. I ate tacos for breakfast and watched daytime TV, never did get dressed. It wasn't until that evening that I noticed that there was a message on my machine. It was a call from Boston, from someone I didn't know, telling me that my childhood friend Elsa had died. She had left me some money, the person said, and a check would be coming to me.

I was surprised by the grief I felt. I had not seen Elsa for many years. As little girls we had been furiously loyal and close, as only seven-year-olds can be, and our friendship had continued all our lives. She had been my first friend. She was the last close friend I had that had been alive. My parents dead, my brothers and sister and all my relatives gone too. Elsa had stood in the way of my own death.

I went back to work the next day but I continued to feel very sad. The days dragged on and on; I had to get out of there. I did not have that much time left in this world. I couldn't spend the remaining days doing Medi-Cal billing and CPT coding.

For several nights I didn't sleep, torturing myself with having wasted all those years, with having nothing to fall back on, nothing to offer anyone. Nothing, in fact, to enjoy.

I forced myself to stop brooding, to try and figure out how I was going to change. One night I cried myself to sleep, change seemed so impossible.

I had forgotten about Elsa's check when it finally arrived. Thirty thousand dollars. A cashier's check. I sat in the kitchen, holding it, almost all night long. Maybe I went crazy that night, or caught Alzheimer's. No, there is simply no explanation or excuse for what I did.

I didn't go to work the next day. I slept late, showered and dressed and went to the bank. I didn't have to deposit the check to have it changed to another cashier's check made out to Jennie Wilson. I had left my wallet at home. All I had now was Jennie Wilson's birth certificate and driver's license, two hundred dollars and her check. I took BART to San Francisco. I opened a bank account in my new name. They asked for all kinds of references and information, but I just acted senile and bereaved, babbling and sniffling, so they didn't pursue it. I checked into the Continental Hotel downtown.

The first few hours I was so scared I stayed in my room, looking down at the street. I wanted to call Marla, but wisely realized that she was the last person to call. I just watched the people from my window. All kinds of people. The world had a miraculous multiplicity of types and races and classes and shapes and hairdos. Finally I just had to go get into it all, so when it got dark I went out and walked through the crowds. Block after block in ever widening circles, seeing the city, seeing each person's face, as if I had never looked at anything before. I was exhilarated, alive, reborn.

Raworth, the police chief, was efficient and reassuring. Jason and Miles went home feeling that everything possible was being done. For the next few days all the hospitals and morgues would be checked, an APB was put out on both sides of the bay. There was no reason yet to have the media in on this. But if they didn't find her in a few days they would have to go public, it was the only chance of finding her. Or, if she had been kidnapped, they would probably hear by then.

Jason and Alexis went over to Miles and Amanda's for dinner. They didn't talk about Millie in front of the children. It was interesting how differently the wives took it than did Millie's sons. Well, of course, she was their mother and what they both felt was fear and worry, remorse. She probably should have been living with one of us, etc. The two women were simply worried for her, less willing to believe in foul play than the men were. They thought she was hurt, unconscious or unable to remember where she was.

If Millie had been very ill or dead, the four of them would have comforted and supported each other. But no one knew what had happened so there were floating feelings of anger and blame, guilt and fear. They were all defensive and edgy, snapped at each other, were short with the children. "Hush up, we're trying to talk!"

After a few days it became clear that she was not in any local hospital or morgue. No one had communicated with them. Chief Raworth said the media had to be told, that they could help.

It was worse than any of them could have imagined. Marla

and Millie's boss and the grandchildren were all hurt and angry that no one had told them right away. Reporters and cameras were at both sons' doors. Jason and Miles insisted that their wives and children be kept away from the camera, which only made things more mysterious. You kept seeing Alexis and Amanda running places with the children, hiding their faces like criminals.

Jason, tense and anxious, handled the interviews, usually on his front porch. More of a pillared entranceway than a porch. As predicted, the media liked the idea of a revenge plot. "Have either of you been threatened by any felons you have helped to imprison?" Extended coverage was given to the Drug Lords and Crime Bosses they had each had a part in convicting. "Were the Bradford Brothers Too Tough on Crime?" asked one headline.

They could not change their phones because Millie might call, so they had to hear the predictable calls from cranks who threatened their wives and children's lives, from six different callers who claimed to have murdered Millie. Amanda and the twins came home crying from the grocery store. The checker had told the man in line in front of them that the brothers looked like the Menendez brothers, only older. "Yeah, they look guilty as heck to me," the man said. "You see the old lady's picture? What a battle-ax. They say the main suspect is always family."

The children enjoyed the excitement, though. Their parents on TV, their own backs on TV. Grandma's picture on telephone poles, in Walgreen's. Their mothers resented not being able to let them walk to school alone or go to the mall or park. Since they didn't know what had happened they weren't really grieving. They desperately wanted to know, to get on with their lives. The women became closer. Both felt their husbands were overreacting and ignoring them and the children. The husbands were hurt because their wives were so unfeeling and so careless about their children's safety. But then they had protected them from the obscene reality of the phone threats. Three times in three days Jason and Miles were asked to identify unclaimed bodies. The bodies weren't Millie, but someone had killed each of those women.

The second day I got my hair cut and permed and dyed mahogany red, had my almost white eyebrows dyed black. I also got acrylic fingernails, painted deep red. I absolutely did not recognize myself; so no one else would either. I realized that before I had been a "handsome" elderly woman. Grey hair in a bun, no makeup. Birkenstocks in summer, boots in winter. Wool and cotton. Comfortable, classic clothes. "Comfortable" means the same as "handsome." Boring.

I bought bright red and green and blue jersey dresses, wedgie-heeled shoes, pant suits with waists and shoulder pads, gold buttons. Blusher and green eyeshadow. Passion and Opium perfumes. Back and forth I went from my hotel to the shops on Union Square. On the last trip home, the one with just a bag of makeup and perfume, I did something I had never done before. I went into a bar by myself.

It was four in the afternoon and there were only a few people in the Beachcomber.

"What's a nice girl like you doing in a place like this?" the bartender asked and grinned at me. I grinned back and ordered a glass of white wine. He said his name was Hal, and he introduced me to Myron and Greg, two older men who were sitting together. Slightly seedy, in frayed polyester suits and Giants baseball hats, but they were respectful, friendly persons, both retired salesmen, both widowed. I said I was a widow too, a retired schoolteacher visiting from Montana, seeing if I wanted to move here.

At one point Greg went out to buy an *Examiner* and Myron went to the restroom. I asked the bartender Hal if these were nice gentlemen.

"Why yes, ma'am," he said. "That's the very reason I introduced them to you. I could tell you were a lady, and new in town, not no bar type. Figured they could keep an eye on you. We bartenders are pretty good judges of people, you know."

I spent the next day visiting Chinatown and Fisherman's Wharf. Back at the hotel I changed into the red jersey. I met my new friends at the Beachcomber Bar at four. We had an early dinner at the Hofbrau, where they ate every night. Then we went to see the movie *Housesitting*, with Goldie Hawn. All three of us just loved it.

They asked me to join them for a nightcap but after all that walking at the wharf I just wanted to hit the hay. I was too sleepy even to think about what I was going to do.

In the morning I had a nice breakfast at Sears. There was nothing about me in the paper. No one even noticed I was gone, I thought, and that was depressing. I tried to concentrate on my future. Should I get a job? An apartment? Should I write my sons? No, not yet. I wanted a little more time being Jennie Wilson. Not thinking about anything but where to go today. The Steinhart Aquarium and the Japanese tea garden. It was early spring, rhododendron and azalea time. I'd save the botanical gardens for a whole day of their own.

Amanda and Alexis had lunch together at Chez Panisse Cafe. This affair had brought the two of them much closer, as it had their husbands, but unfortunately had the women squaring off against the men.

"This is worse than spending too much money on a funeral or a wedding shower. A reward? Jason said it would 'look bad' to offer only ten thousand dollars. Give me a break. I'll get a bloodhound and find her for five thousand dollars. Ten thousand is a lot of money. Don't tell them, but I am sick about it, just sick. We have just barely begun to save any money."

"Well, I feel bad because it's all coming from you guys. We don't have any, and no credit at all. But I can see they have to do it, couldn't forgive themselves if they didn't. I think they're reasoning that whoever has her is going to ask for much more. Anyway, last I heard they were thinking twenty thousand dollars."

"God! On the other hand, if I ever get kidnapped I'll be pretty insulted if all Jason offers for me is twenty thousand dollars!"

They had a second glass of wine, ordered calzone and salads. They both were relaxed. They looked pretty, animated, with the camaraderie women have when they are trashing their husbands.

"I mean, he used to go for weeks and weeks without even thinking about her. Now he's constantly remembering things like her making red and green paper chains at Christmas, or saying '*au contraire*' all the time."

"I know, Miles too! He gets big old tears in his eyes and I'll say, 'You OK, hon?' 'Yeah, just thinking about my Mom.'"

"Well, maybe something horrible has happened, or maybe she's dead somewhere. But we don't know, so I can't seem to get all that upset, and he thinks I'm unfeeling. Accuses me of never liking her."

"Exactly what happens with me and Miles!"

"It's because they never had a father. They always were responsible for her, so now they feel it's their fault. I tried to talk about it but Jason got absolutely furious with me."

"Oh, I know!" Amanda clasped Alexis' hand in sympathy.

"Just imagine Miles when I suggested that maybe Millie wasn't kidnapped. I said maybe she felt, 'What the hell, time to hit the road, Jack,' and took off. Just got on a train and headed for Tijuana. Why not? He was nearly hysterical about me suggesting such a thing, that she would abandon her grandchildren. Shall we share a dessert?"

"No, I can't stand that custom. I want my own bread pudding."

"Ten dollars for bread pudding! I know why you're ordering it. Millie always made it!" Amanda laughed.

Alexis nodded, "You know that's probably true. The bad part is that I do miss her. Oh, hell, I am worried."

"So am I. I love her, don't you?"

The two women clasped hands again and looked with compassion into each other's eyes. They finished their puddings and cappuccinos in relative silence. The leather folder with the check inside was on the white cloth. A folded piece of paper was next to it.

Alexis put her Visa inside the folder and looked at the piece of paper, which was a page from an appointment book, from the middle of May. With a black magic marker someone had scrawled,

"Happy you got rid of Grandma? How will you like it when I get your kids?"

Hal made boilermakers for Myron and Greg. They watched "Real Crime Stories" for a while, one of those programs where all the people have wavery grids instead of faces so you know it is all true.

"So how's our new sweetheart?" Hal asked them.

"She's a sweetheart, that's the truth. Doesn't talk too much, doesn't drink more'n two glasses of wine, gets sleepy at eight."

"Got her figured yet?"

"Not yet," Myron said. He fanned for another shot, like a gambler asking for another card.

"All we know is she says she's from Montana, but has no idea where Butte is. Everything she wears is brand new and she never mentions a word about her life."

"Running from the law?"

"Naw, she's a lady. Some other sort of problem."

"That's where we come in. We'll help her take care of her problems." Greg gave one of his wheezy laughs. "Our specialty, right, Hal?"

"Yeah, you guys will take care of the poor old broad."

"She's not poor. I know that much."

I spent a lovely day at the De Young Museum and the Botanical Gardens. It was exhausting though, so I took a nap when I got back, went later than usual to the Beachcomber. Everyone was watching the six o'clock news. My boys were on it! Jason and Miles looked so handsome and worried. Even my boss, Mr. Harding, looked sad. He said it must be foul play because I hadn't called. That I was the most responsible employee he ever had. Then they showed a photograph of me.

"Check out the car trunk!" Myron said. "Her sons did that old biddy in for sure."

I couldn't even finish my wine. I told them I was feeling sick and ran out and back to the hotel.

For the next three or four days all I did was watch the news and read the papers. Lord, Lord, what a mess I had made. They were worried that I'd been kidnapped by somebody Miles had arrested or Jason had prosecuted. They were worried about harm to the children, to those dear babies. I couldn't think of how to get out of this mess. I was so ashamed. I knew that I should just call and tell them I was all right. I didn't have the courage. They'd hate me so much. They would make me go home.

They arrested a nice-looking Hispanic boy who was an ex-con. Someone said they had seen him in my neighborhood. He was in an orange suit and handcuffs. Then on Channel Four Jason was at his back door saying they were offering a reward of twenty thousand dollars. Oh Lord, Lord.

A New Life

All I did was call room service and watch the news and soaps and talk shows and more news and crime shows and the late news for days.

There was a knock at my door. Oh Lord, Lord. The police. I didn't answer. They knocked again, louder.

"Jennie, it's us! Myron and Greg. Let us in."

I opened the door.

"Jennie, you look awful. You sick? We were worried about you."

"Yes, I've had some kind of flu."

"Looks like more'n that to me," Myron said. "You've been crying. We brought some cans of daiquiris and some cheese and crackers. Let us just sit down here, Greg, and see if there's anything we can do to help this little lady."

At first all I wanted was to get them out of my room. But I had some cheese and crackers and some daiquiris. Then it seemed so good to have somebody to talk to and the drinks made me so calm after those terrible past days and nights. I found myself blurting out the whole shameful story, about what suffering and worry I was causing everybody and how I didn't know how to get out of it.

Myron and Greg listened and were so understanding, especially the part about having a new life. They said they both had done the very same thing, only they hadn't family to think they'd been kidnapped. Then they said they needed to go get us more to drink and some takeout Chinese and we'd have it all figured out by that night.

Seemed like while they were gone they planned the whole thing. The next day we would go to a pay phone and call Jason or Miles. Myron would ask for a hundred thousand dollars for my safe return. He would say that they'd call the next day with instructions. I'd get on the phone and say I was fine and not to worry, but that they'd kill me if they didn't get the money.

That afternoon they'd tape up my hands and mouth, then rip the tape off so there would be marks. Maybe hit me just a little so I'd have a bruise on one cheek. At night they'd let me out of a cab south of Market. As soon as the cab was gone, I'd run and run screaming bloody murder until I found a policeman. I would tell them I escaped from my kidnappers. Since I had been blindfolded I wouldn't know where I had been. I'd say they had disguised me, and they always wore ski masks so I didn't know what they looked like.

They said we'd work out all the details the next day. I couldn't thank them enough, and when they left I slept like a baby for the first night in a long time.

Jason answered the phone in his office. A menacing voice asked if this was Millie's son, and he said yes, frantically gesturing to the policeman across the desk to trace the call.

"I'm calling from a phone booth in the Haight-Ashbury. I know where your mother is. I know her kidnappers, but don't want them to know I snitched. I want the reward money, the twenty thousand, no questions asked. I can get you to her before the kidnappers get back. But I don't want to be involved in any way."

"What do you want me to do?"

"Come to the phone booth on the corner of Haight and Cole. There will be a piece of paper taped above the phone with her address and phone. Call her phone number once and hang up, then call it again. This is how you'll know she's fine. Don't say a word to her, that will blow the whole deal. You got that? Just go to that address and she'll be there under the name Jennie Wilson. That is, she'll be there if, one: You leave an envelope with the money in the phone booth. And if, Two: you don't bring anyone with you. If you do then the arrangement is off. The guys who snatched her will be back tomorrow, and you'll have to pay them. It's a simple choice between twenty and one hundred thousand."

Myron and Greg watched from the window of the laundromat on Haight Street.

"There he is. It's the D.A. son, in the phone booth."

"Yeah, and look who's across the street with two other guys. The cop son, in an unmarked car."

"So what do you think?"

"We wait. Our clothes aren't even in the rinse cycle anyway."

"I'll tell you what I think. Kidnapping is a felony."

"Tell you what else. He's gone. He left an envelope, but the brother's still sitting there. Four cops. Look, have we committed an actual crime, yet?"

"I don't think so. But I think they could get us for intent to do something."

"What say we catch the next bus downtown and get on a Greyhound for Reno?"

"I don't know. I never have abandoned my laundry before, Myron."

"I think she's on drugs, or drunk," Jason said, standing above me. "God, she looks awful, like a bar-maid."

"I think she looks great!" Amanda said.

"She's in some kind of shock. She must have been mistreated." Alexis patted my arm.

"You two still don't get it. She was not kidnapped. She's been gallivanting out there while we've been worried sick. Threatened, in a fucking state of siege," Miles said. "God, Ma, you look disgusting with that kinky red hair. Do you know the trouble and anguish and expense you caused? Have you any idea?"

"Don't attack her!" Alexis said. "She's had some kind of postmenopausal breakdown, that's all. I don't think she realized how we might be feeling."

I nodded, grateful to her, my eyes filling with tears.

"I just wanted to run away," I said. "If I had told anybody it wouldn't have been running away."

"Run away from what?" Jason said. "I mean, your life is not so bad. I could tell you about some bad lives if you want. Chees, we all want to run away, every day. Everybody in the whole world would like to run away. What stops them is some consideration for other people's feelings."

Alexis put her arm around my shoulder. "Opium?" she sniffed. "Mama, I hope you never thought we wouldn't care terribly if you weren't a part of our lives. We are all glad you're safe and are back with us."

"Glad? I feel like I'm welcoming a boa constrictor."

Alexis glared at Jason, who glared back at her. He and Miles were getting madder and madder. I don't understand really why the women weren't mad at me too, since they had been so frightened about their children and all. But they were kind to me, warmer than they had ever been before, really.

Miles went on, "To think of my mother, dressed like a tramp, picking up some sleazeballs in a place called the Beachcomber Bar. Least they didn't get our money."

"Well, be grateful for that. They didn't," Amanda said.

"Thanks for offering that money," I said. I wished I knew if my friends had really meant to take it, and just got scared off.

"Let's act as if none of this ever happened," Amanda said to Miles. "Only now we'll be better about communicating. Millie, if we'd known how you felt, maybe we could have sent you on a Love Boat cruise."

I began to weep. I couldn't stop myself. "Love Boat cruise? Wwaa waaa waa." I cried and cried. Love Boats were the kinds of things I wanted to run away from. I'd rather be in the Beachcomber Bar. I missed the Beachcomber Bar.

A New Life

"Let's leave her alone, come back tomorrow," Amanda said.

"I don't think she should be alone. She should stay at one of our houses."

"Not mine!" Miles said.

Alexis patted my hand. "Pack what you need and come on home with us."

We shoved through the crowds in front of their door to get inside. The phone rang every time the answering machine stopped.

"It's been like this ever since you left," Alexis said. And bless her, that was the closest she ever came to blaming me. I helped her get dinner while Jason spoke with reporters outside. The twins wouldn't get near me but didn't stop staring at me either.

Mr. H, my boss, and Marla were two of the calls. I didn't know how I would ever be able to talk to either of them.

It occurred to me that nobody was ever really crazy. They just decided to go crazy so as not to accept responsibility. I considered acting catatonic or running amok so I could get locked up until this blew over. But somehow I knew that if I ever got locked up anywhere I would never get out.

Alexis made me comfortable with ironed sheets and a bouquet of tulips. Well, anyway, I was glad to be home.

502

502 was the clue for 1-Across in this morning's *Times*. Easy. That's the police code for Driving While Intoxicated, so I wrote in DWI. Wrong. I guess all those Connecticut commuters knew you were supposed to put in Roman numerals. I had a few moments of panic, as I always do when memories of my drinking days come up. But since I moved to Boulder I have learned to do deep breathing and meditation, which never fail to calm me.

I'm glad I got sober before I moved to Boulder. This is the first place I ever lived that didn't have a liquor store on every corner. They don't even sell alcohol in Safeway here and of course never on Sundays. They just have a few liquor stores mostly on the outskirts of town, so if you're some poor wino with the shakes and it's snowing, Lord have mercy. The liquor stores are gigantic Target-size nightmares. You could die from D.T.'s just trying to find the Jim Beam aisle.

The best town is Albuquerque where the liquor stores have drive-through windows, so you don't even have to get out of your pajamas. They don't sell on Sundays either though. So if I didn't plan ahead there was always the problem of who in the world could I drop in on who wouldn't offer a wine cooler.

Even though I had been sober for years before I moved here I had trouble at first. Whenever I looked in the rear view mirror I'd go "Oh no," but it was just the ski racks everybody has on their cars. I have never actually even seen a police car in pursuit or seen anyone being arrested. I have seen policemen in shorts at the mall, eating Ben and Jerry's frozen yogurt and a SWAT team in a pickup truck. Six men in camouflage with big tranquilizer rifles, chasing a baby bear down the middle of Mapleton.

This must be the healthiest town in the country. There is no drinking at frat parties or football games. No one smokes or eats red meat or glazed donuts. You can walk alone at night, leave your doors unlocked. There are no gangs here and no racism. There aren't many races, actually.

That dumb 502. All these memories came flooding into my head, in spite of the breathing. The first day of my job at U——, the Safeway problem, the incident at San Anselmo, the scene with A——.

Everything is fine now. I love my job and the people I work with. I have good friends. I live in a beautiful apartment just beneath Mount Sanitas. Today a western tanager sat on a branch in my backyard. My cat Cosmo was asleep in the sun so he didn't chase it. I am deeply grateful for my life today.

So God forgive me if I confess that once in a while I get a diabolical urge to, well, mess it all up. I can't believe I'd even have this thought, after all those years of misery. Officer Wong either taking me to jail or to detox.

The Polite one, we all called Wong. We called all the other ones pigs, which would never have applied to Officer Wong, who was very nice, really. Methodical and formal. There were never any of the usual physical interchanges between you and him like with the others. He never slammed you against the car or twisted the cuffs into your wrist. You stood there for hours as he painstakingly wrote up his ticket and read you your rights. When he cuffed you he said, "Permit me," and "Watch your head," when you got into the car.

He was diligent and honest, an exceptional member of the Oakland police force. We were lucky to have him in our neighborhood. I am really sorry now about that one incident. One of the steps of AA is to make amends with people you have wronged. I think I have made most of the amends I could. I owe Officer Wong one. I wronged Wong for sure.

Back then I lived in Oakland, in that big turquoise apartment on the corner of Alcatraz and Telegraph. Right above Alcatel Liquors, just down from The White Horse, across the street from the 7–11. Good location.

The 7–11 was sort of a gathering place for old winos. Although, unlike them, I went to work every day, they ran into me in liquor stores on weekends. Lines at the Black and White that opened at six A.M. Late night haggling with the Pakistani sadist who worked at the 7–11.

They were all friendly with me. "How ya been, Miss Lu?" Sometimes they asked me for money, which I always gave them and several times when I had lost my job, I asked them. The group of them changed as they went to jails, hospitals, death. The regulars were Ace, Mo, Little Ripple and The Champ. These four old black guys would spend their mornings at the 7–11 and their afternoons snoozing or drinking in a faded aqua Chevrolet Corvair parked in Ace's yard. His wife Clara wouldn't let them smoke or drink in the house. Winter and summer, rain or shine, the four would be in that car. Sleeping like little kids on car trips, heads on folded hands, or looking straight ahead as if they were on a Sunday drive, commenting on everybody who drove or walked by, passing around a bottle of port.

When I'd come up the street from the bus stop I'd holler out, "How's it going?" "Jes' fine!" Mo would say. "I got my wine!" And Ace would say, "I feel so well, got my muscatel!" They'd ask about my boss, that fool Dr. B.

"Just quit that ole job! Get yourself on SSI where you belong! You come sit with us, sister, pass the time in comfort, don't need no job!"

Once Mo said I didn't look so good, maybe I needed detox.

"Detox?" the Champ scoffed. "Never detox. Retox! That's the ticket!"

The Champ was short and fat, wore a shiny blue suit, a clean white shirt and a porkpie hat. He had a gold watch with a chain and he always had a cigar. The other three all wore plaid shirts, overalls and A's baseball hats.

One Friday I didn't go to work. I must have been drinking the night before. I don't know where I had gone in the morning, but I remember coming back and that I had a bottle of Jim Beam. I parked my car behind a van across the street from my building. I went upstairs and fell asleep. I woke to loud knocking on my door.

"Open your door, Ms. Moran. This is Officer Wong."

I stashed the bottle in the bookcase and opened the door.

"Hello, Officer Wong. How can I help you?"

"Do you own a Mazda 626?"

"You know I do, sir."

"Where is that car, Miss Moran?"

"Well, it's not in here."

"Where did you park the vehicle?"

"Up across from the church." I couldn't remember.

"Think again."

"I can't remember."

"Look out the window. What do you see?"

"Nothing. The 7–11. Telephones. Gas tanks."

"Any parking places?"

"Yeah. Amazing. Two of them! Oh. I parked it there, behind a van."

"You left the car in gear, without the parking brake on. When the van left, your vehicle followed it down Alcatraz during rush hour traffic, proceeded to cross into the other lane, narrowly missing cars and sped down the sidewalk, almost harming a man, his wife and a baby in a stroller."

"Well. Then what?"

"I'm taking you to see then what. Come along."

"I'll be right out. I want to wash my face."

"I'll stay right here."

"Please. Some privacy, sir. Wait outside the door."

I took a big drink of whiskey. Brushed my teeth and combed my hair.

We walked silently down the street. Two long blocks. Damn.

"If you think about it, it's pretty miraculous that my Mazda didn't hit anything or hurt anybody. Don't you think so, Officer Wong? A miracle!"

"Well, it did hit something. It is a miracle that none of the gentlemen were in the car at the time. They got out to watch your Mazda coming down the street."

My car was nuzzled into the right fender of the Chevy Corvair. The four men were standing there, shaking their heads. Champ puffed on his cigar.

"Thank the Lord you wasn't in it, sister," Mo said. "First thing I did, I opened the door and said, 'Where she be?'"

There was a big dent in the fender and the door of the Chevrolet. My car had a broken bumper and headlight, broken turn-signal light.

Ace was still shaking his head. "Hope you got insurance, Miz Lucille. I got me one classic car here what has some serious damage."

"Don't worry, Ace. I got insurance. You bring me an estimate as soon as you can."

The Champ spoke to the others quietly. They tried not to smile but it didn't work. Ace said, "Just sittin' here minding our own business and look what happens! Praise the Lord!"

Officer Wong was writing down my license plate numbers and Ace's license plate numbers.

"Does that car have a motor in it?" he asked Ace.

"This here car is a museum piece. Vintage model. Don't need no motor."

"Well, guess I'll try to back out of here without running into anybody," I said.

"Not so fast, Ms. Moran," Officer Wong said. "I need to write up a citation."

"A citation? Shame on you, officer!"

"You can't be writing this lady no ticket. She was asleep at the time of the incident!"

The old guys were crowding around him, making him nervous.

"Well," he sputtered, "she's guilty of reckless... reckless..."

"Can't be reckless driving. She wasn't driving the car!"

He was trying to think. They were muttering and grumbling. "Shame. Shameful. Innocent taxpayers. Poor thing, on her own and all."

"I definitely smell alcohol," Officer Wong said.

"That's me!" all four of them said at once, exhaling.

"No sir," Champ said. "If you ain't doing the D you can't get the DWI!"

"That's the truth!"

"Sure enough."

Officer Wong looked at us with a very discouraged expression. The police radio began squawking. He quickly put his pad into his pocket, turned and hurried to the squad car, took off with lights and siren.

The insurance check came very soon, sent to me but written out to Horatio Turner. The four men were sitting in the car when I handed the check to Ace. Fifteen hundred dollars.

That afternoon was the only time I sat inside the old car. I had to slide in after The Champ since the other door wouldn't open. Little Ripple, who was little, sat on my other side. They were all drinking Gallo Port but brought me a big Colt 45. They toasted me. "Here's to our lady Lucille!" That's how I was known in the neighborhood after that.

The sad part was that this happened in early spring. Officer Wong still had spring and summer on that same beat. Every day he had to pass by the guys in the Chevrolet Corvair, smiling and waving.

Of course I had other encounters with Officer Wong after that one, not pleasant at all.

Here It Is Saturday

The ride from city to county jail goes along the top of the hills above the bay. The avenue is lined with trees and that last morning it was foggy, like an old Chinese painting. Just the sound of the tires and the wipers. Our leg-chains made the sound of oriental instruments and the prisoners in orange jumpsuits swayed together like Tibetan monks. You laugh. Well, so did I. I knew I was the only white guy on the bus and that all these dudes weren't the Dalai Lama. But it was beautiful. Maybe I laughed because I felt silly, seeing it that way. Karate Kid heard me laugh. Old Chaz has a wet brain now for sure. Most of the men going to jail now are just kids for crack. They don't hassle me, think I'm just an old hippy.

The first view of the prison is awesome. After a long climb you come upon a valley in the hills. The land used to be the summer estate of a millionaire called Spreckles. The fields around the county jail are like the grounds of a French castle. That day there were a hundred Japanese plum trees in bloom. Flowering quince. Later on there were fields of daffodils, then iris.

In front of the jail is a meadow where there is a herd of buffalo. About sixty buffalo. Already there were six new calves. For some reason all the sick buffalo in the U.S. get sent here. Veterinarians treat them and study them. You can tell when dudes on the bus are doing their first time because they all freak out. "Whoa! What the fuck! Do they feed us buffalo? Check them mothers out."

The prison and the women's jail, the auto shop and the greenhouses. No people, no other houses, so it seems as if you're suddenly in an ancient prairie lit by sunbeams in the mist. The Bluebird bus always frightens the buffalo even though it comes once a week. They break into a gallop, stampede off toward the green hills. Like a tourist on safari I was hoping I'd get a view of the fields.

The bus unloaded us into the basement holding cell where we waited to get processed. A long wait and still another butt search. "Chaz, don't be laughin' now," the Karate Kid said. He told me CD was here, had been violated. Jail talk is like Spanish. The cup breaks itself. You don't violate your parole. The police violate you.

Sunnyvale gang shot the Chink. I hadn't heard that. I knew CD loved his brother Chink, a big-time dealer in the Mission. "Heavy," I said.

"No shit. Everybody gone by the time the police come except CD be sittin' there holding the Chink's head. All they had on him was violation. Six months. He'll do three maybe. Then he'll get the motherfuckers."

I lucked out and got the third tier (no view), but a cell with only two surly kids and Karate, who I know from the street. Only three other white guys on the tier, so I was glad Karate was with me. The cells were meant for two people. Usually there are six men in them; we'd get two more in a week. The Kid would spend his time lifting weights and practicing kicks and lunges, whatever he does.

When we got here Mac was the deputy in charge. He's always laying AA rap on me. He knows I like to write though, brought me a yellow pad and a pen. Said he saw I was in for B and E and burglary, would be staying awhile. "Maybe this time you'll do a fourth step, Chaz." That's when you admit all your wrongs.

"Better bring me about ten more tablets," I told him.

Here It Is Saturday

Anything you can say about prison is a cliché. Humiliation. The waiting, the brutality, the stench, the food, the endlessness. No way to describe the incessant ear-splitting noise.

For two days I had bad shakes. One night I must have had a seizure, or else fifty guys beat me up in my sleep. Split my lip, broke some teeth, black and blue all over. Tried to make sick bay but none of the guards would go for it.

"You don't ever have to go through this again," Mac said.

At least they let me stay on my bunk. CD was on another tier but during exercise I could see him down in the yard, smoking with other dudes, listening while they laughed. Most of the time he walked around alone.

Weird how some people have power. Meanest mothers out there deferred to him, just by how they stood back when he passed by. He's not huge like his brother, but has the same strength and cool. They had a Chinese mother and black father. CD has one long pigtail down his back. He is an unworldly color, like an old sepia photograph, black tea with milk.

Sometimes he reminds me of a Masai warrior, other times a Buddha or a Mayan god. He'd stand there not moving, not blinking an eye, for half an hour. He has the calm indifference of a god. I probably sound like a nut or a fag. Anyway he has this effect on everybody.

I met him in county when he just turned eighteen. It was our first time in jail. I turned CD on to books. The first time he fell in love with words was Stephen Crane's *The Open Boat*. Every week the guy from the library would come and we'd give him back our books and get more. Latinos have an elaborate sign language they use in here. Me and CD started speaking in book. *Crime and Punishment, The Stranger,* Elmore Leonard. I was in one other time when he was and by then he was turning me on to different writers.

Out on the street I'd run into him sometimes. He'd always give me money, which was awkward, but I was out there panhandling, so I never said no. We'd sit on a bus stop bench and talk. CD's read more than I have by now. He's twenty-two. I'm thirty-two but people always figure I'm a lot older. I feel around sixteen. I've been drunk since then, so a lot has passed me by. I missed Watergate, thank God. I still talk like a hippy, say things like "groovy," and "what a trip."

Willie Clampton woke me by banging on my bars when the tier got back from the yard. "Yo, Chaz, what's happening? CD says welcome home."

"Say, how you been, Willie?"

"Cool. Couple more Soul Trains I'm gone. You dudes got to sign up for writing class. They got righteous classes now. Music, pottery, drama, painting. They even let them over from the women's jail. Say, Kid, Dixie's in the class. Word."

"No way. What's Dixie doing in county?"

Karate Kid used to pimp Dixie. She ran her own feminist operation now, girls and coke to big-time lawyers, county supervisors. Whatever she was in for she'd be out soon. She was about forty but still looked fine. On the street you'd take her for a Neiman Marcus buyer. She never copped to knowing me but always gave me five or ten bucks and a big grin. "Now, young man, you use this to get a nice nourishing breakfast."

"So what you write?"

"Stories, rap, poems. Check out my poem:

> Police cars rolling back to back
> They don't care
> cause it's black on black

and

> Two wet sugars
> for one cigarette
> Big score."

Karate and I laughed. "Go ahead on, motherfuckers, laugh. Dig this."

Damned if he didn't recite a sonnet by Shakespeare. Willie. His deep voice above the insanity of jail noise.

"'Shall I compare thee to a summers' day? Thou art more lovely and more temperate...'

"Teacher's white, old. Old as my gramma, but she's cool. Ferragamo boots. First day she came in wearing Coco perfume. She couldn't believe I knew it. Now she wears different ones. I know them all. Opium, Ysatis, Joy. Only one I missed was Fleurs de Rocaille."

Sounded like he said it perfectly. Karate and me laughed our heads off about him and his Fleurs de Rocaille.

Actually one sound you hear a lot in jail is laughter.

This is not your normal jail. I've been in normal jails, Santa Rita, Vacaville. A miracle I'm still alive. County #3 has been on "60 Minutes" for how progressive it is. Computer training, mechanics, printing. A famous horticulture school. We supply the greens for Chez Panisse, Stars, other restaurants. This is where I got my G.E.D.

The head of the jail, Bingham, is something else. He's an ex-con, for one thing. Murdered his father. Did serious time for it. When he got out he went to law school, decided to change the prison system. He understands jail.

Nowadays he'd have walked, got self-defense for being abused. Hell, I could get off murder one easy, just tell a jury about my ma. Stories about my father, I could be the fuckin' Zodiac.

They're going to build a new jail, next to this one. Bingham says this jail is the same as the street. Same power structure, attitudes, brutality, drugs. The new jail will change all this. You won't want to come back to it, he says. Face it, part of you likes to get back in here, get some rest.

Signed up for the class just to see CD. Mrs. Bevins said that CD had told her about me.

"That ole wino? Bet you heard plenty about *me*. I'm the Karate Kid. I'll be makin' you smile. Put some pep in your step. Glide in your stride."

A writer called Jerome Washington wrote about this kind of Uncle Tomming. Talking jive to whites. Things like, "I be's so rich I had money in bof my shoes." True, we love it. The teacher was laughing. "Just ignore him," Dixie said. "He's incorrigible."

"No way, mama. Encourage me all you want."

Mrs. Bevins had me and Karate fill out a questionnaire while they read their work out loud. I thought the questions would be about our education and police record, but they were things like, "Describe your ideal room," "You are a stump. Describe yourself as a stump."

We were scribbling away, but I was listening to Marcus read a story. Marcus is a brutal guy, Indian, a serious felon. He wrote a good story, though, about a little kid watching his dad get beat up by some rednecks. It was called, "How I Became a Cherokee."

"This is a fine story," she said.

"The story is fucked. It was fucked when I first read it some-place. I never knew my father. I figured this was the kind of bullshit you want from us. Bet you come all over yourself how you help us unfortunate victims of society get in touch with our feelings."

"I don't give a rat's ass about your feelings. I'm here to teach writing. Matter of fact you can lie and still tell the truth. This story is good, and it rings true, wherever it came from."

She was backing to the door while she spoke. "I hate victims," she said. "For sure I don't want to be yours." She opened the door, told the guards to take Marcus up to the tier.

"If this class goes right what we will be doing is trusting each other with our lives," she said. She told me and Karate that the assignment had been to write about pain. "Read your story, please, CD."

Here It Is Saturday

When he finished reading the story, Mrs. Bevins and I smiled at each other. CD smiled too. First time ever I saw him really smile, little white teeth. The story was about a young man and a girl looking in the window of a junk store in North Beach. They're talking about the stuff, an old picture of a bride, some little shoes, an embroidered pillow.

The way he described the girl, her thin wrists, the blue vein on her forehead, her beauty and innocence, it broke your heart. Kim was crying. She's a young Tenderloin whore, mean little bitch.

"Yeah, it's cool, but it ain't pain," Willie said.

"I felt pain," Kim said.

"Me too," Dixie said. "I'd kill to have somebody see me that way."

Everybody was arguing, saying it was about happiness, not pain.

"It's about love," Daron said.

"Love, no way. Dude doesn't even touch her."

Mrs. Bevins said to notice all the mementos of dead people. "The sunset is reflected in the glass. All the images are about the fragility of life and love. Those tiny wrists. The pain is in the awareness that the happiness won't last."

"Yeah," Willie said, "except in this story he be engrafting her new."

"Say wha, nigger?"

"That's from Shakespeare, blood. It's what art does. It freezes his happiness. CD can have it back any old time, just reading that story."

"Yeah, but he can't be fuckin' it."

"You've got it perfectly, Willie. I swear this class understands better than any class I ever taught," she said. On another day she said that there was little difference between the criminal mind and the mind of the poet. "It is a matter of improving upon reality, making our own truth. You have an eye for detail. Two minutes in a room you have everything and everybody scoped out. You all can smell a lie."

The classes were four hours long. We talked while we wrote, in between reading our work, listening to things she read. Talked to ourselves, to her, to one another. Shabazz said it reminded him of Sunday school when he was a kid, coloring pictures of Jesus and talking away real soft just like here. Shabazz is a religious fanatic, in for beating his wife and kids. His poems were a cross between rap and Song of Solomon.

The writing class changed my friendship with Karate Kid. We wrote every night in our cell and read our stories to each other, took turns reading out loud. Baldwin's "Sonny's Blues." Chekhov's "Sleepy."

I stopped being self-conscious after the first day, reading aloud "My Stump." My stump was the only one left in a burned-out forest. It was black and dead and, when the wind blew, bits of charcoal crumbled and fell away.

"What have we got here?" she asked.

"Clinical depression," Daron said.

"We got us one burnt-out hippy," Willie said. Dixie laughed, "I see a very poor body image." "The writing is good," CD said. "I really felt how bleak and hopeless everything is"

"True," Mrs. Bevins said. "People are always saying 'tell the truth' when you write. Actually it is hard to lie. The assignment seems silly... a stump. But this is deeply felt. I see an alcoholic who is sick and tired. This stump is how I would have described myself before I stopped drinking."

"How long were you sober before you felt different?" I asked her. She said it worked the other way around. First I had to think I wasn't hopeless, then I could stop.

"Whoa," Daron said, "if I want to hear this shit I'll sign up for AA meetings."

"Sorry," she said. "Do me a favor, though. Don't answer this out loud. Each of you. Ask yourself if the last time, or times, you were arrested, whatever it was for—were you high on drugs or alcohol at the time?" Silence. Busted. We all laughed. Dwight said, "You know that group MADD, mothers against drunk drivers? We got our own group, DAM. Drunks against mothers."

Willie left a couple of weeks after I got there. We were sorry to see him go. Two of the women got in a fight so there was only Dixie, Kim and Casey left and six guys. Seven when Vee de la Rangee took Willie's place. Puny, pimply ugly transvestite with blonde permanent, black roots. He wore a plastic bread fastener for a nose ring, about twenty along each ear. Daron and Dwight looked like they might kill him. He said he had written some poems. "Read us one."

It was a lush violent fantasy about the drag-heroin world. After he read no one said anything. Finally CD said, "That's some powerful shit. Let's hear some more." Like CD gave everybody permission to accept this guy. Vee took off from there and by the next class he was at home. You could see how much it meant to him, to be heard. Hell, I felt that way too. Once I even had the nerve to write about when my dog died. I didn't even care if they laughed, but nobody laughed.

Kim didn't write that much. A lot of remorse poems about the child that got taken away from her. Dixie wrote sardonic things to the theme of "Vice is so Nice." Casey was fantastic. She wrote about heroin addiction. Really got to me. Most of the guys in here sold crack but either didn't use it that much or were too young to know what years and years of voluntarily returning to hell can do to you. Mrs. Bevins knew. She didn't talk that much about it, but enough to make it seem pretty cool that she had stopped.

We all wrote some good things. "That's great!" Mrs. Bevins said to Karate once. "You get better every week."

"No lie? So, Teach, am I as good as CD?"

"Writing isn't a contest. All you do is your own work better and better."

"But CD's your favorite."

"I don't have a pet. I have four sons. I have a different feeling for each one. It's the same with you guys."

"But you don't be telling us to go to school, get a scholarship. You're always getting on him to change his life."

"She does that with all of us," I said, "except Dixie. She's subtle though. Who knows, I might sober up. Anyway, CD *is* the best. We all know that. First day I got here I saw him down in the yard. You know what I thought? I thought he looked like a god."

"I don't know about god," Dixie said. "But he has star quality. Right, Mrs. Bevins?"

"Give me a break," CD said.

Mrs. Bevins smiled. "OK. I'll cop. I think every teacher sees this sometimes. It's not simply intelligence or talent. It's a nobility of spirit. A quality which could make him great at whatever he wanted to do."

We were quiet then. I think we all agreed with her. But we felt sorry for her. We knew what it was he wanted to do, was going to do.

We got back to work then, choosing pieces for our magazine. She was going to have it typeset and then the jail print shop would print it.

She and Dixie were laughing. They both loved to gossip. Now they were rating some of the deputies. "He's the kind leaves his socks on," Dixie said. "Right. And flosses before."

"We need more prose. Let's try this assignment for next week, see what you come up with." She handed out a list of titles from Raymond Chandler's notebook. We all had to choose one. I took *We All Liked Al.* Casey liked *Too Late for Smiling.* CD picked *Here It Is Saturday.* "In fact," he said, "I think we should call our magazine that."

"We can't," Kim said. "We promised Willie we were going to use his title, *Through a Cat's Eye*."

"OK, so what I want is two or three pages leading up to a dead body. Don't show us the actual body. Don't tell us there's going to be a body. End the story with us knowing there is going to be a dead body. Got it?"

"Got it." "Time to go, gentlemen," the guard said, opening the door. "Come here, Vee." She blasted him with perfume before sending him back up. The homosexual tier was pretty miserable. Half of it was old senile winos, the rest were gays.

I wrote a great story. It came out in the magazine and I still read it over and over. It was about Al, my best friend. He's dead now. Only she said I didn't do the assignment right because I told about me and the landlady finding Al's body.

Kim and Casey wrote the same horrible story. Kim's was about her old man beating her, Casey's about a sadistic john. You knew that they would end up murdering the guys. Dixie wrote a fine story, about a woman in solitary. She has an asthma attack, really bad, but no one can hear her. The terror and pitch black darkness. Then there is an earthquake. The end.

You can't imagine what it is like to be in prison during an earthquake.

CD wrote about his brother. Most of CD's stories had been about him. When they were little. The years they were lost to each other in different foster homes. How they found each other by chance, in Reno. This story took place in the Sunnyvale district. He read it in a quiet voice. None of us moved. It was about the afternoon and evening leading up to the Chink's death. The details about the meeting of two gangs. It ended with Uzi fire and CD turning the corner.

The hairs were standing up on my arm. Mrs. Bevins was pale. Nobody had told her CD's brother was dead. There wasn't a word about his brother in the story. That's how good it was. The story was so shimmering and taut there could only be one end to it. The room was silent until finally Shabazz said, "Amen." The guard opened the door. "Time to go, gentlemen." The other guards waited for the women while we filed out.

CD was set to get out of jail two days after the last day of class. The magazines would be out the last day and there was going to be a big party. An art exhibit and music by the prisoners. Casey, CD and Shabazz were going to read. Everybody would get copies of *Through a Cat's Eye*.

We had been excited about the magazine but none of us had known how it would feel. To see our work in print. "Where is CD?" she asked. We didn't know. She gave each of us twenty copies. We read our pieces out loud, applauding each other. Then we just sat there, reading our own work over and over to ourselves.

The class was short because of the party. A mess of deputies came in and opened the doors between our room and the art class. We helped set up tables for the food. Stacks of our magazines looked beautiful. Green on the purple paper tablecloth. Guys from horticulture brought in big bouquets of flowers. Student paintings were on the walls, sculptures on stands. One band was setting up.

First one band played, then came our reading and then the other band. The reading went fine and the music was great. Kitchen dudes brought in food and soft drinks and everybody got in line. There were dozens of guards but they all seemed to be having a good time too. Even Bingham was there. Everybody was there except CD.

She was talking with Bingham. He is so cool. I saw him nod and call a guard over. She went and got twenty copies of the magazine and followed the guard out. I knew Bingham had said to let her go up on the tier.

She wasn't gone long, even after all the stairs and six locked steel gates. She sat down, looking sick. I took her a can of Pepsi.

"Did you talk with him?"

Here It Is Saturday

She shook her head. "He was lying under a blanket, wouldn't answer me. I slid the magazines through the bars. It's horrible up there, Chaz. His window is broken, rain coming through it. The stink. The cells are so small and dark."

"Hey, it's heaven up there now. Nobody's there. Imagine those cells with six dudes in them."

"Five minutes, gentlemen!"

Dixie and Kim and Casey hugged her goodbye. None of us guys said goodbye. I couldn't even look at her. I heard her say, "Take care, Chaz."

I just realized that I'm doing that last assignment again. And I'm still doing it wrong, mentioning the body, telling you that they killed CD the day he got out of county.

Elsa's Life

Luna was a state-funded art project where painters, musicians and writers worked with the elderly.

The artists took turns evaluating the new clients, deciding what kind of project they would most enjoy. Clarissa, the writer, was sorry to realize how few of the old people wanted to do oral histories or to write stories. Painting and music were what they liked the most.

Clarissa was assigned two people simply because she could speak Spanish with them. But she was sure Mr. Ramirez had a wonderful story. A Spaniard. Eighty years old, still fit and muscular, with black hair and moustache, broody brown eyes. He had been a sailor and had traveled all over the world.

Every Tuesday morning she would show up at nine. They sat in front of the window that faced the bay. Clarissa opened a world atlas and made them strong coffees with milk and then they would begin.

"Where were we?" he would ask.

"Valparaiso."

"*Muy bien.* Copper. Next port Arequipa. Callao. Guayaquil. Buenaventura. Balboa. Colón."

And that was it. Week after week. Names of every port, with an occasional reference to cargo. Sewing machines, olives, oranges, wire cables. Clarissa and Sr. Ramirez had already been around the world several times.

He was handsome but never had a girl in any port. He never went ashore. He stayed on board in Madagascar, Rio, Marseilles. In every port, all over the world. When asked why, he said it was because he didn't drink. The only romance he told Clarissa of was a three-day affair he had with a whore off a sampan in Singapore. He was alone on the ship, everyone else had gone on leave. She climbed up a rope onto the deck and she refused to leave. She wanted him to marry her and take her to the USA, didn't understand that he wasn't American. It wasn't an American ship. He remembered her fondly. They cooked, just the two of them, in the galley. They danced to music from the shortwave radio. Artie Shaw's "Frenesi." At night they slept on a mattress on the deck, beneath the stars. At last, weeping, she slid down the rope onto a sampan which lay low in the water. The sampan was crowded with her family, all visibly disappointed in her.

Elsa lived in the Mission district, in a small house only blocks from the 16th Street BART. A shabby grey building on a car-lined street, dwarfed by graffitied buildings. The windows and doors had metal bars on them. Inocencia, Elsa's sister, opened the door only wide enough to peer over a metal chain.

It was hot, summer, and they were ironing and cooking food and boiling laundry. The windows were steamed up. Ferns and banana plants and ivies dripped as if it were Veracruz in rainy season. Bright plastic flowers and real plants were everywhere. There were two or three bird cages in every room. Canaries, parrots, finches, macaws, love birds. Juan Gabriel singing "Noche de Ronda" could barely be heard above the cacophony of bird sings. Horns and sirens, pneumatic drills from the street sounded like faraway jungle noises.

"Aaaiii!" wailed a blonde woman in a soap opera on top of the refrigerator. *"Ai Diós mio, me está matando este amor!"*

Elsa's Life

"Ai, Ai, el dolor! Me está matando el dolor!" screamed Elsa from the bedroom.

Elsa was fat and soft, with beautiful strong features. Distorted now with pain, her face resembled stone images of Coatlique giving birth to the world. She screamed in agony until her caregiver Lola gave her an injection. Almost instantly she stopped crying, lay panting, sweating under the sheet. The same soap opera flickered on a television set in Elsa's room. She resumed watching it, her breast still heaving.

Clarissa thought she'd give Elsa some time to feel better before she introduced herself. She went into the kitchen and talked with Inocencia and Lola.

Clarissa explained the arts program to Elsa's sister, told her what different things they had to offer. Inocencia was all for it.

"Elsa is so sad, in so much pain. It will be nice for her to see a new face."

Elsa herself seemed to be depressed by the idea. "What can I tell you about my life? It is a boring story. Pain and loneliness and suffering."

"Suffer! Suffer! Suffer!" Lola said, handing Elsa three pills, spooning water into her mouth. Elsa's arthritis was so painful she couldn't lift her head or use her arms. Of course she couldn't walk, had to be bathed and fed.

"Maybe this lady will get your mind off your suffering!" Lola said. "Tell her all about El Salvador, about the ocean, the flowers." Lola combed Elsa's hair roughly. Elsa cringed. It hurt her to be touched.

"You come," Lola said to Clarissa. "Cheer her up, give me a break."

Elsa smiled weakly at Clarissa. Lola smoothed the bedding, cooled Elsa's face with a damp cloth. She turned off the television, lowered the blind and left the room. Clarissa sat in the sweltering darkness, rocking quietly as Elsa drifted off to sleep. She too almost fell asleep, or rather she was awake but entered into a dream world in the tropical heat with food sizzling in hot lard in the kitchen and *murmullos* from the women, which even in English, *murmurs,* is a mesmerizing sound. Elsa slept peacefully except for an occasional moan. Tango music played and the parrot kept calling, *"Vente, mijo! Vente!"* Where exactly Clarissa drifted in her reverie isn't clear, but it seemed a peaceful, painless place.

The next time she came, Clarissa brought a notebook. She didn't write much down. Elsa spoke very slowly. She seemed to enjoy describing the little house where they lived outside of San Salvador, at the end of the tram lines. Their father had been killed in a mill accident when Ivan was eight and the others all younger.

"How terrible. What did your mother do then?"

"Well...you see the woman we call our mother, she was really our aunt. She was a saint, a blessed person." As Elsa spoke, her hands cramped into claws, her body arched in pain.

"When our father died. When. When he died our mother left us. When. One day she was gone. We waited for her. A long time. Our aunt, our true mother, came and she fed us. She was our mother then. When.

"We helped her cook food to sell on the street. My brother, Ivan. He. I made drinks from pineapple and mango and cucumber. Oh yes, cucumber makes a lovely drink." Elsa rang her bell. "Bring me and Clarissa an *agua* of cucumber."

The life she described was hard. They went to a small school in the mornings. They worked the rest of the day, until late into the night. Elsa and her family weren't Catholic. But her religion was one of the things that, when mentioned, caused her pain, literal pain. Her hands would curl up and she would thrash like a baby dragon in the bed.

Elsa's Life

Clarissa's notes were meager. It was painful to write the repetition of work work work. Clarissa asked Elsa if she had ever seen her birth mother. Elsa was silent and then she nodded.

"But don't write her down. She was not part of my life."

The mother had come in the night and had taken her three daughters. She had thin eyebrows and smelled of perfume and dry-cleaned clothes. They went on a train. Far. It was hot, midday, when they got to the town where she lived. As Elsa described this she began to writhe in pain and to cry.

"Please stop. Never mind," Clarissa said, although she did mind. "You didn't stay there, no?"

"No, Marta stayed. She wanted to stay. It was bad place, bad. She. Inocencia and I ran away in the night. We walked by the train tracks all night long. There was no moon. Just the boards and the shine of the track. In the morning I fell down. I was very sick. Typhus. I was asleep in the grass. Cool grass. A woman put me in a shed by her house. Inocencia kept on walking and walking day and night until she found our home in San Salvador. One day my mother, my aunt-mother, came with a man from the church. They took me home in a car."

"My brother, Ivan. He. He was very bad. He hit us. He hurt us. He. We stopped school because there was no money. We cooked food starting very early and took it by tram to sell outside factories. No, Ivan didn't work. He."

"When I was fifteen my mother sent me here to live with an aunt and uncle. Inocencia stayed. She came much later. Ivan? No. He."

Clarissa saw that Elsa was in terrible pain. She rang the bell for Lola to come give her an injection.

"Let's listen to the radio for a while," Clarissa said. "When you fall asleep I'll leave."

It was easy for Clarissa to assume that painful memories exacerbated Elsa's very real physical pain. But the stories she told about her difficult early years in the United States did not seem to upset her or cause her any physical distress, no matter how terrible they were. She slept on a cot in the kitchen of her relative's apartment. It was hard to sleep as many people lived there and the men drank most of the night. Elsa worked in a laundry in the Mission district, on the mangle, doing sheets for $3.00 an hour, ten hours a day. After work she would come home, eat and go to bed, year in and year out for five years. She didn't learn English or go out anywhere, had never been to Golden Gate Park or to the Wharf or even to movies in the neighborhood.

"No, I never went anywhere after work. I wasn't pretty. I was. I," she said.

It wasn't that her sentences trailed off but simply as if that was all she could bear to say. "One day I closed my eyes because I felt sick. My boss shook me. Then he."

Another day she was so tired she fell asleep standing up, burned her hand badly on the mangle. She was off work for weeks but didn't get any disability. When her hand healed they didn't give her back her job. Olivia, a woman in the Mission, got her another job ironing coveralls in another laundry, where she stayed for four years. But she began slowing down because of the arthritis in her neck and hands. Her knees hurt standing all day. She got fired for not doing enough coveralls in one day. This time though, the woman Olivia helped her get disability compensation. She taught her how to apply for medical insurance and food stamps, took her to the places she needed to go. In all those years Elsa had never been on a bus, had lived in the Mission as one would in an isolated mountain town. When Inocencia decided to move to the United States, Olivia helped the two of them find this little house that at first they shared with an old widower they cooked and cleaned for. He left them the house when he died.

Olivia found them a wonderful job, working in the laundry of the Mark Hopkins Hotel, ironing sheets. How happy they had been! Their boss, Mr. Whipple, was kind to them, always made a special effort to speak to them. He called Elsa his canary because she sang so sweetly. A few times, when the laundry was short-handed, they were allowed to deliver towels or hand laundry to people's rooms in the hotel. To ride in the beautiful elevator and knock on the doors. Smell the rooms. Once a man gave them a twenty-dollar bill. He laughed when they went back, said no, it wasn't a mistake.

Elsa was beginning to get very sick then. Inocencia worked even harder. She put sheets she had ironed on Elsa's pile so she would not get fired. Mr. Whipple caught her doing that. The sisters had begun to cry, thinking they would both be fired. But he was a good man. He was a saint. He said, "Now, even sick as you are, Elsa, you work harder than most girls I've had here. I don't want Inocensense knocking herself out and making herself sick too, got that? You two just do what you can. Long as you keep on singing, I won't complain about your work."

Elsa said that had been the happiest day of her life.

After work the sisters took the bus home. They did grocery shopping in the neighborhood. They did not ever go out, but watched TV in Spanish at home. Every night before they went to sleep they talked about their mother, remembered her and prayed for her.

"And then our mother died. She. I. *Ai ai!*" Elsa cried out, convulsed with pain, buckling under the damp sheet. Lola and Inocencia came in. Lola gave her a shot. Clarissa told them that Elsa had been talking about her mother's death.

"When Mama died, Ivan called us from El Salvador. The minute she heard it, Elsa became paralyzed. We had to call the ambulance. She was in the hospital for several months. This was three years ago. She has not been able to walk since."

"Is the paralysis real, physical?"

"Oh yes. Her X-rays show deterioration, huge swellings in all her joints. It is very real. I believe that the pain is always there but that only sometimes, to punish herself, she allows herself to feel it."

Clarissa looked down at Elsa, in a morphine sleep now on the bed. Salty tears had dried like tiny pressed flowers on her cheeks.

Inocencia asked Clarissa to join her and Lola at the table. They ate soup and good hot bread. Clarissa loved sitting there, listening to the birds. It was hard to tell them that she was leaving.

"Talking about her past is too hard on her. It is just the opposite of what we mean to do in our program. I'm going to have Angela come with her guitar tomorrow. You'll see, this will make her happy, all of you happy, even the birds."

On the way home to Oakland on BART, Clarissa decided to have Angela see Mr. Ramirez too. They would both like music much better.

As the train rumbled beneath the bay, Clarissa leafed through the notebook titled, "Elsa." Almost nothing was written down. One page was blank except for, "I always liked oranges." It was so pitiful that when the train arrived at her station she threw the notebook into the trash.

Several months later, the staff got together to bring one another up to date. Clarissa was glad to hear how good Angela was with Elsa and Sr. Ramirez. She and Elsa sang boleros for the entire hour of her visit. Every week, Mr. Ramirez played to Angela on the accordion.

Shortly after this, Clarissa left the program and went to work full time in the East Bay. She was very busy, and gave little thought to the old people, except for Mr. Ramirez, whenever she saw a map.

Over a year had gone by when Clarissa got a phone call from

Will Marks, the director of Luna. He told her that Elsa was in San Francisco General, that she was dying. Clarissa said she was was very sorry, that she would go to visit her.

"Well, no," Will said. "Actually she doesn't want visitors. The slightest movement or effort is excruciatingly painful for her. But she keeps talking about one thing, obsessively. She says you promised to write her life story. She wants it before she dies. She probably has about another week, the doctor said. I was surprised, I must confess. It wasn't like you to promise something and not do it."

"Oh," Clarissa said.

"This is vitally important to her. She feels she must have something to leave behind. Whenever she talks about it, she gets very ill."

"Oh."

Clarissa giggled, her hand over the mouthpiece. I'm talking just like her, she thought. He. When. Oh.

"Will, the first day I did say something about writing her life story. But it was incredibly hard to get material. For the last thirty years she went to work and came home. There is very little to work with."

Like, nothing, she remembered. But she said, "I'll bring you her story as soon as I can. In Spanish for her, because that's how she told it. An English one for you. I do want to see her, though."

Clarissa called in sick at work the next day, and the day after that.

She opened a computer file called "Elsa's Life." Damn, that's it. *Tabula rasa*. The worst part was that she had forgotten details like which saints were given festivals, what food the mother cooked to sell on the street.

What Clarissa did remember was only conjecture. All she carried with her, all her "material" was her own fiction. What she imagined about the actual mother with the plucked eyebrows. What she suspected about the brother Ivan.

The details which were vividly clear to Clarissa, the children walking along the railway tracks in the moonlight, the men fighting in the kitchen her first night in the US, were things Elsa wouldn't want in the story at all, had even said, "Don't write that down!"

Clarissa went to the library, looked in atlases and travel books to get names of trees and birds. The name of the beach where the sisters must have gone. Twice. She looked in books of saints. She called the Salvadoran consulate. She bought international cookbooks and went to record stores in the Mission district. She went to the Mark Hopkins Hotel and asked to see the manager. She told him she was a mystery writer, got permission to look at the laundry.

She called in sick another day and still another, as she desperately worked on page one, then page two. Three and four were Christmas in El Salvador. Five, six and seven were Elsa's mother. Expressions she used. How she french-braided their hair every morning. The dishes, with ingredients, she had taught them to cook, how she made them kneel to pray at night. Page eight was the beach and what they saw from the streetcar. Nine and ten were neighborhood festivals and New Year's Eve, with details Clarissa got from questioning waitresses and busboys in Salvadoran restaurants.

The story of Elsa's life was finally finished. Twenty-two pages, as long as she could possibly stretch it. The last page was about the birds, with their names, in the little house in the Mission. How their song expressed the love of Inocencia for her sister Elsa, who used to sing like a canary.

Clarissa took the story to Elsa on a Sunday morning. She got to the hospital early but there were already many ambulances and police cars, crowds in the emergency room. Clarissa's heart was beating, her mouth dry as she rode elevators and walked the maze to Elsa's room. Inocencia sat by the bed, dozing. Elsa was asleep, thin and tiny on the bed. It was a special bed, with a sand mattress, which caused less pain to all her bones.

Clarissa embraced Inocencia, kissed Elsa lightly on her forehead. Elsa smiled but didn't speak.

"Did you bring her story?" Inocencia whispered.

Clarissa nodded, frightened.

"Please, read it," Inocencia said.

"Some things may not be quite right…you just tell me and I'll change them right away."

"Don't worry. Please, read," Inocencia said.

Elsa's brown eyes did not move from Clarissa. She cried out in pain only once, when Clarissa read about the death of their mother.

Inocencia wept softly throughout the reading. *"Que bonito,"* she said about the festivals and the trips to the beach. She especially liked the parts about the laundry and Mr. Whipple, how he used to call her Inocensense.

When Clarissa finally finished reading, Inocencia embraced her, sobbing, "It is so beautiful! Thank you, thank you. I will cherish this forever!"

Clarissa was dizzy with relief. She bent over Elsa, brushed her lips with a kiss.

"I hope you liked it," she said to Elsa.

Elsa's eyes were closed now but she spoke to Clarissa.

"That was not the story of my life. No. My life."

Wait a Minute

Sighs, the rhythms of our heartbeats, contractions of childbirth, orgasms, all flow into time just as pendulum clocks placed next to one another soon beat in unison. Fireflies in a tree flash on and off as one. The sun comes up and it goes down. The moon waxes and wanes and usually the morning paper hits the porch at six thirty-five.

Time stops when someone dies. Of course it stops for them, maybe, but for the mourners time runs amok. Death comes too soon. It forgets the tides, the days growing longer and shorter, the moon. It rips up the calendar. You aren't at your desk or on the subway or fixing dinner for the children. You're reading *People* in a surgery waiting room, or shivering outside on a balcony smoking all night long. You stare into space, sitting in your childhood bedroom with the globe on the desk. Persia, the Belgian Congo. The bad part is that when you return to your ordinary life all the routines, the marks of the day, seem like senseless lies. All is suspect, a trick to lull us, rock us back into the placid relentlessness of time.

When someone has a terminal disease, the soothing churn of time is shattered. Too fast, no time, I love you, have to finish this, tell him that. Wait a minute! I want to explain. Where is Toby, anyway? Or time turns sadistically slow. Death just hangs around while you wait for it to be night and then wait for it to be morning. Every day you've said goodbye a little. Oh just get it over with, for God's sake. You keep looking at the Arrival and Departure board. Nights are endless because you wake at the softest cough or sob, then lie awake listening to her breathe so softly, like a child. Afternoons at the bedside you know the time by the passage of sunlight, now on the Virgin of Guadalupe, now on the charcoal nude, the mirror, the carved jewelry box, dazzle on the bottle of Fracas. The camote man whistles in the street below and then you help your sister into the sala to watch Mexico City news and then U.S. news with Peter Jennings. Her cats sit on her lap. She has oxygen but still their fur makes it hard to breath. "No! Don't take them away. Wait a minute."

Every evening after the news, Sally would cry. Weep. It probably wasn't for long but in the time warp of her illness it went on and on, painful and hoarse. I can't even remember if at first my niece Mercedes and I cried with her. I don't think so. Neither of us are cryers. But we would hold her and kiss her, sing to her. We tried joking, "Maybe we should watch Tom Brokaw instead." We made her *aguas* and teas and cocoa. I can't remember when she stopped crying, soon before her death, but when she did stop it was truly horrible, the silence, and it lasted a long time.

When she cried sometimes she'd say things like, "Sorry, it must be the chemo. It's sort of a reflex. Don't pay any attention." But other times she would beg us to cry with her.

"I can't, *mi Argentina*," Mercedes would say. "But my heart is crying. Since we know it is going to happen we automatically harden ourselves." This was kind of her to say. The weeping simply drove me crazy.

Once while she was crying, Sally said, "I'll never see donkeys again!" which struck us as hilariously funny. She became furious, smashed her cup and plates, our glasses and ashtray against the wall. She kicked over the table, screaming at us. Cold calculating bitches. Not a shred of compassion or pity.

"One *pinche* tear. You don't even look sad." She was smiling by now. "You're like police matrons. 'Drink this. Here's a tissue. Throw up in the basin.'"

At night I would get her ready for bed, give her pills, an injection. I'd kiss her and tuck her in. "Good night. I love you, my sister, *mi cisterna*." I slept in a little room, a closet, next to her, could hear her through the plywood wall, reading, humming, writing. Sometimes she would cry then and those were the worst times, because she tried to muffle these silent sad weepings with her pillow.

At first I would go in and try to comfort her, but that seemed to make her cry more, become more anxious. The sleeping medicine would turn around and wake her up, get her agitated and nauseous. So I would just call out to her, "Sally. Dear Sal *y pimienta*, Salsa, don't be sad." Things like that.

"Remember in Chile how Rosa put hot bricks in our beds?"

"I'd forgotten!"

"Want me to find you a brick?"

"No, *mi vida*, I'm falling asleep."

She had had a mastectomy and radiation and then for five years she was fine. Really fine. Radiant and beautiful, wildly happy with a kind man, Andrés. She and I became friends, for the first time since our hard childhood. It had felt like falling in love, the discovery of one another, how much we shared. We went to the Yucatan and to New York together. I'd go to Mexico or she would come up to Oakland. When our mother died, we spent a week in Zihuatanejo where we talked all day and all night. We exorcised our parents and our own rivalries and I think we both grew up.

I was in Oakland when she called. The cancer was in her lungs now. Everywhere. There was no time left. *Apúrate.* Come right now!

It took me three days to quit my job, pack up and move out. On the plane to Mexico City, I thought about how death shreds time. My ordinary life had vanished. Therapy, laps at the Y. What about lunch on Friday? Gloria's party, dentist tomorrow, laundry, pick up books at Moe's, cleaning, out of cat food, babysit grandsons Saturday, order gauze and gastrostomy buttons at work, write to August, talk to Josee, bake some scones, C.J. coming over. Even eerier was a year later clerks in the grocery or bookstore or friends I ran into on the street had not noticed that I had been gone at all.

I called Pedro, her oncologist, from the airport in Mexico, wanting to know what to expect. It had sounded like a matter of weeks or a month. "*Ni modo*," he said. "We'll continue chemo. It could be six months, a year, perhaps more."

"If you had just told me, 'I want you to come now,' I would have come," I said to her later that night.

"No, you wouldn't!" she laughed. "You are a realist. You know I have servants to do everything, and nurses, doctors, friends. You'd think I didn't need you yet. But I want you now, to help me get everything in order. I want you to cook so Alicia and Sergio will eat here. I want you to read to me and take care of me. Now is when I'm alone and scared. I need you now."

We all have mental scrapbooks. Stills. Snapshots of people we love at different times. This one is Sally in deep green running clothes, cross-legged on her bed. Skin luminescent, her green eyes limned with tears as she spoke to me. No guile or self-pity. I embraced her, grateful for her trust in me.

In Texas, when I was eight and she was three, I hated her, envied her with a violent hissing in my heart. Our grandma let me run wild, at the mercy of the other adults, but she guarded little Sally, brushed her hair and made tarts just for her, rocked her to sleep and sang "Way Down in Missoura." But I have snapshots of her even then, smiling, offering me a mud pie with an undeniable sweetness that she never lost.

In Mexico City the first months passed in a flash, like in old movies when the calendars flip up the days. Speeded up Charlie

Wait a Minute

Chaplin carpenters pounded in the kitchen, plumbers banged in the bathroom. Men came to fix all the doorknobs and broken windows, sand the floors. Mirna, Belen and I tore into the storeroom, the topanco, the closets, the bookcases and drawers. We tossed out shoes and hats, dog collars, Nehru jackets. Mercedes and Alicia and I brought out all Sally's clothes and jewelry, labeled them to give to different friends.

Lazy sweet afternoons on Sally's floor, sorting photographs, reading letters, poems, gossiping, telling stories. The phone and doorbell rang all day. I screened the calls and visitors, was the one who cut them short if she was tired, or didn't if she was happy, like with Gustavo always.

When someone is first diagnosed with a fatal illness, they are deluged with calls and letters and visits. But as the months go by and the time turns into hard time, less people come. That's when the illness is growing and time is slow and loud. You heard the clocks and the church bells and vomiting and each raspy breath.

Sally's ex-husband Miguel and Andrés came every day, but at different times. Only once did the visits coincide. I was surprised by how the ex-husband was automatically deferred to. He had remarried long ago, but there still was his pride to consider. Andrés had been in Sally's room only a few minutes. I brought him in a coffee and *pan dulce*. Just as I set it on the table, Mirna came in to say, "The señor is coming!"

"Quick, into your room!" Sally said. Andrés rushed into my room, carrying his coffee and *pan dulce*. I had just shut him in when Miguel arrived.

"Coffee! I need coffee!" he said, so I went into my room, took the coffee and *pan dulces* from Andrés and carried them in to Miguel. Andrés disappeared.

I got very weak, and had trouble walking. We thought it was *estress* (no word in Spanish for stress), but finally I fainted on the street and was taken to an emergency room. I was critically anemic from a bleeding esophageal hernia. I was there several days for blood transfusions.

I felt much stronger when I got back, but my illness had frightened Sally. Death reminded us it was still there. Time got speeded up again. I'd think she was asleep and would get up to go to bed.

"Don't go!"

"I'm just going to the bathroom, be right back." At night if she choked or coughed, I'd wake up, go in to check on her.

She was on oxygen now and rarely got out of bed. I bathed her in her room, gave her injections for pain and nausea. She drank some broth, ate crackers sometimes. Crushed ice. I put ice in a towel and smashed it smashed it smashed it against the concrete wall. Mercedes lay with her and I lay on the floor, reading to them. I'd stop when they seemed to be asleep, but they'd both say, "Don't stop!"

Bueno. "I defy anyone to say that our Becky, who has certainly some vices, has not been presented to the public in a perfectly genteel and inoffensive manner..."

Pedro aspirated her lung, but it still became more and more difficult for her to breathe. I decided we should really clean her room. Mercedes stayed with her in the living room while Mirna and Belen and I swept and dusted, washed the walls and windows and floors. I moved her bed so that it lay horizontally beneath the window; now she could see the sky. Belen put clean ironed sheets and soft blankets on the bed and we carried her back in. She leaned back on her pillow, the springtime sun full on her face.

"*El sol,*" Sally said. "I can feel it."

I sat against the other wall and watched her look out her window. Airplane. Birds. Jet trail. Sunset!

Much later I kissed her goodnight and went to my little room. The humidifier on her oxygen tank bubbled like a fountain.

Wait a Minute

I waited to hear the breathing that meant she slept. Her mattress creaked. She gasped, and then moaned, breathing heavily. I listened and waited and then I heard the clink clink of curtain rings above her bed.

"Sally? Salamander, what are you doing?"

"I'm looking at the sky!"

Near her I looked out my own little window.

"*Oye*, sister…"

"Yes," I said.

"I can hear you. You are crying for me!"

It has been seven years since you died. Of course what I'll say next is that time has flown by. I got old. All of a sudden, *de repente*. I walk with difficulty. I even drool. I leave the door unlocked in case I die in my sleep, but it's more likely I'll go endlessly on until I get put away someplace. I am already dotty. I parked my car around the corner because there was someone in my usual spot. Later when I saw the empty spot I wondered where I had gone. It's not so strange that I talk to my cat but I feel silly because he is totally deaf.

But there's never enough time. "Real time," like the prisoners I used to teach would say, explaining how it just seemed that they had all the time in the world. The time wasn't ever theirs.

I teach in a pretty, *fresa*, mountain town now. The same Rocky Mountains Daddy used to mine, but a far cry from Butte or the Coeur d'Alene. I'm lucky though. I have good friends here. I live in the foothills where deer walk dainty and modest past my window. I saw skunks mating in the moonlight; their jagged cries were like oriental instruments.

I miss my sons and their families. I see them maybe once a year and that's always great, but I'm no longer really a part of their lives. Or of your children's either. Although Mercedes and Enrique came here to get married!

So many others have gone. I used to think it was funny when someone said, "I lost my husband." But that is how it feels. Someone is missing. Paul, Aunt Chata, Buddy. I understand how people believe in ghosts or have seances to call the dead. I go for months without thinking of anyone but the living, and then Buddy will come with a joke, or there you vividly are, evoked by a tango or an *agua de sandia*. If only you could speak to me. You're as bad as my deaf cat.

You last arrived a few days after the blizzard. Ice and snow still covered the ground, but we had a fluke of a warm day. Squirrels and magpies were chattering and sparrows and finches sang on the bare trees. I opened all the doors and curtains. I drank tea at the kitchen table feeling the sun on my back. Wasps came out of the nest on the front porch, floated sleepily through my house, buzzing in drowsy circles all around the kitchen. Just at this time the smoke alarm battery went dead, so it began to chirp like a summer cricket. The sun touched the teapot and the flour jar, the silver vase of stock.

A lazy illumination, like a Mexican afternoon in your room. I could see the sun in your face.

Lost in the Louvre

As a child I would try to capture the exact moment that I passed from awake to asleep. I lay very still and waited, but the next thing I knew it was morning. I did this off and on as I grew older. Sometimes I ask people if they have ever tried this, but they never understand what I mean. I was over forty when it first happened, and I wasn't even trying. A hot summer night. Arcs from car headlights swept across the ceiling. The whirr of a neighbor's sprinklers. I caught sleep. Just as it came quiet as a cool sheet to cover me, a light caress on my eyelids. I felt sleep as it took me. In the morning I woke up happy and I never needed to try it again.

It certainly had never occurred to me to catch death, although it was in Paris that I did. That I saw how it comes upon you.

I'm sure this sounds melodramatic. I was very happy in Paris, but sad too. My lover and my father had died the year before. My mother had quite recently died. I thought about them as I walked the streets or sat in cafes. Especially Bruno, talking to him in my head, laughing with him. My childhood friends, girls lying around on the grass, on the beach, talking about going to Paris someday. They were dead too. So was Andrés who had given me *Remembrance of Things Past*.

The first few weeks I explored every tourist destination in the city. L'Orangerie, the lovely Sainte Chapelle on a sunny day. Balzac's house, Hugo's museum. I sat upstairs at the Deux

Magots where everyone looked like a Californian or Camus. I went to Baudelaire's grave in Montmartre and thought it was funny for feminist Simone de Beauvoir to be buried with Sartre. I even went to a museum for medical instruments and a stamp museum. I loitered on the rue de Courcelles and walked the Champs Elysées. Napoleon's tomb, the Sunday bird market. La Serpente. Some days I took random combinations of Metros and walked and walked in each new quarter. I sat in the square beneath Colette's apartment and walked in the Luxembourg gardens with everybody from Flaubert to Gertrude Stein. I went to Boulevard Hausmann and to the Bois de Boulogne with Albertine. Everything I saw seemed vividly *déjà vu*, but I was seeing what I had read.

I took the train to Illiers, to see the Aunt's house and the village Proust used for much of Combray. I took a very early train and got off at Chartres. It was a stormy day, so dark no light came through the stained glass windows. An old woman prayed at a side chapel and a boy was playing the organ. No one else was there. It was too dark to see the stone floor but it was worn smooth as satin. A dim light that came through the dirty clear glass windows showed the intricate carvings in sharp relief. The exquisite stone figures seemed especially striking with no color anywhere, the way black and white films seem true.

The little train to Illiers was exactly as I had imagined. The dull relentless landscape, the workers and country women, the cane seats. The spire of the church! The train stopped long enough for me to get off. Eerily, there were no cars to be seen, only a bicycle leaning against the wall of the train station. I knew where to go, down the avenue de la Gare under the lime trees, almost bare now in October, the wet leaves muffling my footsteps. Right at rue de Chartres, Florent d'Illiers to the town square. I saw no one at all.

Lost in the Louvre

I walked around the village, waiting for the tour of the house, which began at ten. I did finally see some people, dressed in such an old-fashioned way that I could have been back in time.

At the gate to Aunt Amiot's house was an elderly German couple. They rang the bell and smiled and I rang it and smiled too. It sounded just as it was supposed to. Muttering at us through his cigarette, an old man came to let us in. He spoke too quickly for me or the Germans to understand, but it didn't matter. We followed him through the tiny house. So few stairs for Marcel's mother to climb! A begonia on the landing seemed out of place. The moldy windowless kitchen not at all "a miniature temple of Venus."

The three of us stayed for a long time in Marcel's bedroom, silent. We smiled at one another, but I could tell they too felt a deep sadness. The pitcher, the magic lantern, the little bed.

I stood in the cemented garden. I tried to see the house as a drab, tacky little place, and the town as a typical village, but they kept turning into the garden, the house, the village of Combray and were dear to me.

The dining room was truly ugly. Flocked green wall paper and massive furniture. It was now a museum, with postcards and books. In a glass-covered stand was a page of original manuscript written in a spidery hand, the ink sepia now, the paper amber. The "page" was several inches thick because each sentence had additional sentences pasted on, like ruffles, with still more clauses pasted on top of those and here and there a word pasted onto a phrase. These appendages were neatly folded down like an accordion, but so dense they fanned apart. The case was sealed but the pasted papers opened and closed, slightly, as if the page were breathing.

Finis, the old man said, and showed us to the door. I understood that the German woman was inviting me to walk with them to the "Mereglise way." I thanked them and said that there wasn't that much time before the train, which they didn't understand, but when I said the church of St. Jacques, they nodded. We shook hands, warmly, in the freezing drizzle, and later we turned back to wave.

It was raining hard by the time I got to the church and I was disappointed to find that it was locked. I had started to look for a café when an arthritic, ancient woman called out to me, waving her stick. *"J'arrive!"* She unlocked a creaking side door and let me into the church. It was dark, lit only by votive candles. She crossed herself and took a feather duster from behind the communion rail, flicked it everywhere as she led me around, talking softly without teeth. I understood that she was Matilde and eighty-nine. She was the caretaker of the church, swept it and dusted it and put flowers on the altar. Her pale gray eyes could barely see me and fortunately didn't see the cobwebs on the cross or the dead Michaelmas daisies. She told me about the church as we walked around. I caught "Eleventh Century, rebuilt in the Fifteenth." I put some money in the alms box and lit three candles. Then I lit another one, for me or for her. I knelt on the cold wood and said a Hail Mary. I was exhausted and hungry now. But there it was, the pew of the Duchesse of Guermantes. I wanted to sit there quietly. To be, well, *perdu,* but instead I got lost with Matilde. She crossed herself again, genuflected before the altar and knelt next to me. Suddenly she grabbed my arm and cawed, "Berenice! Petite Berenice!" She embraced me then and kissed both my cheeks, happy to see me again and how was my mother, Antoinette. She hadn't seen us for many years. She thought I lived in Tansonville, where she was born. She kept telling me about people in Illiers (my mother was from Illiers), asking me about my family, not waiting for answers. She heard so poorly that she didn't notice my poor French. She asked if I had married. *"Oui. Mais il est mort!"* She was so sorry to hear this, her eyes swam with tears. When I told her I had to leave for the train, that I lived in Paris now, she kissed my cheeks again. She didn't cry, stated matter-of-factly that she would never see me again, that she would be dead soon, probably.

I cried unreasonably on the way to the train station. I had a very bad lunch at the town's only inn.

On the train to Paris I tried to remember any bed from my own childhood, but I couldn't. I couldn't really remember my own children's beds. So many bassinets and cribs and bunk beds, trundle beds, hide-a-beds, waterbeds. None seemed as real to me as the little bed in Illiers.

The next day I went to see Proust's grave at Père Lachaise. It was a beautiful clear day and the old tombs clustered together like Nevelson sculptures. Old women knitted on benches and there were cats everywhere. Perhaps it was because it was so early I saw few people, only caretakers and the knitters, a stocky man in a blue windbreaker. I had a map, and it was fun searching for Chopin and Sarah Bernhardt, Victor Hugo and Artaud, Oscar Wilde. Proust was buried with his parents and his brother. Poor brother, imagine. There were many bouquets of Parma violets on Proust's black grave. His shiny black tomb seemed vulgar against the pale worn stone throughout the cemetery. It must take about a hundred years to look aged and beautiful, like Eloise and Abelard's or the man whose tomb said, "IL A FROID."

I started walking quickly down the tree-lined paths, partly because it was getting cold and windy but also because the man in the windbreaker was always about half a block behind me. The wind blew my map away just as rain began pouring down. I ran toward where I thought the exit was, but finally had to jump a railing and find shelter inside a mossy crypt. Except for being cold it was wonderful watching the yellow and red leaves blowing in whirlwinds from the trees, the silver sheets of rain darkening the stones. But it kept getting darker and colder, and I heard not just the wind howling but moans, anguished cries. Mournful dirge-like songs, diabolical laughter. I told myself

I was crazy, but I was very frightened and I became convinced that the man in the windbreaker was death, come for me. Then the band of Jim Morrison fans ran past, their boombox playing, "This is the end, my friend!" I felt pretty ridiculous. I left the crypt and tried to follow the sound of their voices since now I was hopelessly lost. It would seem logical to catch death, that hour in Père Lachaise as I ran and ran and there was no way out. I could hear traffic and horns from afar, but there was not a soul to be seen, not any cats or birds, not even the man in the windbreaker.

No, it wasn't where I caught death, although when I sat down to rest I did wonder. What if I died there of exposure? I had no papers, no ID at all. Should I write my name down and add, "Please bury me here in Père Lachaise?" But I had no pen. I decided to walk in a completely straight line on one path. I would at last come to a wall and would luckily choose the direction which led outside. I was faint with hunger, my beautiful Italian shoes had stretched in the rain and were making blisters. I came in sight of a wall just as I also saw a familiar sad and unkempt grave in the middle of the well-tended ones with fresh flowers. This had been close to Colette, who was near the gate and the flower vendors. Dear Colette, she was still there. The gates were locked and death crossed my mind again, but a man came out of a booth and let me out. The flowers were gone, but a taxi was at the curb.

I ate in a Greek restaurant near my hotel, then had espresso and a pastry, two espressos and pastries. I smoked and watched people passing by and that's when I first wondered if I could catch death, the way I had caught sleep. When people died, were they aware of it, the moment it came for them? As he was dying, Stephen Crane told his friend Robert Barr, "It isn't bad. You feel sleepy—and you don't care. Just a little dreamy anxiety about which world you're really in, that's all."

Croissant and café crème the next morning and then I went to the Louvre. They were building the pyramid so it was as hard to get into the museum as it was to get out of the cemetery. At last I have seen the Louvre. Just walking miles trying to get in was thrilling. It is monumental. I never knew anything so vast. Maybe the first time I crossed the Mississippi.

The inside of the Louvre was as elegant and grand as I had ever imagined. I had seen beautiful photographs of the Victory of Samothrace. And of course I love her because of Mrs. Bridge. But nothing had prepared me for the enormity of the hall. For the way she stands, so regal, so, well, victorious, above the crowds in that space.

The first day I went very slowly, reverently. Not because of the art, although the Victory and Ingres made me shiver, many things did, but because of the grandeur of the place, the history of it. Although there were mummies and Anubi and caskets, I wasn't preoccupied with death. In fact, an embracing couple on an Etruscan sarcophagus was so beautiful I felt better about Jean-Paul and Simone.

I walked from room to room, upstairs and downstairs and back upstairs again, walking with my hands clasped behind my back as I imagined Henry James might. I thought of Baudelaire, who had seen Delacroix himself here, showing an old lady around the museum. I loved everything. Saint Sebastian. Rembrandts. I never saw the Mona Lisa. There was always a line in front of her and she was behind a window just like they have in liquor stores in Oakland.

I sat outside at a cafe in the Tuilleries. The waiter brought me a crocque monsieur and a café crème. He said he would be inside if I needed him; it was too cold to stay out there. I sat there wishing I could talk to somebody about everything I had seen. It was hard not being able to have a real conversation in French. I missed my sons. I felt sad about Bruno and my parents. Not sad because I missed them, but because I really didn't. And when I died it would be the same. Dying is like shattering mercury. So soon it all just flows back together into the quivering mass of life. I told myself to lighten up, I'd been alone too long. But still I sat there, looking back on my life, a life filled with beauty and love actually. It seemed I had passed through it as I had the Louvre, watching and invisible.

I went inside and paid the waiter, told him he was right, it was too cold out there. On my way back to the hotel, I stopped at a beauty salon and had my hair washed. I asked the hairdresser to rinse it still another time, so desperately I wanted to be touched.

The second day at the Louvre I enjoyed going back to the works I had really liked. Bronzino's sculptor. Géricault's horses! "Derby at Epsom." To think he died falling from a horse, only thirty-three years old. I turned into a Flemish room and then somehow I was back with Rembrandt, and when I took the stairs down I was in the mummy room. Then I got really lost, like in the cemetery, even though there were thousands of people around me. I took some stairs I had not seen before. I sat on the landing to rest. The strange thing is that I knew that outside there were some people in the streets. Maybe five or six tables with coffee drinkers at the cafe in the Tuilleries. But inside the Louvre there were hordes of people. Thousands and thousands, going upstairs, downstairs, streaming past the pharaohs and the Apollos and Napoleon's salon.

Perhaps we were all caught inside a microcosm. What a laughable word to use about the Louvre. Perhaps we were all part of a performance piece that had been lovingly placed in someone's tomb, along with the jewelry and slaves, all of us mummified but moving cleverly upstairs and downstairs past all the works of art whose creators were long dead. Past the Rembrandts and Fragonard's "The Bolt," whose poor lovers were long dead too. Probably they were only models, having to earn their wages for hours and days in that uncomfortable position. Stuck that way for eternity! I had no idea where the staircase was going to lead me. Oh, good, Etruscans. Since no one spoke to me or even looked at me, it added to the illusion that we were all performers for eternity in the Immortality piece, so I ignored them also as I took my random turns and stairways until I was in a near hypnotic trance and, it felt, at one with the goddess of Hathor, with the Odalisque.

At last I would force myself to leave, have oysters and pâté at the Apollinaire and go fall into bed and sleep without reading or thinking. I went back to the Louvre three or four more times, each time seeing new sculptures or tapestries or jewelry, but also losing myself until I felt as if I were flying out of time.

An interesting phenomenon was that if I took a wrong turn and came upon the Nike herself I was immediately restored to reality. The last day I was in the Louvre, I suspected that a staircase would lead me to her, so to avoid that I crossed the room and went through a narrow hall, down some unfamiliar stairs.

My heart was beating. I was excited, but wasn't sure why. I came upon a new hall. A wing entirely unknown to me. I had read nothing about it, seen no photographs. It was an odd and charming assortment of everyday artifacts from different periods. Tapestries and tea sets, knives and forks. Chamber pots and dishes! Snuff boxes and clocks and writing desks and candelabras. Each little room contained lovely mundane objects. A footstool. A watch. Scissors. Like death, this section was not extraordinary. It was so unexpected.

Homing

I have never seen the crows leave the tree in the morning, but
every evening about a half an hour before dark, they start flying
in from all over town. There may be regular herders who swoop
around in the sky for blocks calling for the others to come home,
or perhaps each one circles around gathering stragglers before
it pops into the tree. I've watched enough, you'd think I could
tell by now. But I only see crows, dozens of crows, flying in
from every direction from far away and five or six circling like
over O'Hare, calling calling, and then in a split second suddenly
it is silent and no crows are to be seen. The tree looks like an
ordinary maple tree. No way you'd know there were so many
birds in there.

I happened to be on my front porch when I first saw them.
I had been downtown and was on my portable oxygen tank,
sitting on the porch swing to look at the evening light. Usually
I sit out on the back porch where my regular hose reaches.
Sometimes I watch the news at that time or fix dinner. What
I mean is I could easily have no idea that that particular maple
tree is filled with crows at sundown.

Do they all leave together then for still another tree to sleep
in, higher up on Mount Sanitas? Maybe, because I'm up early,
sitting at the window facing the foothills, and I have never seen
them come out of the tree. I see deer though going up into the
hills of Mount Sanitas and Dakota Ridge and the rising sun

glowing pink against the rocks. If there is snow and it is very cold, there is alpenglow, when the ice crystals turn the color of the morning into stained glass pink, neon coral.

Of course it is winter now. The tree is bare and there are no crows. I'm just thinking about the crows. It's hard for me to walk so the few blocks uphill would be too much for me. I could drive, I suppose, like Buster Keaton having his chauffeur drive him across the street. But I think it would be too dark then to see the birds inside the tree.

I don't know why I even brought this up. Magpies flash now blue, green against the snow. They have a similar bossy shriek. Of course I could get a book or call somebody and find out about the nesting habits of crows. But what bothers me is that I only accidentally noticed them. What else have I missed? How many times in my life have I been, so to speak, on the back porch, not the front porch? What would have been said to me that I failed to hear? What love might there have been that I didn't feel?

These are pointless questions. The only reason I have lived so long is that I let go of my past. Shut the door on grief on regret on remorse. If I let them in, just one self-indulgent crack, whap the door will fling open gales of pain ripping through my heart blinding my eyes with shame breaking cups and bottles knocking down jars shattering windows stumbling bloody on spilled sugar and broken glass terrified gagging until with a final shudder and sob shut the heavy door. Pick up the pieces one more time.

Maybe this is not so dangerous a thing to do, to let the past in with the preface "What if?" What if I had spoken with Paul before he left? What if I had asked for help? What if I had married H? Sitting here, looking out the window toward the tree where now there are no branches or crows the answers to each "what ifs" are strangely reassuring. They could not have happened, this what if, that what if. Everything good or bad that has occurred in my life has been predictable and inevitable, especially the choices and actions that have made sure that I am now utterly alone.

But what if I were to go way back, to before we moved to South America? What if Doctor Mock had said I couldn't leave Arizona for a year, that I needed extensive therapy and adjustments to my brace, possibly surgery for my scoliosis? I would have joined my family the following year. What if I had lived with the Wilsons in Patagonia, went weekly to the orthopedist's in Tucson, reading *Emma* or *Jane Eyre* on the hot bus ride?

The Wilsons had five children, all of them old enough to work at the General Store or the Sweet Shop the Wilsons owned. I worked before and after school at the Sweet Shop with Dot, and shared the attic room with her. Dot was seventeen, the oldest child. Woman, really. She looked like a woman in the movies the way she put on pancake makeup and blotted her lipstick, blew smoke out of her nose. We slept together on the hay mattress covered with old quilts. I learned not to bother her, to lie quiet, thrilled by her smells. She tamed her curly red hair with Wildroot oil, smeared Noxzema on her face at night and always put Tweed on her wrists and behind her ears. She smelled of cigarettes and sweat and Mum deodorant and what I later would learn was sex. We both smelled like old grease because we cooked hamburgers and fries at the Sweet Shop until it closed at ten. We walked home across the main street and the train tracks quickly past the Frontier saloon and down the street to her folks' house. The Wilson house was the prettiest house in town. A big two-story white house with a picket fence and a garden and a lawn. Most of the houses in Patagonia were small and ugly. Transient mining town houses painted that weird train station mining camp butterscotch brown. Most of the people worked up the mountain at the Trench and Flux mines where my father had been superintendent. Now he was an ore buyer in Chile, Peru and Bolivia. He hadn't wanted to go, didn't want to leave the mines, working down in the mines.

My mother had convinced him to go, everybody had. It was a big opportunity and we would be very rich.

He paid the Wilsons for my room and board, but they all decided it would be good for my character for me to work just like the other kids. We all worked hard too, especially Dot and me, because we worked so late and then got up at 5: 00 A.M. We opened up for the three buses of miners going from Nogales to the Trench. The buses arrived within fifteen minutes of one another; the miners had just enough time for one or two coffees and some donuts. They'd thank us and wave on their way out, *Hasta luego!* We'd finish washing up, make ourselves sandwiches for lunch. Mrs. Wilson got there to take over and we'd go to school. I was still in the grade school up on the hill. Dot was a junior.

When we got home at night she'd sneak back out to see her boyfriend Sextus. He lived on a ranch in Sonoita, had left school to help his dad. I don't know what time she got back in. I was asleep the minute my head was on my pillow. The minute I hit the hay! I loved the idea of a hay mattress like in *Heidi*. The hay felt good and smelled good. It always seemed like I had just closed my eyes when Dot was shaking me to wake up. She would already have washed or showered and dressed, and while I did she brushed her hair into a pageboy and made up her face. "What are you staring at? Fix up the bed if you got nothing else to do." She really didn't like me, but I didn't like her back so I didn't care. On the way to the Sweet Shop, she'd tell me over and over I better keep quiet about her seeing Sextus, her daddy would kill her. Everybody in town knew about her and Sextus already or I would have told somebody, not her folks, but somebody, just because she was so mean. She was just mean on principle. She figured she should hate this kid they put up in her own room. The truth was we got along well otherwise, grinning and laughing, good teamwork, slicing onions, making sodas, flipping burgers. Both of us fast and efficient, both of us enjoyed people, the kind Mexican miners mostly, who joked and teased us in the mornings.

Homing

After school, kids from school and town people came in, for sodas or sundaes, to play the jukebox and the pinball machine. We served hamburgers, chili dogs, grilled cheese. We had tuna and egg salad and potato salad and coleslaw Mrs. Wilson made. The most popular dish though was chili Willie Torres' mother brought over every afternoon. Red chili in the winter, pork and green chilis in summer. Stacks of flour tortillas we'd warm on the grill.

One reason Dot and I worked so hard and so fast was we had an unspoken agreement that after we did all the dishes and cleaned the grill, she'd go out back with Sextus and I'd handle the few pie and coffee orders between nine and ten. Mostly I did homework with Willie Torres.

Willie worked until nine at the assayer's office next door. We had been in the same grade together at school and I had made friends with him there. On Saturday mornings I'd come down with my dad in the pickup to get groceries and mail for the four or five families that lived on the mountain by the Trench mine. After he did all the buying and loading, Daddy would stop by Mr. Wise's Assay Office. They'd drink coffee and talk about ore, mines, veins? I'm sorry, I didn't pay attention. I know it was about minerals. Willie was a different person in the office. He was shy at school, had come from Mexico when he was eight, so even though he was smarter than Mrs. Boosinger, he had trouble reading and writing sometimes. His first valentine to me was "Be my sweat-hart." Nobody made fun of him though, like they did of me and my back brace, yelling, "Timber!" when I came in because I was so tall. He was tall too, had an Indian face, high cheekbones and dark eyes. His clothes were clean but shabby and too small, his straight black hair long and raggedy, cut by his mother. When I read *Wuthering Heights*, Heathcliff looked like Willie, wild and brave.

In the Assay Office he seemed to know everything. He was going to be a geologist when he grew up. He showed me how to spot gold and fool's gold and silver. That first day my father asked what we were talking about. I showed him what I had learned. "This is copper. Quartz. Lead. Zinc."

"Wonderful!" he said, really pleased. During the drive home I got a geological lecture on the land all the way up to the mine.

On other Saturdays Willie showed me more rocks. "This is mica. This rock is shale, this is limestone." He explained mining maps to me. We'd paw through boxes filled with fossils. He and Mr. Wise went out looking for them. "Hey, this one! Look at this leaf!" I didn't realize I loved Willie since our closeness was so quiet, had nothing to do with the love girls talked about all the time, not like romance or crushes or ooh Jeeny loves Marvin.

In the Sweet Shop we'd close the blinds, sit at the counter doing our homework for that last hour, eating hot fudge sundaes. He could trip the juke box to keep playing, "Slow Boat to China," "Cry," and "Texarkana Baby" over and over. He was good at arithmetic and algebra and I was good with words so we helped each other. We leaned against each other, our legs hooked around the stools. He even hooked his elbow onto the part of my back brace that stuck out and I didn't mind. Usually if I saw that anybody even noticed the brace under my clothes I'd feel sick with embarrassment.

More than anything else we shared being sleepy. We never said, "Gee, I'm sleepy. Aren't you sleepy?" We were just tired together, leaned yawning together at the Sweet Shop. Yawned and smiled across the room at school.

His father was killed in a cave-in at the Flux mine. My father had been trying to get it shut down ever since we got to Arizona. That was his job for years, checking on mines to see if the veins were running out or if they were unsafe. They called him "Shut-'em-down Brown." I waited in the pickup truck when he went to tell Willie's mother. This was before I knew Willie. My father cried all the way home from town, which frightened me. It was Willie who later told me my father had fought to get pensions for the miners and their families, how much that helped his mother. She had five other children, did washing and cooking for people.

Willie was up as early as I was, chopping wood, getting his brothers and sisters breakfast. Civics class was the worst, impossible to stay awake, to be interested. It came at three o'clock. One endless hour. In the winter the wood stove steamed up the windows and our cheeks would be blazing red. Mrs. Boosinger blazed under her two purple spots of rouge. In summer with the windows open and flies buzzing around, bees humming and the clock ticking so drowsy so hot she'd be talking talking about the first amendment and whap! bang her ruler on the table. "Wake up! Wake up! You two jellyfish have no backbone! Sit up! Open your eyes. Jellyfish!" She once thought I was asleep but I was only resting my eyes. She said, "Lulu, who is the Secretary of State?"

"Acheson, ma'am." That surprised her.

"Willie, who is the Secretary of Agriculture?"

"Topeka and Santa Fe?"

I think we both were drunk with sleepiness. Every time she'd whack us on the head with the Civics book we'd laugh harder. She sent him to the hall and me to the cloak room, found us both curled up fast asleep after class.

A few times Sextus climbed up to Dot's room. I'd hear him whisper, "The kid asleep?"

"Out like a light."

And it was true. No matter how hard I tried to stay awake to watch what they did, I'd fall asleep.

A weird thing happened to me this week. I could see these small quick crows flying just past my left eye. I'd turn but they would be gone. And when I closed my eyes, lights would flash past like motorcycles on the highway zoom by. I thought I was hallucinating or had cancer of the eye, but the doctor said they were floaters, that lots of people get them.

"How can there be lights in the dark?" I asked, as confused as I used to be about the refrigerator. He said that my eye told the brain there was light so my brain believed it. Please don't laugh. This merely exacerbated the crow situation. It brought up the tree falling in the forest all over again too. Maybe my eyes just told my brain about crows in the maple tree.

One Sunday morning I woke up and Sextus was sleeping on the other side of Dot. I might have been more interested if they had been a more attractive couple. He had a buzz cut and pimples, white eyebrows and a huge Adam's apple. He was a champion roper and barrel rider though and his hog had won three years in a row at 4-H. Dot was homely, just plain homely. All the paint she put on didn't even make her look cheap, it only accentuated her little brown eyes and big mouth that prominent eyeteeth kept open in a permanent semi-snarl. I shook her gently and pointed to Sextus. "Oh Jesus wept," she said and woke him up. He was out the window, down the cottonwood and gone in seconds. Dot pinned me against the hay, made me swear not to say a word. "Hey, Dot, I haven't so far, have I?"

"You do, I'll tell on you and the Mexkin." I was shaken, she sounded like my mother.

It was nice not worrying about my mother. I was a nicer person now. Not surly or sullen. Polite and helpful. I didn't spill or break or drop things like at home. I never wanted to leave. Mr. and Mrs. Wilson kept saying I was a sweet girl, a good worker and how they felt I was one of the family. We had family dinners on Sundays. Dot and I worked until noon while they went to church, then we closed up, went home and helped make dinner. Mr. Wilson said grace. The boys poked each other and laughed, talked about basketball and we all talked about, well, I don't remember. Maybe we didn't actually talk much, but it was friendly. We said, "Please pass the butter." "Gravy?" My favorite part was that I had my own napkin and napkin ring that went on the sideboard with everyone else's.

On Saturdays I got a ride to Nogales and then a bus to Tucson. The doctors put me in a medieval painful traction for hours, until I couldn't take it any more. They measured me, checked for nerve damage by sticking pins in me, hitting my legs and feet with hammers. They adjusted the brace and the lift on my shoe. It looked like they were coming to a decision. Different doctors squinted at my X-rays. The famous one they had been waiting for said my vertebrae were too close to my spinal chord. Surgery could cause paralysis, shock to all the organs that had compensated for the curvature. It would be expensive, not just the surgery, but during recovery I would have to lie immobile on my stomach for five months. I was glad they didn't seem to want surgery. I was sure that if they straightened my spine I would be eight feet tall. But I didn't want them to stop checking me; I didn't want to go to Chile. They let me have one of the X-rays that showed a silver heart Willie gave me. My S-shaped spine, my heart in the wrong place and his heart right in the center. Willie put it up in a little window in the back of the Assay Office.

Some Saturday nights there were barn dances, way out in Elgin or Sonoita. In barns. Everybody from miles and miles would go, old people, young people, babies, dogs. Guests from dude ranches. All of the women brought things to eat. Fried chicken and potato salad, cakes and pies and punch. The men would go out in bunches and hang around their pickups, drinking. Some women too, my mother always did. High school kids got drunk and threw up, got caught necking. Old ladies danced with each other and children. Everybody danced. Two-step mostly, but some slow dances and jitterbug. Some square dances and Mexican dances like *La Varsoviana*. In English it's "Put your little foot, put your little foot right there," and you skip skip and whirl around. They played everything from "Night and Day" to "Detour, There's a Muddy Road Ahead," "*Jalisco no te Rajes*" to "Do the Hucklebuck." Different bands every time but with the same kind of mix. Where did those ragtag wonderful musicians come from? *Pachuco* horn and *guiro* players, big-hatted country guitarists, be-bop drummers, piano players that looked like Fred Astaire. The closest I ever heard anything come to those little bands was at the Five Spot in the late Fifties. Ornette Coleman's "Ramblin'." Everybody raving how new and far-out he was. Sounded Tex-Mex to me, like a good Sonoita hoedown.

The staid pioneer-type housewives got all dressed up for the dances. Toni permanents and rouge, high heels. The men were leathery hard-working ranchers or miners, brought up in the depression. Serious God-fearing workers. I loved to see the faces of the miners. The men I'd see coming off a shift dirty and drawn now red-faced and carefree, belting out an "Ah ha San Antone!" or an "*Ai, Ai, Ai*," because not only did everybody dance, everybody sang and hollered too. At intervals Mr. and Mrs. Wilson would slow down to pant, "Have you seen Dot?"

Willie's mom went to the dances with a group of friends. She danced every dance, always in a pretty dress, her hair up, her crucifix flying. She was beautiful and young. Ladylike too. She didn't dance close on slow dances or go out to the pickups. No, I didn't notice that. But all the Patagonia women did and mentioned it in her favor. They also said she wouldn't be a widow for long. When I asked Willie why he never came, he said he didn't know how to dance and besides he had to watch the kids. But other children go, why couldn't they come. No, he said. His mother needed to have fun, get away from them sometimes.

"Well, how 'bout you?"

"I don't care that much. I'm not being unselfish. I want my ma to find another husband as much as she does," he said.

If diamond drillers were in town the dances really livened up. I don't know if there still are diamond drillers, but in those mining days they were a special breed. Always two of them roaring into the camp ninety miles an hour in a cloud of dust. Their cars were not pickups or regular sedans but sleek two-seaters with glossy paint that shined through the dust. The men didn't wear denim or khakis like the ranchers or miners. Maybe they did when they went down in the mines, but traveling or at dances they wore dark suits and silky shirts and ties. Their hair was long, combed in a pompadour, with long sideburns, a mustache sometimes. Even though I saw them only at western mines, their license plates usually were from Tennessee or Alabama or West Virginia. They never stayed long, a week at the most. They got paid more than brain surgeons, my father said. They were the ones who opened a good vein or found one, I think. I do know they were important and their jobs were dangerous. They looked dangerous and, I know now, sexy. Cool and arrogant, they had the aura of matadors, bank robbers, relief pitchers. Every woman, old ones, young ones, at the barn dances wanted to dance with a diamond driller. I did. The drillers always wanted to dance with Willie's mother. Somebody's wife or sister who had had too much to drink invariably ended up outside with one of them and then there was a bloody fight, with all the men streaming out of the barn. The fights always ended with some-body shooting a gun off in the air and the drillers high-tailing off into the night, the wounded gallants returning to the dance with a swollen jaw or a blackening eye. The band would play something like, "You Two-Timed Me One Time Too Often."

One Sunday afternoon Mr. Wise drove me and Willie up to the mine, to see our old house. I got homesick then, smelling my daddy's Mr. Lincoln roses, walking around under the old oaks. Rocky crags all around and views out into the valleys and to Mount Baldy. The hawks and jays were there and the ticky-tick drum cymbal sound of the pulleys in the mill. I missed my family and tried not to cry, but I cried anyway. Mr. Wise gave me a hug, said not to worry, I'd probably be going to join them once school was out. I looked at Willie. He jerked his head at me to look at the doe and fawns that gazed at us, only a few feet away. "They don't want you to go," he said.

So I probably would have gone to South America. But then there was a terrible earthquake in Chile, a national disaster, and my family was killed. I went on living in Patagonia, Arizona with the Wilsons. After high school I got a scholarship to the University of Arizona where I studied journalism. Willie got a scholarship too, and had a double major in geology and art. We were married after graduation. Willie got a job at the Trench and I worked for the *Nogales Star* until our first son, Silver, was born. We lived in Mrs. Boosinger's beautiful old adobe house (she had died by then) up in the mountains, in an apple orchard near Harshaw.

I know it sounds pretty corny, but Willie and I lived happily ever after.

What if that had happened, the earthquake? I know what. This is the problem with "What ifs." Sooner or later you hit a snag. I wouldn't have been able to stay in Patagonia. I'd have ended up in Amarillo, Texas. Flat space and silos and sky and tumbleweeds, not a mountain in sight. Living with Uncle David and Aunt Harriet and my great-grandmother Grey. They would have thought of me as a problem. A cross to bear. There would be a lot of what they would call "acting out," and the counselor would refer to as cries for help. After my release from the juvenile detention center it would not be long before I would elope with a diamond driller who was passing through town, headed for Montana, and, can you believe it? my life would have ended up exactly as it has now, under the limestone rocks of Dakota Ridge, with crows.